I0780887

Also by

Please enjoy these other titles by Mike Vance. They are available where books are sold and also at www.mikevancewriter.com

Non-Fiction

Undertold Texas Volume 1

Getting Away With Bloody Murder

Mud & Money: A Timeline of Houston History

Murder & Mayhem in Houston (with John Nova Lomax)

Houston Baseball: The Early Years, 1861-1961

Houston's Sporting Life

Stand-Up Stories: Tales from Behind the Microphone

Brenham

Fiction

Wingo: The Remarkable Story of an Unremarkable Man

Wingo's Redemption

Zeke Gets Glasses. Jungleburgh Children's Reading Community (with John Swasey)

The Devil's Lease

Mike Vance

LCCN TXu 2-444-998

ISBN (hardback) 978-1-965272-04-6

ISBN (paperback) 978-1-965272-03-9

ISBN (ebook) 978-1-965272-05-3

This is a work of fiction. Although its form is that of an autobiography, it is not one. All the names, characters, businesses, places, events and incidents in this book are either the product of the author's imagination or used in a fictitious manner. With the exception of public figures, any resemblance to actual persons, living or dead, or actual events is purely coincidental. The actions and words of public figures or businesses described in this book are completely fictitious and were created from the whole cloth of the author's imagination for the purposes of entertainment and humor. The opinions expressed are those of the characters and should not be confused with the author's.

Printed in the United States of America

Part One

Will

Chapter 1

Houston, Texas

March 1901

"Mike, give us another round over here, will you? And add one for our young scribe. We're celebrating. I've set another murderer free."

Ninety minutes in, and J.B. Duckworth was just getting rolling. One wave of laughter was subsiding from his previous story, and Duckworth, with an actor's timing, was letting his friends, admirers and hangers on catch their breaths before he waded in for the next one.

Not that Duckworth ever required an excuse for making merry with friends, but earlier in the afternoon, he had secured an easy not guilty verdict for his client in a case of murder. The act, perpetrated on Christmas Day in First Ward, had almost devolved into a race riot, but today, Frank Montalbano walked free, and his lawyer drank.

Mike Callaghan, the proprietor and primary server at the Acme Saloon, set six mugs of beer and six shots of Old Taylor on the crowded table. He grabbed a round's worth of empty mugs and glasses in his two beefy hands.

"You drunks are going through all my glassware."

Duckworth lifted a sip of the whiskey to his lips, losing nary a drop.

"You recollect the Jim Gompert case back in '96? Well, there was one witness I didn't get to call," he chortled. "Old Mr. Gompert had a young mistress, a redhead half his age, and she was hiding naked in the armoire during the entire incident. When the missus busted in unexpectedly, he had just enough time to throw on a dressing gown and shoo the girl into the closet. Sure, the old lady was screaming like a lunatic and waving a pistol around, but the room must have been reeking of hijinks while they had their tussle."

As the howls swelled, Duckworth took a big swig of his beer and gave a twinkling wink at the new reporter who had joined the group. He wiped some foam from his walrus moustache and pointed at the young man across the table,

"That's off the record, son."

Judd Lewis, an established columnist at the *Houston Post*, clapped his colleague on the shoulder and responded on his behalf.

"Hooper understands the etiquette with the legal community around a barroom table, isn't that right?"

The wide-eyed young man nodded. Next to him, Harris Peterson waved a hand at his friend in the next chair.

"Oh, I promise that if you keep your mouth closed and your bar tab open, you'll get quite the education from Mr. Duckworth."

J.B. responded over the noise.

"No, no. Since it's his first time celebrating with us, I'm willing to waive the rules just for a minute or two. Then it's back to bald faced lies and dirty jokes. Anything you want to know, Mr..."

"Hooper, sir. John Hooper."

"Mr. John Hooper, then. I'll grant you three questions."

Duckworth offered a pompous and kingly wave of his hand. It was at least partially a joke.

"Well, the first is do you do this after every case you win?"

"Ha! The lad wants to know when to show up, J.B.! He's already got you pegged for an easy mark," Walter Malsch, a local Justice of the Peace jumped in.

"Mr. Hooper, ..."

The rest of Duckworth's answer was parroted by at least three of the men at the table in a less than perfectly timed chorus.

"...always celebrate a victory or drown a defeat!"

The men laughed raucously at their own joke. Malsch turned to the cub reporter.

"Mr. Hooper, hundreds of lawyers pass through my little court, and while several of them make more money than J.B. here, none of them are half as ornery or bloody-minded. And most assuredly, none of them are more worthwhile to drink with."

"Thank you, Judge. I will take all of that as a compliment," Duckworth toasted in Malsch's direction. "I'll note that I might have more money if you didn't cheat at poker."

J.B. spoke over the rowdiness to address John Hooper again.

"Second question, Mr. Hooper."

"Yes, sir. This Montalbano case that you won today, did you ever have any doubt that the jury would buy your self-defense argument?"

Suppressed titters came from several of the men. Walter Malsch slapped the table.

"J.B. Duckworth will not brook doubts!"

"Exactly right, Walter. A good lawyer must never doubt his case, Mr. Hooper. You simply build it stronger. But Montalbano is old news."

Duckworth pointed straight at his new acquaintance.

"Use your final question on something more interesting."

Hooper paused, any nerves now gone thanks to the warming qualities of the Old Taylor. While not exactly a member of the club, he reckoned that he was not going to be shooed away.

"Okay. How did you end up in Houston?"

This time his question brought good natured groans all around. Even Duckworth's brother slowly shook his head.

"Oh, but you have pulled at the tangled web this time," lamented Peterson. "I hope there is no Mrs. Hooper keeping your dinner in the warming oven. If you brought a bed roll, now's the time to unfurl it. This could take a while."

Even Duckworth himself laughed at this before he put on a serious face and segued into monologue mode. Hooper had seen the same look as the lawyer delivered his summation that very noon. The attorney's voice had a soft rasp to it, even as it produced a sneaky force.

"I was born in Cobb County, Georgia. My brother John here,..." Duckworth patted the shoulder of the man on his right. "... he was two years old when I came along. When Sherman marched through, I had just turned seven. My brother was a month shy of nine. That was not quite old enough to be conscripted into the ragtag rebel army in those parts, but close. Our daddy had gone away, volunteered for Cobb's Legion at the start of the war, and he got shot down at Crampton's Gap, Battle of South Mountain. The Federals under Henry Slocum had already won, but the Stephens Rifles, with whom my daddy had signed on, were sent in as reinforcements. It was a sucker move for the rebs, but a regular parlieu for Slocum. They killed the first few dozen, of which my daddy was one, and captured the rest."

John Duckworth, who had said almost nothing for the previous hour, looked genuinely ill at ease as he stared at the table top. He certainly knew that his brother was just getting up a head of steam.

"Our farm, such as it was, sat southwest of Big Shanty Spring, not far from Butler's Creek. Our brother Monroe was old enough to work it, as did our sister Julia, but John and me behind a plow were not overly dangerous to the dirt. Since daddy died, our mama had not exactly been a house afire."

John motioned silently for another round. The other men, having heard the tale before, were respectfully quiet if not rapt.

"It was middle of June of '64. Sherman didn't yet realize just how badly he outnumbered Joe Johnston, so there was dancing, feeling out, poking, prodding as he tried to disengage them from Kennesaw Mountain. Hood, Hardee, Loring, Polk, Wheeler, they were all dug in solid. Sherman would patiently send brigades this way and that looking to make ground on the flanks. He used artillery, brilliant artillery, to gain position. Spraying canister and case through the length of the Southern trenches. It made the positions untenable, and little by little, he forced his enemies back. Skirmishes, that's all they were. Nothing of consequence to most folks, unless you happened to be underneath one of those shells. Well, Mr. Hooper, that's where my poor family found themselves. Not on purpose mind you. A load in one of those 12-pound Napoleons went wrong. Too much, too little, too wet, I don't know. But a single case round, that's the ones filled with shrapnel, landed in our derelict little barnyard. It tore my sister Ferlie, she was five, to bloody pieces. I escaped with nary a scratch, but John here lost half his foot and a chunk of his calf. My mother, who was near Ferlie, trying to rush our last two remaining chickens into their coop, was struck right across the face. She lived, but never saw light of day again. Never saw her children again. Or snow on the hills or buds in springtime. Made a snoring noise with every further breath she ever took. That was on account of most of her nose being gone."

"I for one vote to convict that damned Sherman!"

Walter Malsch pounded his hand on the table again. His remark broke the tension with laughter just as Mike Callaghan brought the next round of drinks. J.B.'s story, however, was not yet ready to be dislodged.

"After the war, ..."

Judd Lewis groaned again. Duckworth shot him the cutty-eye as he repeated himself.

"After the war, we all tried to stay together, but things were just too poor in that quarter of the world. While we were still in our teens, John and I took our disabled mother north in hopes of all settling with a sister of hers at Portsmouth, Ohio."

Lewis interrupted.

"Wasn't it Geneva, New York last time?"

"Canandaigua, I think," snickered Harris Peterson.

"It was Portsmouth, Ohio."

Peterson threw his hands in the air.

"I give up. The Duckworth's mother no doubt had many sisters. Pray continue."

"In any case, while residing there,..." J.B. tossed a mock scowl at his friend Peterson. "In Portsmouth, Ohio, I became a protégé of sorts to an old lawyer who saw a spark of intelligence in me."

"You've got something in you," offered Peterson who quickly followed the remark with a placating hand gesture. "All right, all right. I'll concentrate on my beer."

"The short of it is that I caught the legal bug from that fine man. After our mother passed, I moved to Cincinnati, and eventually began to distinguish myself in law. John and I believed Houston to be a city of opportunity, and we both relocated here in 1895. It was the wisest decision we ever made, right brother?"

John Duckworth lifted his eyes toward Hooper long enough to nod while his brother summed up.

"As horrid as was the toll that Sherman inflicted on Georgia, I hold the unpopular opinion that those rebels brought it on themselves. Smart men foresaw the inevitable outcome, our city's namesake Sam Houston among them. A wily David can always whip a slow Goliath, but when you're outnumbered by Goliaths three to one, you are a fool to challenge them. Make smart choices, Mr. Hooper. I made two vows to myself in that squalid barnyard of ours back in Cobb County. First, that the late war is well past and should not define me or anyone else, and second, that I would not be any man's victim."

Harris Peterson, on J.B.'s left, gripped his pal's shoulder.

"That I can solemnly attest to. You are no one's victim. You are, however, a full mug of beer in arrears thanks to flapping your gob about Georgia. Now. I heard a fine one the other day about a priest in a convent."

John Duckworth had excused himself over an hour ago, followed closely by Lewis and Hooper, the two scribes from the *Post*. Harris Peterson lasted one beer past that. The last forty minutes had been left to Walter Malsch and J.B. Duckworth, relocated to the bar, to solve the problems of the world. They leaned there in comfort, each with one booted foot resting on the brass rail. Almost a dozen other drinkers were still scattered about, including the four playing dominoes at a back table.

When a long enough lull in conversation presented itself, Duckworth pulled his watch from a pocket, a Waltham in a gold case that had been given him by one of the more notorious clients he ever had. It was almost certainly pilfered swag, but that just added to its cachet. He wiped the face on his pant leg, gave the stem a twist or two, then carefully snapped the cover shut. He turned toward the barman.

"It's gone midnight, Mike. I was planning to put in another hour of work, but these reprobates have forced me to imbibe past my curfew. Now, I need to hot foot it to catch the last car."

"Ain't it always the way?"

J.B. took his final swallow of beer.

"What's my tab? Just in case I'm run down by a dray."

"Fourteen sixty-five, J.B.. Not even to 300 glasses of Magnolia yet," the barman said with a smile.

Duckworth fished a heavy coin from his pocket and laid it on the white marble bar.

"That's twenty dollars for you, Mike. Take out one more glass for Walter, here. We'll start a new total next time. Meanwhile, it's always smart to catch me when I'm flush."

J.B. shook hands with Callaghan and Malsch in turn before he pushed through the swinging doors, paused in the vestibule to put on his hat, then stepped out onto Preston Avenue and turned right. On a clear, cool night, two days away from a full moon, there was plenty of light to see where he was headed. That natural blue glow easily outshined the dim electric street lamps in some blocks. Duckworth had always considered himself a nocturnal creature at heart. He did his best thinking then.

A few wagons, one with a squeaky axle, headed toward the *Post* building to collect newspaper bundles for suburban delivery. One or two restaurants were still serving, and lights blazed in several downtown bars. The gamblers were still at it in their dens. A few of the dedicated drinkers had already met their limit and were sleeping it off in an alley here and there, oblivious to the likelihood of being rousted by the next foot patrolman. One of the night's drunks headed west toward the City Hall block hugging his horse's neck with all his might in hopes of staying mounted.

The Kiam store was dark, but J.B. glanced in the window as he turned north on Main. He needed a few new shirt collars and made a mental note to take care of that. His footing slipped a tad crossing the street, but J.B. put that down to horse shit on wet paving stones, not the almost four hours' worth of beer and whiskey.

Like every man, he had his habits, but Duckworth was not entirely mired in routine. He rotated his watering holes, for one. Share the wealth and expand your circle of friends was the thinking. He also varied his routes as he walked through the city. Every person he greeted was a potential client. Tonight, he stairstepped up Main and Congress and Fannin Streets as he worked his way northeast.

The Montgomery Line streetcar was waiting up ahead at San Jacinto and Franklin as he rounded the corner by the post office. Its deep red color reduced to a shiny gray. By mid-block, he could see Joe Russo sitting in the motorman's chair, but there were no passengers aboard. Light and laughter spilled out from the Crown Bar at the corner.

"I have a feeling you might come along, Giacomo. I give it a couple of extra minutes."

"Much appreciated, Giuseppi."

Duckworth took pride in his prominent, bushy moustache, but he still got a pang of envy looking at the artwork on Jolly Joe Russo's upper lip.

"The evening paper say you win your trial. That's good. Signore Montalbano is a rat bastard, but his brother is nice. I'm happy he is not going to prison."

Duckworth liked the Italian immigrants, and his regular streetcar driver was probably top of the list. He dropped his fare in the box and snagged the first bench behind Russo. The car eased forward, electric wires humming and sparking overhead. The street angled to the left, over Buffalo Bayou and onto Willow Street. They were now in Fifth Ward.

"What big case will I read about next, Giacomo?"

"Right now, Joe, my desk is piled high with humdrum business. Same for Henry and Sonny. I have half a dozen killings scattered about. They'll be coming to trial over the next few weeks. I'm off to Bellville on Thursday for a man who may or may not have bludgeoned his neighbor over a borrowed bow saw. As far as the next new thing, it'll be along directly. Never you fear. People never tire of murdering one another."

Chapter 2

June 1901

To a connoisseur, Texas in the summer offered several distinct kinds of heat. Along the Red River, where George Purdy grew up, it was the unforgiving sun that burned your skin until your face felt like cracklins fresh from the pot. On those summer afternoons, you labored on in increments that your mind could accept, your lunch having long since deserted you. Time, and the number of rows worked, was marked from one dipper at the water bucket to the next, but you always knew that at nighttime, things would get tolerable again.

Here in Fort Bend County, where the Brazos widened out and started its final run to the Gulf, summer was a suit of clothes you couldn't take off. You slept next to naked on the porch murmuring a vain prayer of catching a wind, but the blanket of hot air never left you. You took a bath in the river, but the water was no cooler than the air. Before you crawled out onto the bank and put on your work pants, you were sweating again. In fact, your clothes never felt dry from April to October. The hot stayed in your mouth and dripped from your ears. When you were lucky enough to catch a breeze, you spread your arms wide like a sail so not a single breath of that cooling air would be wasted.

Still, Purdy loved the smell of a June Texas night. There was something comforting about that warm embrace, and George imagined that he got a whiff of fish from the river. In this single week when the cotton flowers bloomed, it was the smell of reassurance that life was going to be all right. The crop had reached a milestone, and rain gods willing, you would not go hungry this year. Those pale blossoms were not exactly roses, but sixty acres of them could produce a powerful perfume. Part of the perfume of the countryside is how he imagined it. Even the distant scent of a skunk's spray or wind blowing from the cow lot was something to be enjoyed.

George lingered on the edge of his porch. He needed to get down the road to the Mabin's place, but his thoughts held him there, feet dangling over the dirt, smelling the night and trying to remember when he was little. He wanted to call it home, but he had moved so often in his 32 years, that he could not fathom where that would be.

His first thought when he got the letter was that his mother had even selected a convenient time to be dying. The cotton and corn were both well established. If the Mabins would do him this favor, he could get up to Montague, settle whatever needed to be settled and be back a good month before there was any picking to be done. Their kids all got along, and his two would handle the weeding and chopping of their rows while he was away. His head told him that it was a big request of a man he'd known for barely two years and whose margin of living was as razor sharp as his own. His heart hoped that his neighbors were willing to help him out. He sighed and eased himself down off the porch.

The Mabin's cabin was identical to his. George, having built it, knew that better than anyone. The inside, though, was notably more domestic. That was what a woman's touch would do for you. Sewn curtains. A table cloth. The Mabins probably ate a little better than the Purdys. George had never learned to bake. Still, he was a deft hand with a cane pole, and wagered that he was better than Charlie Mabin at pulling fish out of the river. If Sarah and Arthur were getting tired of eating fried catfish, they were not saying anything about it.

Even though it was pitch black, the children, three Mabins and two Purdys, were playing outside. Charlie's wife Polly fussed with sewing to the right of the cottage door while the men visited to the left. Charlie hauled a rickety-looking chair out from inside, and he let his guest take advantage of the spare ladder back, after all, it was Purdy who had gifted it to them. Both men had the chairs leaned back just right against the wall.

George Purdy had grown up farming, but his trade the last decade had been carpenter. He was no fancy furniture maker, but he could build a house, a table, a chest or a chair to be as sturdy and functional as the best of them. His hands were good at turning spare lumber into a place to sit, and he had made two extra chairs this past January and given them to his neighbors, mostly as a thank you to Polly Mabin for the occasional half of a fruit pie or the big basket of squash and potatoes that had helped tide them through the cold months before their own garden got going.

This was Purdy's first year tenant farming. He liked Fort Bend County well enough, and wanted to try his hand at something that would let him stay put. Carpentry work paid better, but moving his two children from town to town every few months could not be good for them, so he signed a contract to farm 120 acres. It was to be 80 in cotton and 40 in corn. The house and a couple acres of garden did not count against him.

His introduction to Sartartia was not as a sharecropper, at all. Will Ennis hired him in the late fall of 1899 to construct 30 cabins for tenant farmers. It was to replace those destroyed by the great Brazos flood that summer. Folks said that 12,000 square miles flooded, and over 200 people died. Dozens of people on the place were pulled out in skiffs. Whole fenceposts were under water, and as for the cane on the north side of the tracks, only the top foot was showing.

The work took Purdy just over a year, and an occasional convict helper, but he was proud of them. When the big storm came through, only three of the completed ones even required a major repair. More than two dozen other buildings on the plantation had taken severe damage. Two were blown off their foundation, and six of the out buildings were turned to kindling, but George Purdy's houses had held up fine.

They were simple houses, two rooms and a sleeping loft. George had built shuttered openings in each side wall of the loft to allow a little airflow. Like the rest of the houses' windows, there was no glass. There was the occasional breeze, but there was also the occasional raccoon or possum.

The back room had a built-in shelf on the left hand wall. Will Ennis had sprung for 40 number 2 washtubs, and those sat atop the shelves and served as the kitchen sink. One of George Purdy's luxuries was a sausage grinder mounted on the back room wall. He scavenged it from a job he did once up in Falls County. The man was prepared to throw it into the trash pile, but that meat grinder had lots of life left in it.

Each tenant cottage had a front porch that ran the width of the house. Like every dwelling in Texas, big or small, it was the primary living space for most evenings of the year. That's where George found himself now, on the Mabin's porch, asking for his favor. It was not a comfortable feeling.

"It was my Aunt Addie who wrote me. I suppose she is my mama's cousin and not my real aunt at all. Anyhow, that's where mama's been staying."

Polly Mabin, though a generous soul, was a talker and perhaps a bit of a gossip, and that did not make things any easier on George.

"Poor thing. I hope she ain't suffering too much. What happened to your daddy?

"He died a few years back."

"So young. What was it?"

Charlie Mabin quietly scolded his wife.

"Now, Polly, mind your business."

"It's all right, Charlie. I'm not trying to hide anything. Daddy blew his brains out with a shotgun. They had lost their farm after the Panic. Owed too much on their note. The night before the bank was set to run them off, he went out to the barn and done it."

The three of them listened to the crickets and frogs for a time. Charlie Mabin broke the silence.

"What do you aim to do, George?"

"Well, there's no one else. I suspect I have three sisters living, but none of them close to Montague. The next one above me is married and living up near Lenexa, Kansas. She has seven children of her own. I ain't heard from the two oldest ones in years. They both got married and moved out west someplace. I can't tell you if mama had kept up with them or not. I reckon not."

Polly made a soft clucking noise.

"I can't understand people like that. No offense, George. Families may squabble, but you should love your mama and daddy enough to stay in touch with them. Mine are still farming up near Pattison. Charlie and I went to visit this Christmas last. They got oranges for each of the young ones, excepting the baby here. Mamas and daddies are to be honored just like the Lord says."

"Oh, I guess that my sisters love mama in their own way. It's just that opportunity took their lives someplace else. We were never a sentimental bunch, but we were hard workers. I figure that's what wore my daddy out. That hard work, only to discover there was no reward."

"It sounds like you're going up there, then?" Charlie asked softly.

"I know it makes no sense, Charlie, and I know I was never seeing her much no way, but it feels like I deserted her when I moved off down this direction. That's where the jobs were, though. I'm not second guessing myself, mind you, but at the least, I owe her trying to say goodbye, don't you think?"

"What about the farming?"

George knew that Charlie understood what had gone into his choice, but it needed to be talked out. One poor man's burden was great enough in life without a neighbor adding to it, but Charlie was probably the closest friend he had anymore.

"I sure do hate to ask y'all, but could you look after Sarah and Arthur for a little bit while I go up to Montague. I've been showing Arthur how to weed in the garden, and Sarah is already a top hand with the hoe. So, I ain't asking y'all to do any work on my place. I want to be clear about that. Just give them a spot of floor to sleep on at night and keep an eye on them. As far as feeding them, I'm a bit beggared like everyone else about now, but I got six chickens laying real good, and there is okra and onions a plenty. Those will need to be eaten while I'm away, anyhow. So, that'd be my contribution. I know this is gonna fall mostly on you, Polly."

Purdy paused for a few seconds, considering whether he had anything else to add.

"I reckon that's my piece. I hope you'll consider it."

With that quiet pronouncement, he turned out toward the dark and the sounds of the kids playing.

Charlie Mabin looked at his wife, still mending clothes on her lap. They had been together long enough to hold a conversation without words when it was required. After about a minute, Polly was the one who answered.

"Your little ones can stay with us, George. Ours will love having the company. And if they get done with their chores here, we can sure see to it that Junior and Anita and Earl help Sarah and Arthur out over at your place. I know Sarah has wanted to learn how to make a cake, at least she's mentioned a time or two while she and Anita were around here playing. So maybe I can show her a thing or two. We'll have a fine time, and you shouldn't worry yourself."

Fireflies were putting on quite a show, and the parents could hear their kids laughing as they tried to catch the bugs in a lidless jar.

"You going to take the train, I suspect?"

"Train would cost me better than ten dollars, though it could get me to Bowie, and that's only a dozen miles from Aunt Addie's place. But no, I don't have that kind of money until the crops are sold and we settle up. No. That gray horse is mine, and he's a real good one. I reckon it'll take me seven or eight days each way to ride up to Montague and back. That's as long as I can get him water and a spot to graze every night. That should be easy enough after a wet spring. So that's two weeks of riding, plus a few days to spend with my mama. Make sure her business is in order, though there won't be much of that to take care of. Thank goodness

I won't have to deal with the bankers. I don't suspect there's any way I'll be gone more than three weeks."

Charlie nodded thoughtfully before he spoke.

"Will Ennis, hell, his whole family... Pardon me, Polly... That whole family can be prickly to deal with, but when a man's mama is dying, that can't be helped. No, it can't."

Chapter 3

The two men sat on the front top gallery of the big, white house, looking south across a vast expanse of Texas coastal prairie. It was as open as land and sky could get. Miles of agricultural palette scraped bare of trees. Any arboreal traces marked a water course. Birds and wildlife seeking a home must make do with those patches. They were not welcome on the rest of the landscape. Those wide dirt vistas served a single purpose – to make money for its owner.

This time of year offered hot, hazy and often dusty days. Southeast Texas would not see a blue sky until Christmas. A nice breeze tousled their hair, though, or at least the hair that the older man had left. The line of trees more than a mile distant, almost the only trees in view aside from the young oaks planted around the house, marked the near bank of the Brazos River. Behind the men, out of sight from the front of the house, the Galveston, Harrisburg & San Antonio Rail Road tracks, recently purchased by mighty Southern Pacific, stretched to the horizons east and west. They were the life line that let the Ennis plantation breathe.

On the surface, they appeared to be old friends, these two gentlemen a generation apart, but they had met only a single time before. That had been eighteen years earlier when Will Ennis was a lowly junior cashier at the Savings Bank in Houston. They had met for a polite drink, and Will, who imagined himself a worldly 24 at the time, had thought that it might offer an important political and social connection to have under his belt. That idea had never borne fruit.

A decade after that whiskey in Houston, Will was summoned home to Sartartia so he could prepare to take the reins of the plantation. His father, ever the taskmaster, even in failing health, had driven the lessons of business into Will like so many railroad spikes. According to Littleberry Ambrose Ennis, the rules of running a large agricultural operation, and a successful man's life, were iron clad. His three younger brothers received some of the curt instruction, but the brunt of the old man's wrath, stoked by painful ailments, had fallen on Will. These days, however, Will rarely missed a chance to remind others that he was now in charge.

The older man on the upstairs porch, Albert Gallatin Clopton, had commanded L.A. Ennis in Company D of the First Texas Infantry, Hood's Brigade. Though Ennis never officially surpassed the rank of lieutenant, he was known after the War as Captain. Major Clopton's rank was earned during the Battle of Eltham's Landing in Virginia. The two men had become friends during the first year of the conflict, and when Clopton, a Louisiana educated doctor, transferred to the Confederacy's Medical Department, they remained devoted correspondents.

After the two separated in the summer of 1862, Littleberry Ennis had seen fighting during the Seven Days and at Second Bull Run. He was lucky enough to be in hospital with dysentery during Antietam when the regiment lost 82 percent of its men to injury or death. He returned to action in time for Gettysburg, Chickamauga, Chattanooga, the Wilderness and Cold Harbor. Comrades and their replacements fell around him with what seemed like every step of the march. Emaciated but carrying the scars of only two minor wounds, Ennis and the other final 149 men of the First Texas were included in the surrender at Appomattox.

For his part, Dr. Clopton's wartime horrors may have been even worse. He endured over three solid years of immersing his bloodied hands into thousands of festering wounds and sawing through hundreds of legs and arms as the men parting with them, restrained by strong hands in the absence of painkillers, screamed endlessly for a reprieve. Neither Albert Clopton nor L.A. Ennis had ever shared those stories with their children.

Clopton's hometown was Jefferson, in the northeast part of the state, but he had taken a professorship in physiology at the University of Texas Medical School in Galveston. He had his bona fides, both as an important man in Texas and in the art of civility. The latter skill allowed him to maintain a perfectly mannered exterior toward his late friend's eldest son, a man he already regarded as tiresome.

The feeling came as no surprise. Like many veterans of the late war, he found it difficult to embrace a man who did not fight, and he both envied and pitied them their ignorance. In spite of the fact that he had promised to stay the night, Clopton tried to recollect if the next eastbound train through Sartartia stopped at four or four-thirty.

"It's roughly 6,000 acres in cultivation right now. Cotton, corn and cane. We've been having a little annoyance with the cotton lice, but the cane is much better than it was last season. Still recuperating from the flood. But this year is promising. Should get us 30 to 35 tons to the acre. That's provided we can get a few more days of rain this next month or so."

Clopton nodded at Will Ennis' narrative and took another sip of his Armagnac. The liquor, imported from France, was indeed top notch. Ennis started a new subject.

"We got a telephone wire four years ago. It is an amazing convenience. It's not even thought about in town, of course, but out here, well, it is a sockdolager. My clerk can order whatever we need and have it run out on the train. Seven weeks ago, I reached Anton Stelzig in downtown Houston direct from our little station over there and described three saddles I had in mind. On Thursday last, they arrived along with all the tack."

Another nod. Another sip.

By mid-afternoon, Clopton had resigned himself, perhaps even embraced his visit to Sartartia to some extent. He guessed his relaxation came courtesy of the good brandy. He and Ennis were outside the stable, in the midst of a cluster of outbuildings that sat to one side of the big white house. Though mostly unpainted, they were in ship shape. Two storage sheds of some sort, a smokehouse, privy, a small servant cottage and even a pigeonnier, one of the few Clopton recalled seeing this far into Texas.

The stable hand, a middle aged Black man whose name he had not learned, was saddling two horses so that Ennis could show his visitor some of the highlights of the property. The offer had been made to take a buggy, but Dr. Clopton had suggested going horseback. He knew that at age 73, he would be consigned to buggies soon enough. He wanted to enjoy sitting astride a good horse while he still could, even if he did now require a mounting block.

"Goddamn it, Tom," Ennis suddenly thundered. "I was just telling the doctor about those new saddles. Why the hell would you put this old thing on for our guest?"

"I'm sorry, Mr. Ennis. I was not aware of that conversation. Fact is that your brothers have pretty much laid claim to those other two new ones."

Dr. Clopton spoke up, especially startled by the outburst since his back was to the stable door.

"This saddle looks fine, Will. Sturdy and functional. It'll certainly do."

"Nonsense. I paid for new saddles." He turned back to Tom's impassive face. "Are they currently using them? What they want is not my concern."

"Mr. Cass took one when he rode over to Richmond this morning."

Will cut him off.

"Emmett's in San Antonio. So, he sure as shit isn't using one."

"Yes, sir," Tom Ward was already leading the gentle bay horse back into the stable. "I will fetch that one and swap it out on old Micah here. Be back directly."

Ennis and Clopton rode farther west to inspect the old Field's sugar mill. L.A. Ennis had been shrewd, buying out three of his biggest neighbors after key deaths or economic downturns. Those purchases had brought him two intact sugar mills, each with a nearby cotton gin. Those were also the locations of the convict camps a decade before. Today, those camps were still intact, but much quieter than what Clopton expected to find.

"I've modernized a great many aspects of the operation," Will Ennis offered in way of explanation. "There is much to be learned by keeping up with modern agriculture. We still use Paris Green, but there are some newer chemicals that work well against the weevils and beetles. Seeds are better than they used to be. Expensive of course, so we introduce them sparingly and mostly use our own any given year."

"I'm sure your father would be proud of your ingenuity."

"I doubt that seriously."

The statement came out so harshly that it left a bitter taste even in the mouth of its speaker. The two men rode the next quarter mile in silence before Ennis continued.

"As for labor, I've spent the last four years getting rid of about two-thirds of the convict lease system that he used and replacing it with share croppers. Even placed advertisements for them in the newspapers. See those houses off yonder? I ordered almost four dozen of those built all across this old Cartwright League, and much of the Battle League, too. They are tidy little houses, don't you think? Much better than the ones we already had."

"Quite handsome. I was under the impression, though, that convict labor had done very well for your family. Your father wrote me extensively when he and Ed Cunningham took over the whole business from the state. Of course, that was 20, 25 years ago now. My goodness. I just remember him being most enthusiastic."

"Yes, you recall correctly." Ennis turned in the saddle to make better eye contact. "There is no doubt that it made the family rich, but the simple truth is that one kind of man wants to work and the other doesn't."

"No doubt. Still, your father did so well that the state took the whole prison system back in order to keep those profits for themselves. That was good money. At least that was my understanding of the situation. I certainly don't intend to speak out of turn."

If Clopton was bracing for another spout of temper, he did not get it.

"Some of it will stay because you can't pay a man to work those sugar fields, not a White man. The work will kill you. Sooner than later, at least. Water moccasins every ten feet in that cane, and mosquitoes so thick you turn your palms blood red slapping at them. Almost makes you feel sorry for the darkies until you remember that they come here because they robbed somebody or chose to make a life of shiftless vagrancy."

They rode another two hours to see more fields and peek inside some of the buildings at what might generously be called the town. The plantation office stood there, a sizable storage shed for equipment and two even larger ones for product and merchandise going in and out by rail. There were five small houses, a carpentry shop, forge, mule barn, capacious corn crib and an open cook's house. The prize was the two-story station. Downstairs was the store for general merchandise complete with post office cubbies. Will's little brothers, Caswell and Emmett, had been getting the monthly stipend as Sartartia's postmaster. Upstairs was a plain, open hall that hosted social events on some Saturday nights and church services most Sunday mornings.

When they returned to the house, a most welcome and savory smell greeted the riders. The bachelor household was eating well. Letha, the cook, who doubled as housekeeper, had made a beef stew that would have been creditable in the best restaurants of Houston or Galveston. Clopton was certain he detected rosemary, thyme and bay leaf. The claret served with it was most passable, too. The next youngest brother, Caswell, had returned from whatever business he had in Richmond. Leigh, the baby of the family was a typical hungry teener, but it still seemed to be a great deal of food for just four men.

As the dessert plates were cleared away, the host suggested that they adjourn to the parlor for some brandy, but Clopton demurred.

"Will, I am worn out by the day. Not used to sitting horseback that long anymore. Rigors of old age. I'm going to head up to my room, if you don't mind. I need to catch the early train back toward Houston and make my connection. Thank you so much for the kind hospitality. It was good meeting you, Caswell, Leigh."

Clopton took a few steps toward the staircase before turning back with one more thought.

"You may not realize it, Will, but I see a great deal of your father in you. He taught you well. Good night. And thank you again."

The old man did not look back to see Will Ennis' stony stare.

Chapter 4

September 1901

The sidewalks were busy on a hot Saturday evening. The working men of Houston, looking forward to their sole day of rest come Sunday, were setting off for their weekly blowout. Bars were filling. Gambling halls readied for the busiest night. The celebration was building, and J.B. Duckworth had a bit of a head start.

For the firm of Duckworth & Fein, Saturdays meant fewer hours in the office. On the months when court was in session, Sunday was inevitably filled, every employee busily prepping for cases. The weekdays were solid with a seemingly endless bustle of clients and other lawyers. Saturday was the firm's only day of flexibility.

Law partner Henry Fein's Saturdays, like Friday nights, were observed as the sabbath. J.B. Duckworth's Saturday translated into time with his wife and daughter. This morning, they had breakfasted on eggs, bacon and toast. J.B. liked two eggs sunny side up. His wife Lola was in the habit of scrambling an extra for Maizy, the dog. Their daughter, Katherine, who had turned a year old only five weeks prior, preferred oatmeal.

Duckworth had brought Maizy home one evening during his daughter's fourth week of life. She was a skinny puppy who had been scavenging the streets, and he couldn't leave her to that sentence of death. He deftly made the case that Katherine and dog could grow up together and be the best of friends. Lola, married to J.B. less than two years, was forced to admit that the pup, an energetic retriever mix, was interminably cute. Within hours, it became clear that Katherine's dog was in fact J.B.'s.

J.B. and Maizy left the house at 573 Waverly Street on the North Side, walked seven blocks to the streetcar line, and rode into town. He was meeting a bailed client for lunch at the Turf Exchange, a nice restaurant and saloon with an even nicer casino upstairs. They'd eaten and talked until two, and as they said their goodbyes on the street corner of Main and Prairie under a merciless sun, Duckworth, in an ebullient mood, had decided that one more drink couldn't hurt.

Lawyer and dog stopped for a couple at the "66" on Main, then followed that with a beer and a shot at the Metropolitan on Preston, then two, or maybe three, more at Burt Dodge's little hole in the wall next door. He was going to stay for just one there, but Burt had a few bites of sausage for Maizy, and the conversation was convivial.

J.B. was standing on the sidewalk. It was well past five o'clock. He really should be getting home for supper, but perhaps he could fit in a last beer. There was a bar directly opposite his car stop, after all. Passersby broke around him like water in a stream as he weighed his options. Suddenly, his daydreaming was interrupted by a motion to his left.

"Git!"

A middle-aged man in a mediocre suit was half-heartedly kicking at Maizy. In a flash, J.B. pulled a small gun from his waist band and shoved it into the man's nostril. The fellow recoiled in fear, trying to back away, but Duckworth's left hand had firm hold of the man's shirtfront. The gun barrel up his nose did not make it easy, but the man was trying to talk. J.B. beat him to it.

"What the holy fuck do you think you're doing to my dog?"

"He tried to bite me."

"Bullshit. She tried to smell you, though why she needed to get so close is beyond my ken."

The cornered man tried a small show of bravado, though Duckworth's gun made it less than convincing.

"Well, then, I just don't want dogs sniffing me."

"Then you shouldn't ever leave the house, you stinky son of a bitch."

"Duckworth!"

The shout came from five store fronts down. J.B. gathered himself and quickly stuck the pistol back into his waistband. Officer Liam Byrne was trotting in his direction.

"Duckworth! Take your hands off that man."

Liam Byrne was six feet tall, but gangly. With his weak chin and eyes that were too close together, he did not offer a first impression built on fear, or even healthy respect. He was Duckworth's least favorite member of the Houston force, and that took some doing.

A criminal defense attorney's relationship with law enforcement was tenuous at every turn. Most on the police force were unconvinced that anyone accused of a crime deserved a vigorous defense. For their part, a common defense attorney tactic was to question the validity of an arrest from the get-go. Duckworth took things a step further than many of his cohorts. He was unafraid of getting personal with police officers on the stand. Byrne had been a target of what he considered blue baiting on several occasions. J.B. often managed to egg the officer into swearing at him from the witness stand. Each time, the defendant on trial had walked free.

Adding to the special animosity between him and Byrne was the fact that the officer had twice hauled Duckworth in for carrying a firearm, an offense in most Texas cities. In one of those cases, Byrne had even pushed a complaint for attempted murder. It had not gotten far, but among J.B. Duckworth's many attributes was a very long memory.

"Plain as day, I saw you assaulting this man."

Byrne was out of breath from his jog down Preston Avenue. Judging by outward appearances, J.B. had collected himself fully.

"This man had assaulted my dog, and I was acting in defense of my property."

As if to recreate the crime, Maizy was sniffing at Officer Byrne's pants.

"Maizy. Come here."

J.B. pointed to the ground at his feet, and the dog complied.

"Defending his dog? The son of a bitch pulled a gun on me."

The one who had set the affray in motion was still visibly shaken, but the mention of a weapon brought a smile to the policeman's face.

"A gun, you say? Well, now, that does put a mark on things. Yes, that raises the ante, indeed."

Byrne's County Wicklow accent, which he generally downplayed, had reemerged in full.

"That's his word against mine, Office Byrne. I say that it was only my finger in his face, and being that you were almost a block away, at the other end of a crowded sidewalk, you certainly were in no position to say."

"That's absurd! The man had a gun."

The aggrieved dog kicker was unprepared for a legal argument to be posed on the street, but Byrne was expecting it.

"Do you wish to file a complaint, sir?"

"You're damned certain, I do."

"And what is your name?"

"Johnson. Marcus."

"That's fine, Mr. Johnson. I'll just ask you and Attorney Duckworth here to accompany me back to the police station."

"Attorney? A lawyer pulled a gun on me?"

"That would seem to be the situation, Mr. Johnson. And to make certain that was the case, I'm going to ask Attorney Duckworth here to submit to a search of his person."

Byrne took a step toward Duckworth, but J.B. held up his hand, palm out.

"I most certainly will not consent to your search of my person," J.B. deliberately raised his voice to a level just shy of shouting. "I most certainly will not."

The one or two onlookers had at least quadrupled in number.

"I suspected as much. In which case I am arresting you for assault, and likely more."

The Irishman's smug look was pushing Duckworth toward the edge.

"You have no grounds to arrest me. You have only this alleged gentleman's accusation. You were too far away to see anything for yourself. For all you know, I was brushing crumbs from his lapel. If you wish to arrest me, you will first produce a warrant."

"Oh, you'll be going with me, Duckworth. Warrant or no."

J.B. dropped his arm and put a plaintive expression on his face.

"Mr. Byrne, are you armed?"

The policeman instinctively felt for his pistol and holster, but they were not there. Though the policy was not universally enforced, it was frequently the case for foot patrolmen to walk the beat without any weapon save their truncheon. To the great chagrin of Officer Liam Byrne, this was one of those times.

"That's what I thought." Duckworth was mostly successful in keeping a straight face. "Now, I am in no way saying that I am carrying a firearm. We both know that would be illegal. But hypothetically, that means for the sake of argument, let's say that I was. Would it be a smart move for an unarmed man to attempt to force a search of an unwilling man with a gun? I suggest that it would not. On top of that, I am accompanied by a vicious dog."

Maizy's tail thumped loudly on the sidewalk at the mention of the word "dog."

Liam Byrne's patience was a short thread long since snapped. He turned on his heel and stomped up the block toward Fannin Street leaving both Duckworth and the open-mouthed Mr. Johnson standing in his wake. J.B. called after him.

"If you want to serve that arrest warrant, Maizy and I will be stopping for a glass at the Crown Bar on Franklin before we catch the car home."

He turned to the man he had been threatening ten minutes earlier.

"Good afternoon to you, Mr. Johnson."

The custom in Texas was for most lawyers to stick together. They often referred clients to one another, so it made perfect sense. Prosecutors and defense men, excepting a handful of real, deep-seated grudges, viewed each other as friendly adversaries. In a few special instances, a good defense lawyer might be hired to supplement the district attorney's team. When the court day was done, it was not at all uncommon for them to clink glasses at one of the city's many saloons. Those outside the profession might even sense a general air of condescension that wafted toward the non-attorney.

Late on a Saturday afternoon, though, when the offices of both the city and county attorneys were locked up tight, the police often saw an opportunity to take a stand and let the vaunted lawyers sort it on Monday.

J.B. was standing at the Crown Bar facing the mirror. He saw Officer Byrne and Officer Lee walk in together. He took the last third of his beer in one gulp then turned to face the two policemen with a smile and with both hands raised to head height. He had wisely handed his pistol to Jimmy Viglini, one of the bar's two owners, as soon as he had arrived.

"Officers. What an unexpected pleasure. Am I to assume that you have procured a warrant for my arrest?"

"You know good and well that ain't happening on a Saturday night," said Officer Henry Lee through gritted teeth.

His colleague Byrne had a smirk nonetheless.

"Chief Blackburn would still like a word." He patted his hip. "And this time we are both of us armed. So, you'll spin around and be patted. For our protection, you understand."

"Certainly."

Duckworth placed his hands on the dark wood. He smiled and gave a tiny shake of the head to the scowling Jimmy Viglini. When the rough frisking was concluded, he pulled a silver dollar from his pants pocket and laid it in front of him, keeping his back to the two coppers.   "That's for the beer, Jimmy, and draw one for yourself. If you could find a lad willing to roust my brother from wherever he's got himself off to, four bits of it is for him. This time of day, I'd have him start with Max Koepnick's place. He lives upstairs. Just tell him where to find me."

Duckworth turned to face Byrne and Lee and extended a hand toward the San Jacinto Street door.

"Shall we?"

"The dog stays here," Lee growled.

"I'll keep a watch on her, J.B.. See you soon." Viglini's dark visage was expression free, as were those of the other twenty men in the Crown.

Belying that a tidal wave of drunks and rowdies would soon be taking every square foot of space, the police station on Caroline Street was relatively calm. A diminutive Black woman was anxiously describing her missing grandson to the disinterested desk sergeant as they passed. Somewhere out of sight, an argument was going on, but whether it was entirely contained within a single person was indeterminate.

"An overachiever, that one," Byrne said to Lee before he steered Duckworth to the left with a hearty nudge. "You know the way."

Chief of Police John Blackburn's office was not grand. File cabinets lined two walls. Stacks of paper towered atop them. On the wall behind his cluttered desk hung a calendar advertising Hill's Cascara Quinine and a portrait of Robert E. Lee. Blackburn motioned Duckworth to one of the visitor chairs. Liam Byrne took the other.

"Officer Byrne is willing to swear an affidavit that he saw you assaulting a gentleman on Preston right in front of the Metropolitan. I was just about to send a man to find Justice Mathews to sign an arrest warrant that would land you a spot with the sheriff until Monday, but I thought I'd talk to you first."

"That is most thoughtful, Marshal."

"My title is Chief of Police, Mr. Duckworth."

"A title you single handedly selected for yourself from what I've heard. Personally, I'm thinking about becoming a maharajah. What are your thoughts on that?" Duckworth held up a finger as he continued. "In any case, though, your officer is mistaken."

Blackburn began to fume, but Byrne could contain himself no longer.

"Bullshit. I saw you roughing the fellow up. Saw it with my own eyes."

Byrne twisted in his seat to face Duckworth as he spoke. The lawyer glibly answered.

"That might have carried some weight if you hadn't left the complainant standing on his own in the middle of the street."

"You sorry son of a bitch."

Chief Blackburn interrupted the building banter, cutting his subordinate short. The chief was pudgy, especially his fleshy face, but there was no mistaking the stoutness that he had acquired from an earlier career as a blacksmith. When he rose halfway from his chair and leaned across the desk toward the lawyer, it was meant to intimidate.

"We feel certain that the complainant will surface. We also have every confidence that we will soon have an arrest warrant, maybe one that takes into account your use of a deadly weapon. So, I have decided that the department can save itself a bit of legwork by holding you in the cells while those events take place."

"Is this what you had in mind by a talk?"

"It sure as hell satisfied me. And while you cool your heels, you can think about your smart mouth and the respect that I am due. Officer, lock this shyster up."

J.B. Duckworth had barely managed to get his body comfortable on the metal shelf, or relatively so, when Herman Youngst poked his grizzled face around the edge of the bars. Youngst was the oldest officer on the Houston force, north of 60, and he walked the daytime beat that included the courthouse and the law offices of Duckworth & Fein across the street. J.B. had staked Officer Youngst to an afternoon beer on many an occasion.

"J.B., your brother is in the marshal's office. Just passing the word."

"Thanks, Herman, but you mean the chief of police, don't you?"

Youngst laughed with an easy croak.

"Only when he's within hearing distance."

John Duckworth was an anomaly, a contradiction. Most men around Houston thought of John as J.B.'s shadow, but he was not a follower. With his limp and quiet demeanor, he was uniformly judged to be the weaker one, but he was in fact a defender. He thought nothing was more important than family, but he was bound by family in the abstract, by the idea of a family that he and his younger brother never had.

After the war had taken their father and a sister and turned their mother into an invalid, the remaining children wasted little time fooling themselves. With no prospects to hold his older sister near, she had married at the first opportunity, whether she thought the man a good fit or not. Their older brother, Monroe, disappeared one night, presumably to join the army in the last gasping days of the war, but who knew. J.B. summed it up thusly to his older brother one night: "Nothing scatters the seeds of family faster than the winds of poverty."

John and J.B., mere children, cared for their mother for the few remaining years of her life. They were street dogs, relying on their wits. As much as J.B. enjoyed inventing and reinventing his fantastical background, there had been no mentors, no shining fortuity. There was only the Duckworth party of two, busking across America and facing all comers.

When John walked into the station to bail his younger brother, he was reprising a well-worn role. It had played out in dozens of city jails. When words or temper failed James, who the world had picked to be the star, there was shy John to supply either muscle or quiet assurance. Facing an entire police department, John hoped today would require only the latter.

"Mr. Duckworth, your brother assaulted a man on the street. Pulled a gun on that man. Carrying firearms is illegal, and this is far from the first time we've caught him at it."

Chief Blackburn was leaned back in his chair. He would have had his feet on the desktop, but his belly made that uncomfortable. John remained standing, hat literally in hand.

"You're right about that last part, Chief. I sure do appreciate that. On the other hand, I just spoke to him, and he denies assaulting anyone or having a pistol. Nobody found a gun on him like they have before. And your man was almost a block away down a busy street. That's not the best of cases, you know."

"My man saw enough. Certainly enough to catch Judge Mathews' fancy."

"Yes, sir. That may be. May very well be. Still, and Lord knows I'm not a lawyer, but I just don't see these charges holding much water in court."

"Courts can be damned, Mr. Duckworth. It may just be that my goal is nothing more than seeing your brother rest his derriere in my cell for a couple of nights."

"Chief, between you and me, he may have that coming. J.B. does have a temper. That's not unlike your officer who hauled him in from what I hear."

For the first time during the conversation, the chief sat up straight before answering.

"My officer is not your concern."

"Well, it's just that as much as J.B. loves talking to reporters, I can just picture what he'd be telling them about the incident. A small misunderstanding blown up into this, and one of the best known lawyers in town thrown in the hoosegow without any evidence whatsoever."

John added a low whistling noise for emphasis before continuing.

"That story would be in the *Post* tomorrow, and that Sunday paper is probably seen by 40,000 pairs of eyes, don't you think?"

Chief Blackburn pursed his lips and looked unseeingly at his desk top. There was a pulsing in his jaws as he ground his back teeth. After a half minute, he spoke. The words were explosive even if the manner behind them lacked conviction.

"Goddamn it, Duckworth. I am sick to death of my department being made the fool."

"If there was to be some sort of fine for disturbing the peace, that would make the police blotter. I might have a word with J.B. suggesting that it was best to let the entire matter drop."

"What kind of fine?"

"Let's see, I have…"

John Duckworth made a small show of fishing in his front pocket for a silver money clip. He removed two worn bank notes bearing James Garfield's engraved image.

"Ten dollars in currency. It's all I have on me. With the banks being closed, it will leave me stone broke till they open Monday, but we could all put this behind us."

The chief shook his head, defeated.

"Goddamn it," he said again. "I'll have the desk write it up. And keep that son of a bitch out of trouble for the rest of the night."

"Oh, I will."

"And you be sure your brother understands that if the other guy presses an assault charge, there's not a damn thing I can do about it. He still keeps his mouth shut."

Blackburn stood up in a half-hearted attempt to retain his air of menace.

"Now get him out of my building."

The two brothers walked north on Caroline Street. It was mostly residential for the two blocks until they reached Congress Avenue, and James spent much of it laughing and thanking John for a job well done.

"Not that I doubted you, brother."

"I just wish you could have seen him gulp when I mentioned the newspaper."

They laughed yet again. At the intersection, James motioned toward the bar that occupied a downstairs corner of the Eagle Hotel. It was an unremarkable two-story wooden building owned by Max and Lena Koepnik. The bar was his domain, and she oversaw the rooms. Number three was where John Duckworth lodged. Though his little brother could be profligate at times, John enjoyed hanging on to his dimes. He had gotten the ten dollars back within the first block. Between the coins in his other front pocket and a few notes in a wallet, John had three times that left on him after paying the fine, but he would never let J.B. get the better of him financially.

"Do you have time to buy me a short one before you catch a car home?"

"Only one, though you'll have more coming. I'll be obliged to buy two more drinks at the Crown when I stop to pick up Maizy. Plus, they'll all be itching to hear the story. And somewhere along the line, I'll need to concoct a sanitized version to get me out of Dutch with Lola."

The Duckworth brothers were still laughing as they stepped up to the bar.

Chapter 5

Sartartia, Texas

September 1901

"Don't speak ill of the dead, William."

Mamie chided her older brother. She and her husband, Marshall Lyons, had come from San Antonio to stay with family for a few days. She had been looking forward to it for weeks, and thought Marshall had, too. In her book, he and her older brother were thick as thieves.

These dances were about the biggest gaiety to be found in Sartartia, but the shock of national events was what had tongues wagging on this Saturday night. President William McKinley had died that morning, eight days after being shot by an assassin at the Pan-American Exposition in Buffalo, New York. The news of his death spread like wildfire down the nation's telegraph wires, even causing a furor in a Texas backwater like the Ennis family's town. The outlier, who brushed off the bulletin as if it was nothing more than a mule stuck in mud, was their patriarch, Will.

"No need to be a hypocrite. I was a Bryan man in '96 and a Bryan man last fall. He was our president, but that didn't mean I had to like him. Why should I shed false tears?"

"McKinley won this very county," Marshall Lyons playfully reminded him. "I thought you would want to respect your neighbors, Will."

"He won courtesy of my colored neighbors. Don't know what's good for them." Will Ennis offered a sly smile. "And no, him carrying this county does not alter my opinion of that Yankee bastard."

The doctor laughed.

"Will, that is downright un-Christian," Mamie said with limited conviction.

The oldest Ennis leaned close to his brother-in-law and affected a conspiratorial whisper.

"I've always felt that the money lenders in the temple were highly underrated."

The two men laughed heartily.

"I thought he was improving," Mamie said. Her husband, a physician, followed her conversational lead in changing the subject.

"He may have been for a while, but they never found the bullet. It cut right through his middle, ripping through God knows what vital organs, and apparently hid. Or not so apparently. According to the reports in the *Express*, the doctors sewed things up the best they could, but unless a person is extremely lucky, a dirty little bullet left alone in the abdomen will fester into gangrene. And there's no cure for that. You can't amputate a man's belly."

Mamie sighed.

"It is a sad occasion for everyone. He was still a man. Think of his poor, afflicted wife."

The three of them contemplated that for a moment. Marshall took a few steps to his right and snagged two fresh cups of Fish Club Punch for him and Will. Mamie was not drinking the rum and brandy concoction as fast as the men.

"So, Will," Marshall asked. "What do you expect now that we have a young war hero as president?"

Mamie was not ready to give up the banter with her brother. Perhaps she had consumed more punch than everyone realized.

"Mr. McKinley was also a war hero."

She tried to summon some small indignity. Her brother was not having it.

"The man was promoted for driving a wagon full of food."

"It was in the midst of the deadliest battle of the war."

"I would counter, dear sister, that our good Southern boys did not require a snack in the first place."

"It is generally remembered that our good Southern boys lost at Sharpsburg. Perhaps they should have eaten."

Mamie smiled at her small victory.

The three were not particularly interested in talking to anyone else, but since the dance was being held in a building and town that they owned, there was a certain level of obligation. Some sixty people, roughly the usual turnout, were enjoying themselves. Will tried to keep the interactions short as he made his way clockwise around the big room.

The hall was neat and unadorned. The beadboard on the walls was painted bright white, and the pressed tin ceiling, installed 15 years earlier, still looked respectable. Windows were propped open, and there was what an optimist might call a light breeze. The front five feet of the room were raised to serve as a stage for Saturday dances or Sunday preaching. A long table in the back, covered with a passably clean linen cloth, held the drinks and refreshments. The Ennis family supplied a big bowl of spiked punch or a keg of beer for every dance. There was always a platter of barbecued meat. Though a few of the local men freely shared from a jug of their homemade shine, the dances were largely reputable affairs.

Being Saturday night, almost everyone in attendance had bathed and put on clean clothes. At least a clean shirt. Their jackets and street pants were brushed and aired. Most men and all the ladies had availed themselves of a splash or three of what was commonly known as dime store toilet water. It was not perfect, but eight o'clock on a Saturday night was as close to smelling good as South Texas ever came. Local decorum dictated that no man dared shuck his jacket until about ten. Even then, those were mostly the daring youngsters.

Five of the local men made up the band. Ennis paid them a dollar each, usually twice a month, sometimes more often, to come play reels, waltzes and popular tunes. The Sartartia dances drew people from neighboring farms and even from the few nearby hamlets that dared to call themselves towns. Everyone knew everyone else. They might not always like each other, but trouble was not tolerated.

Tim Guillory, the curly-haired Cajun who ran Sartartia's general store, waved Will over. He tended to try too hard to curry favor with the Ennis men, and though he was pleasant enough, he was not a man Will would seek out for socializing. Guillory was a burly fellow, a man's man who was said to be bedding more than one of the sharecroppers' wives. The trysts probably took place in this very building, Will thought fleetingly.

"Good week just past."

Ennis smiled blankly. He was unsure what that weak attempt at a conversation starter was supposed to mean. He did not believe that he deliberately set out to be intimidating to those beneath him, but he never minded having that effect.

"You mean sales at the store?"

"Yep. Money from the early bales. We had almost a dozen farmers pay down on their tabs. A few others are banking on the good crop and put the odd pair of boots or a half bolt of cloth down on credit."

"I assume they're still eating, too."

Guillory laughed at the boss's joke.

"Yes, sir. That they are. We are still selling beans and flour."

"That's good news."

Will made to move along, but Guillory was just getting to the gossip.

"That Daugherty woman came in Wednesday last. My, she is a corker."

"I can't say that I've noticed her. This is their first year on the place. I do recall that her husband struck me as rather non-descript."

"If you'd seen her, you'd remember. Worth you riding over toward Field's Gin. Sure as shooting."

The two men watched the dancers for a few minutes. Guillory was sure that Will Ennis was being an uppity liar about never noticing the Daugherty woman.

That any man could miss her was more than he could fathom. For his part, Will was thinking that he had no intention of going any further into this topic. He had no objections to base speculation, but was damned if he would engage with the likes of Tim Guillory. He concluded that more mingling was in order.

"Nice visiting with you, Guillory. I'll be around Monday."

The two men nodded at each other, but Ennis turned back for a final thought.

"By the way, Guillory, when you get a chance, make sure that George Purdy's expenses are all in order. Totaled up. If he comes in, next few days, you might steer him away from any big purchases."

Ennis slapped Guillory on the bicep and continued on his turn around the hall.

Tom and Letha Ward stood dutifully at the refreshment table quietly observing the merriment. Though the African population of Fort Bend County outnumbered Whites by a large margin, theirs were the only Black faces in the large upstairs room. Their usual work revolved around the big white house and its outbuildings, but on Saturday dance night, they became servers and cleaners for the area public. Letha had baked some sweets, as she always did, and the smoke roasted pig was Tom's work.

He was an expert at barbecue. He maintained a permanent trench underneath a two-sided shed that sat to the east of the stables, and it was the one place where Tom Ward was truly and solely in charge. He could split a hog's backbone or butcher a cow or goat well enough. He could coax the coals to the perfect temperature for even, slow cooking, but the magic lay in his sauce. When asked, Tom proudly stated that it was a family secret brought from Africa, though exactly which people had brought it, he could not say. An astute diner could easily discern butter, vinegar, salt and pepper, but Tom combined those with a paste of herbs and roots that he grew next to their house. It was the best meat in East Fort Bend County. Tom had stashed several slices in a towel and put them in the dance hall storage closet for himself and Letha. It would not be accepted for them to eat off the big platter.

The Wards were both in their early forties. Though they were the children of enslaved parents, they had no vivid memories of the institution themselves. They had worked for the Ennis family for right at two decades, and their place in society had changed dramatically in that time. The push for rights and equality had never been accepted in the South, but it had often been tolerated. A deadly gun battle between political factions on the streets of the county seat had brought an abrupt end to those dreams in Fort Bend. In the aftermath, Black elected officials were told to resign and leave or face a violent end. The Wards knew full well that the dancers and drinkers they waited on judged them to be either invisible or downright problematic. Their lot in life was stoic service, though they both felt that the bulk of their personal dignity remained intact. The Ennises, at least, supplied them with a house, food and a tolerable wage.

People at the dance were lively. Having a topic of conversation beyond the weather and local gossip had sparked a bit of electric buzz around the room. Up north tonight, such occasions would be subdued or even bereft, but the news brought less of a dampening effect in Texas. Will reserved his true political opinions for his family and offered ambiguous commiseration to his neighbors and employees when they inevitably brought up McKinley's death. The one or two men whom he genuinely liked were busily engaged in other conversations as he made his rounds. They would be privately joking over drinks soon enough. There was no need to interrupt now. Soon he had completed what he viewed as his obligatory circuit and was back to his comfortable corner.

Cass Ennis was much less aloof. Perhaps it was his youth. He sought out several of the male guests to give the glad hand. They swapped their dirty jokes and laughed a bit too loud. The men's wives did admirably at pretending not to overhear. It took well over an hour, but he gravitated back to his family.

Caswell was several cups of punch further along when he ambled into the conversation group that included Will, Mamie and Marshall. Requisite mingling accomplished for the moment, the elder Ennis children were circled in the back corner of the hall. Cass clinked his little glass against his brother-in-law's.

"Don't tell me. Will is still denigrating our president even in the face of national tragedy."

"As a matter of fact, I was just reiterating to Mamie and Marshall that y'all can save your attempts at reason. My opinion of the man will not be changed," Will responded.

Caswell's initial mocking tone turned ever slightly less jocular. These political talks between the brothers always started civilly, but had been known to get louder when mixed with whiskey, or in this case, rum, brandy and lemon. Propriety was almost always maintained when others were around, even those as familiar as Mamie and Marshall.

"Will, we can't just have our elected leaders shot willy-nilly, whether you agree with them or not."

Those who knew him best could look at Will's gray eyes and the enlarged pupils and know that pontification was imminent. The adult members of the Ennis family might say it was the way in which he was most like their father. Will did not disappoint.

"Do you know what I like best about William Jennings Bryan? It's not that vaunted silver policy of his. Not his saving America from crucifixion on the cross of gold. Not even that famously defiant chin. I like his youthful energy. He cares about the farmers. The little man. That is the primary difference between Republicans and Democrats. Democrats appreciate the plight of the masses."

Caswell Ennis responded with a snort that sent a tiny dribble of punch onto his chin.

"Hogwash. And from a man who once managed a bank, prattling on about the plight of the masses like some anarchist."

Will grinned as he responded.

"You can tell Cass is only a half-sibling. Amanda must have been a meaner mother."

"Sod you!"

Mamie slapped her brother's arm again, but Will already had his other big arm hugging Caswell's neck.

"I'm joshing you, little brother. You know I valued sweet Amanda."

Cass, though a full grown 24 years old, pushed and squirmed from his brother's clinch. At six feet, the elder brother was four inches taller and had been the stronger of the two their entire lives. Will released Cass with a final, playful shove but kept talking.

"Yes, banks are important. We owe them, har har." With no smiles acknowledging his weak pun, he continued. "I'm talking about those northern industrialists, which you know good and well. The Morgans and Schiffs of the world. Even people as wildly influential as the Ennis clan must pay our tribute to the Robber Barons. And they had McKinley secured in their very full pockets."

"Hell, Will, you'd jump at the chance to be a Robber Baron. I think you were born for it. You just don't like Yankees," Cass answered.

"You're not quite old enough to remember dad dressed in his old uniform, going to those veteran's meetings. He put a lot of stock in those times, and I am not going to sell those memories of his short. Maybe he didn't blow his own trumpet to the world, but his time in the army should mean something beyond that they just lost. How can you deny that?"

Cass clinched his lips and shook his head with mock sadness as he addressed his brother-in-law.

"Marshall, consider yourself fortunate to live far away from Sartartia. I must endure this claptrap every night."

Will let out a chuckle.

"At least we have good drinks while we argue," he said.

He patted his younger half-brother on the back then fondly roughed his oiled hair. Cass ducked away and smoothed it back with annoyance.

Chapter 6

George Purdy was not sure what his body had left to sweat out. He needed to take a break and drink some water, but he wanted to finish all the work in the garden before he lost daylight. The morning had been spent weeding through the cotton, the last time he would need to do that task before picking the last of it, a task which would soon be upon him. Chopping cotton at this point in the season was not the delicate work that it was in the late spring. Still, a body did not want pigweed or some wild grass stealing moisture and nutrients. That chopping extended well past the dinner hour. The late afternoon was devoted to the garden plot.

He was working alone today. The little school had started up at Sugar Land, and he wanted to make sure that Sarah and Arthur got some days in at the outset. Come picking time, he, like almost every other parent in the county, held them out for a couple of weeks so that they could help with the work. It was the one time during the year that George felt a twinge of envy toward those big families with six or more children. He would never want to feed them the other eleven months, but at harvest time, they were a God-sent work force.

His children had done their best during the 22 days that he was gone, but the skies had blessed them with rain only once. It was not the little ones' fault, but he did not find the garden rows in the same promising shape as he left them. As arranged, the Mabins picked what was ripe, but the output had slowed considerably during his absence. The drought-withered parts of plants had sapped strength from the good parts, but there was nobody there to cut them away. That two acres provided a goodly portion of the food on the table. Now he was babying the vegetables along as best he could.

George had hauled buckets of water for the remaining plants, and he optimistically thought that he had managed to save more than half of them. The heat had gotten the best of his tomatoes weeks ago, but a scattered handful of plants were still throwing fruit. Some years it rained so much that farmers cried over their fruit that split, but that was not the case after a dry July. There was still some life in the green and yellow squash. His pickling cucumbers were no bigger than his thumb, and he suspected that the last of the sweet potatoes would be scrawny, as well. The black eyed peas and pole beans were still doing all right, and from his experience, okra was damn near impossible to kill until the first frost. Luckily, he had planted enough of those to get him by until the winter seeds he had recently put in the ground had started to rise and produce.

The hard work and unforgiving sun felt good on his muscles. The feel of the hoe handle against stiffening hands, the ache in his shoulders. He did not mind it one bit. Farming brought a different soreness than carpentry work, an all over reminder that it took hard labor to coax a healthy plant from the soil. He had not felt the sense of ownership when he was working the family farm as a child, but he did now. Eating what your own hands grew was the same as the first night's sleep in a bed you made. Purdy had just about decided that it suited him.

Part of his joy came from shedding that sorrow that enveloped him in Montague County. He had figured the days for the trip just about right. He paced his gray horse well, and the countryside had been good to them. The ponds and creeks had plenty of water and the grass was green and lush. Not a single farmer along the way offered any objection to him throwing out a hobble and a bedroll on the edge of a pasture.

Purdy had chosen a route that roughly paralleled the Texas Central tracks, trying to maintain a distance of about two miles to the west. From Waco, he picked his way around to the far side of Fort Worth. The contents of his pocket book did not allow for those big town prices. His assumption that country folks were more apt than city dwellers to let him sleep on their property free of charge had been proven out. One man, a total stranger near the outskirts of Meridian, not only offered to accommodate him, but offered him part of his evening meal.

George, who had been subsisting mostly on day old bread he bought along the way and a bag of salt beef that he brought from Sartartia, happily accepted the generous offer. The man, a tall and wiry fellow with an unruly shock of gray hair, was a widower just like Purdy. He made a decent pot of chicken stew, though Purdy found himself hunting and pecking for the strands of meat like the hen herself looking for barnyard bugs. Still, he was very grateful. The two men talked well into the dark hours. That night George slept in the old man's barn, and the gray horse was treated to sweet hay. Purdy figured that it was loneliness that made the man insist on offering the same hospitality on the return journey, and George gave his word to stop again in two weeks.

It was a promise he regretted breaking, but the road home was much more gloomy. His mother was already gone by the time he reached Montague. In fact, she had died before George ever even got the letter telling of her decline. It was a small consolation to know that even had he borrowed money for a train ticket, he would not have reached her bedside in time to say goodbye. All he could do was hold his regrets and hope that she did not think too harshly of him in her last earthly thoughts.

His mother's body was of course in the ground when he arrived at her cousin's farm. They had found a spot near the back of the Methodist churchyard, an acre that was quickly reaching the tree line. He was not much for praying, but he squatted down beside the fresh mound of earth for what may have been a half hour and let his mind roam through his childhood. He discovered that he possessed relatively few memories to unpack. He kept returning to dewberry pie fresh from the wood stove and cooling on the farm table. His mother did make a good pie. When George stood up, his knee and ankle joints complained. He blamed it on seven full days in the saddle.

She had been sick so long, and she didn't own much to begin with. Her distant cousins, two spinsters named Addie and Dorothy said that they had been taking care of his mother for more than nineteen months. Her rare letters put the time at closer to a year, but he had no way of knowing for certain. The crux of it was that the two old maids figured that they were due for what she had left behind, and George guessed they likely were. He knew that he had neglected to do his part.

The estate amounted to a few changes of clothes, a brass bedstead, two small paintings, some sundries and a sterling silver bowl. He took her wedding band, bought when things had been good. It was simple and unembellished, but George figured the ring could be passed on to Sarah or to Arthur for his future girl. It was not sentimentality, just that family legacy should count for something.

He visited what few kin he had left around there, suspecting at each stop that it would be his last time to ever see them. He had little to do, but did not wish to seem disrespectful of his mother's memory. In all, he lingered around Montague for five nights, accepted some fruit, cheese and a tin of saltine crackers from Addie and Dorothy, and rode out just after breakfast on a Sunday.

In solitude on the trek south, he realized that he was depressed in spirit. A full life lived by his mother, and father, come to that, and what was left to show for it? No material belongings save a few trinkets. Four children scattered across the country, and only one of them who summoned the gumption to bid her farewell. Grandkids that she had never even met, his youngest included. The melancholia soon got in his bones like a winter damp.

He even got down thinking of the poor old farmer near Meridian who was probably sitting on his porch looking forward to a return visit from his new friend, but the prospect of that much conversation was more than George could stomach. He gave the town a wide berth. Better to be a mystery than for the old man to know he was deliberately avoided. The blues had stuck to him long after he got home, but he was determined to work his way out of them.

Purdy was sitting alone on the front porch one night, about eight weeks after coming back from North Texas, when he heard the crunch of someone approaching on the hard dirt track. Charlie Mabin quietly hallooed the house. It was the smart thing to do in the blackness of night.

"Come on up, Charlie. Sit a while. The young ones are asleep. Or they're supposed to be."

George spoke softly. The door and windows were open on the hot night.

"Evening, George. Sorry to disturb you."

Mabin eased himself into an empty rocker. It was a sturdy, well-fitting chair that was no doubt built by Purdy.

"George, I won't stay long, but I heard something at the store this afternoon that troubled me, and it's been festering. I reckoned that I needed to come and talk to you, and Folly finally shooed me on my way."

"Well, what can I do to help?"

"No. It ain't like that. It's that I heard Ed Bertrand talking about all the work he has facing him this week, and one of the things he listed was bringing a gang over here to pick your corn. I know you and I had planned to swap hands for that picking. I couldn't see any reason that you'd have asked Ed Bertrand for extra hands knowing that it would eat up your share."

George did not immediately know what to make of the news. He cocked his head a bit like a hound.

"Hell, no, I didn't ask for any picking gang. My profit margin is already thinner than the seat of my skivvies. And that goes double after my ride up to Montague."

"That's what I figured."

The possibilities percolated for a few minutes before Purdy spoke again.

"I can't find any good angle on this.

"No, sir."

"I really appreciate you coming to me Charlie. I'll go talk to Bertrand first thing and find out what it's all about."

"Whatever is brewing, I doubt it's Ed's doing. Will Ennis can be a snaky son of a gun."

"I suspect you're right."

The next morning, the three Purdys ate eggs for breakfast. Sarah had been trying for months to make biscuits, but they still felt more related to hard tack. Or lumber. Everyone ate them, keeping any complaints locked away. The two children then set off through the fields, picking their way over the crop rows toward school. As soon as they were gone, George saddled the gray horse and rode toward the plantation office.

George was still 300 yards west of the Sartartia Store when he spotted Ed Bertrand, the plantation foreman, driving an empty wagon north toward Convict Camp #1. Though Will Ennis had moved decidedly away from relying on leased prisoners, there were any number of tasks around Sartartia that still employed them. Through a combination of design and unfilled tenant properties, some of the cotton and corn crops still belonged entirely to the Ennis family. All of that acreage was tended by convicts.

The biggest amount of work for convicts lay in the sugar operations. The family had two of their three sugar mills still going, and the unskilled labor at those plants were Black convicts. Though some of the raw sugar was now imported from Cuba and elsewhere, several hundred acres of Sartartia plantation were still planted in cane. Working those fields was labor intensive, thus more convicts.

Purdy urged the gray into a trot and managed to close on Bertrand well before he reached the camp. Bertrand pulled his wagon to a stop.

"Morning, Mr. Bertrand."

"Purdy."

Ed Bertrand was an average-sized man with an earnest face. He had run the operations at Sartartia for several years, and had established a reputation for honest dealings. Many people in the area believed that his first duty was to round the sharp edges off some of the Ennis family directives. Looking at George Purdy this morning, his expression was impassive.

"I won't keep you, but I'm a tad anxious about something that Charlie Mabin told me yesterday evening. He said that he overheard talk that you had plans to come pull my corn crop."

Bertrand's eyebrows moved up his already high forehead, and he scratched at his left sideburn.

"Well, yes, I was told to schedule just such a thing. I have it written down to get started this Friday morning."

"I didn't ask for any such help. Charlie and I, and maybe Ken Harvey, are gonna work each other's corn. Cotton, too."

"George, you know I just do as I'm told."

"So, this is Will Ennis' idea? What the Sam Hill is he up to?"

Bertrand cast his eyes downward for a bit. Whatever itch he had moved a bit farther up his scalp.

"George, you know I try to be a straight shooter, but I just don't feel like that is my question to answer. Mr. Ennis ought to be in the yard office this afternoon."

"I'm here now, Ed. I got work to do this afternoon, and it takes me a good half hour each way to get here. I'm of a mind to just ride over and talk to him at his house."

"I can't recommend that. Can't even guarantee that he's there. I ain't seen him this morning."

"I will keep you out of it as best I can."

George Purdy wheeled the gray horse to his left. The big white house was about half a mile distant, just across the railroad tracks.

Ed Bertrand's instinct had proven correct. Ennis was not at all happy to see his uninvited visitor. George had tried to lessen the affront by coming around to what he believed was the kitchen door that sat to the left side of the back porch. At this time of the morning, it was completely in shadow. A plump Black woman had answered, listened and then closed the door to leave him alone outside. It took well more than ten minutes before Will Ennis opened it again, still pulling on his coat. He met Purdy's eyes for a moment then stepped outside and closed the door behind him.

"Yes? Why are at my door, Mr. Purdy?"

"I was told that you have a convict gang lined up to pull my corn starting this Friday."

"I don't recollect the particulars, but the basic answer is yes."

"But I didn't ask for any help with my crop, and I don't have the money to pay for it. I've got it all arranged."

"Per our agreement, our signed agreement, it is no longer your crop. You have forfeited it. It is now mine."

George's jaw dropped a little, leaving him with an open-mouthed expression that was much less than flattering. It took a few loud beats of his heart to recover the power of speech.

"What the hell are you talking about? I planted 40 acres of that corn, raised it, tended to it, and I surely intend to pick it. Half the money from that crop belongs to me."

"And I furnished the land, the tools, the seeds, two mules, a plow, and a place for your family to live for the year. The difference is that I honored my side of the bargain."

"That makes no sense! I kept my side! That corn is thriving. It'll be as good a yield as you're likely to find on this whole plantation."

Will Ennis shifted his weight to his left side and put both fists on his hips.

"It is in your contract, Mr. Purdy that you must tend to your allotted acreage throughout the entire growing season. I discovered that you left for a significant amount of time."

"So, you think you can just take my corn?"

"Your corn and your cotton, too. Both are now mine. It's in our deal."

"The hell you say. That is my income for the year, and I've put in all the work."

"Clearly not all of the work, since you left and violated our terms."

"You didn't even bring that contract around until my crops was sprouting from the ground. How is that even legal?"

"It's legal. You signed it. Maybe you should've read it."

"You didn't give me any choice. You told me at the time that it was a formality, and was required if I wanted to stay. Like I said – no choice."

George was trying his level best to maintain control of his voice and his fists, but as aggrieved as he now was, he was not finding it easy. Ennis' smugness was striking him like an open palm to the face.

"People sign contracts for a reason, Mr. Purdy. I've been doing this for a long time. Contracts are necessary to avoid misunderstandings. I don't see how there can be any confusion here. The terms of the agreement are clear. I can't be expected to honor it when you leave for two months."

"I was gone for 22 days. My mother died, Goddamn you. You've been through the same thing from what I hear."

Ennis now raised his voice to just short of shouting, and for the first time, Purdy noticed another figure standing inside behind the lacy curtains. This was not the time to make a stand.

"I have nothing more to explain to you, Purdy. I have your signature, and you have my decision. Now you get the fuck off my porch!"

With that, Will Ennis turned on his heel, entered the house and slammed the door hard enough to rattle glass. George heard low voices on the other side.

He stood there for no more than half a minute before deciding there was nothing to gain here. Purdy descended the steps, untied the reins, and mounted the gray horse. He had no choice but to ride back home.

Chapter 7

Ed Bertrand's wife nudged him lightly in the ribs, trying to make it seem accidental. First, he kept her awake with his tossing and flipping, and now that he had finally fallen asleep, he had done so on his back. He always snored on his back. She pulled the feather pillow tight against her left ear, but holding it there was uncomfortable. If she let it go, it made little difference in stopping the horrible noise. She swore that with every bearish intake of breath, she could hear her china jumping on the shelf. She nudged him again.

"What?"

"You're snoring."

There was enough moonlight that Bertrand could see his wife leaning up on one elbow. Their words came in whispers even though they were alone in the foreman's house.

"Sorry. I just now fell off to sleep. A lot on my mind."

She rubbed her hand lightly back and forth on his bare shoulder. His heavy, gritty eyes closed again, hoping that their brief conversation was over.

"Will Ennis?"

Bertrand sighed loudly.

"He's taking George Purdy's corn crop in the morning on account of Purdy leaving to bury his mother."

"That's horrible. Why would he ever do such a thing?"

"Because he can, I reckon."

"Well, just the same. That is evil."

"We can talk through it in the morning. I want to try to go back to sleep. So quit elbowing me."

He leaned over and kissed the top of her head then rolled onto his side with his back toward the middle of the bed.

A mile and half to the west in the wee hours of that Friday morning, George Purdy was not sleeping either. Ed Bertrand had told him that Friday was the day. Since Will Ennis had ordered George off his back porch, he had heard nothing more. He had spent the last two days going about his business as usual. Though he held out no such hope, he kept dreaming that someone would come to their senses and just leave things as they were.

George had been working as hard as always. Wednesday, after he got home from Ennis' place, he pulled a good acre of corn and stowed it in the little crib he had built in his backyard for chicken feed. Yesterday, he and Charlie helped Ken Harvey pick close to four acres. They filled three wagons and hauled them into Sartartia at dusk. He certainly should be plenty tired enough to sleep.

Over a year prior, Sarah had tamed one of the mousers that patrolled the place. Around the start of spring, she had gotten in the habit of sneaking the thing into her bed at night. George had fought against the notion nightly for maybe three weeks, using fleas as the reason. Sarah countered by rising earlier to sweep the house first thing of a morning then sprinkle alum around her bed. Once the cat got comfortable in the house, it had developed a routine of bed hopping. That was why George grudgingly petted a purring tabby as he stared toward the ceiling.

He must have dozed some, but he would not swear by it. He tried counting, concentrating on each breath, repeating the word sleep in his head. He had cursed the gods before he finally gave up and moved silently to the porch rocker. The first cool front of the year had blown through the previous day, and the temperature was enough to make him wish he had a blanket.

When the first hint of dawn appeared in the sky, George grabbed his fishing rig from the shed. It was a twelve foot bamboo cane pole that he bought years ago at a second hand shop in Houston. He inspected the line, hook and cork and looked inside his canvas fishing bag for spares. The bag also held a stringer, a small spade and a fine gauge net. He briefly considered leaving a note for his sleeping children, but figured that they knew where he was most likely to be. With the bag slung over his shoulder, George began walking southwest, cutting through fields toward the river. He kept his eyes on the ground, watching for snakes.

A mix of trees lined the banks of the Brazos River – various oaks, cottonwoods, pecans, and some woody trash that grew almost as tall. Many of the branches still held residue, boards or dead limbs left from the great flood on the river. Even that detritus did not deter from the peaceful beauty. A few native persimmons sprouted here and there, the fruit edible after the first frost. It was underneath one of those that George used the little spade to dig for earthworms. He soon found a trove, and scrambling ten feet down the embankment got himself a prime spot to fish.

Fishing was the one gift George could trace to his mother's father. He pictured the old man as ancient, but that probably meant about 60. His grandfather was a Mexican War veteran from Kentucky who had left for cheap land in Texas. From what George could piece together, the old fellow brought with him three skills – making moonshine, drinking moonshine and fishing. Some of his earliest memories were baiting hooks with that old toothless man.

Purdy slung his hook and worm sidearm into a deep pool that had been good to him many times before. Within ten minutes, he yanked out two small catfish and then a crappie about the size of his hand. He threw them all back. That many small bones were not worth dealing with unless you had to. After a walk back to get another handful of worms, he landed a good medium-sized blue cat. He debated for a minute before removing the hook and slipping that one back into the river. If he could get one over two feet long, it would be enough for supper.

George loved the peace and solitude of the river. Without the potential catastrophe looming, he would linger, but as morning presented itself in full, he knew it was time to get back. The big fish was not going to show today. Two more little crappie got tossed back before he brought in a channel cat in the 18 inch range. He slipped it onto his stringer and lowered him back into the water. The next fish that bit was the same blue catfish he had turned loose 15 minutes earlier.

"Just not your day, little fellow."

George slipped the other one off the stringer and killed and gutted them both on the bank. It would be food for possums or raccoons directly. He would rather leave the innards here than outside his house. He pulled a towel from his fishing bag, saturated it with river water and used it to wrap his two cleaned catfish. His short reverie at the riverbank ended, George headed back home expecting trouble any minute.

Things were still quiet at mid-morning. His kids had gone to school, and he was glad of that. Whatever may come, and George had no idea what that might be, was better without his children watching.

He took a dollop of bacon grease from the old crock that sat on his counter and pan fried the fish in his well-traveled black iron skillet. Through all the moves from one short-lived carpenter job to the next, that skillet had come along. He bought it new as a Christmas present for his wife in their first year of marriage. Some day he might sit and try to figure the number of meals that had been prepared in that trusty thing.

George tidied up a bit. He was still deciding where he wanted to work today. His main worry was getting too far from his corn field. He could fill his lone wagon, but if the clerks at Sartartia had been told not to credit him for his crop, that seemed pointless. It might just provoke confrontation. He needed to think this through.

He stooped and picked up Arthur's brown pull horse. The poor thing had seen better days. Whoever owned it before his boy had taken a toll, and Arthur followed suit. The wood skeleton was sturdy, but the cloth body was getting threadbare. Both push pin eyes remained, but part of the saddle was missing. It still had most of its worn yarn mane, but the matching tail was long since gone. So was one of the little iron wheels on the platform. George laughed ruefully and spoke out loud.

"That's just how I feel today, horsey. Missing a wheel and tail. You work for the better part of a year, then they want to come take your whole livelihood."

It was not yet ten in the morning, and he had already been holding conversations with a catfish and a stuffed horse.

George was tired from no sleep. If he could just shut his eyes for ten or fifteen minutes, he would be set to go work. He woke with a start an hour or more later still sitting on his bed with his back against the wall.

The morning was quiet. A few distant voices or dog barks floated on the wind. He grabbed the top of the door frame and stretched his back. It had been a completely wasted day aside from the fish for supper. He had to salvage something. He stepped outside and breathed in the unseasonable air.

George walked around to the back of his house and headed east down the track that bisected his big corn field. He wanted to be certain there was no activity. He had gone about 300 yards when could make out the front edge of a wagon and a single mule. The rear of it was backed into his corn. He kept walking at a steady pace. As he got closer, he saw a second wagon, empty and parallel to the corn to the north of the wide path.

Two voices were laughing and joking. When George reached the wagon, he could see that it was two convicts. They were standing in the back of the wagon pulling corn from both sides and tossing the cobs into the bed. From the ground, it looked to George if it was already two thirds full.

He recognized one of the Black men. He was a short, dark skinned man, perhaps still in his teens, who had been sent out as his carpenter's helper a time or two. He remembered the fellow's unusual name – Thirsty. The bare facts unknown to George was that Thirsty Davis had been picked up for beating a white railroad brakeman outside a Houston bar. The fact that the trainman had thrown the first punch did nothing to sway the judge from awarding Davis four years in the state prisons.

The other man, who George could not recall seeing before, was older. About the same height, but stocky. His hair was starting to recede. The man's name was Moss Gordon, and he was in the system for the third time for vagrancy. He had been picked up for sleeping behind a feed store in Marlin, one of the towns that Purdy had skirted on his ride to Montague County and back.

The workers both looked over at George when he stepped into view next to the mule. Thirsty Davis smiled and nodded at him.

"Boss."

The two then resumed their picking and talking.

To his right, George heard hooves on the dirt and turned to see Ed Bertrand riding toward him at a trot. It was hard to read his expression, but when he pulled to a stop, George thought he could see a touch of shame.

"I'm sorry, Purdy. You know this is nothing I wanted to see."

At the approach of the plantation foreman, the two convicts had ceased their joking. George looked at Bertrand without speaking.

"I argued for you as best I could, but that rarely does much good with Mr. Ennis."

Bertrand wore brown trousers and a gray long sleeved cotton shirt that looked fairly clean. His hat, a nice wide brimmed Stetson, was heavily sweat-stained. He sat easy on his big chestnut, a fine looking horse with a blaze of white. A Colt pistol that he carried in the field, a defense for snakes, was holstered on his right hip. He looked back at Purdy, standing in front of him, and shook his head once.

"I'm sorry."

George broke his stare away from Bertrand and looked hard at the ground in front of his own boots. After a time, he raised his eyes back to the foreman and gave a him a few slight nods. Then he turned and headed back in the direction of home having never spoken a word.

Purdy stepped back into his house and pulled his rifle out from under his bed. They had a wagon almost loaded. They truly meant to do it. They intended to steal all the product of his labor. When he awoke this morning, he was still unsure of the course that things would take. Seeing the thieves in action had given him some clarity.

He stayed to the left side of the dirt track as he walked forward, hugging the edge of his tall corn and trying to tread softly. The wind was blowing from his back, so he was certain that sound of his footfalls was carrying, but the rhythm of the work held its pace. If Ed Bertrand interpreted his retreat as surrender, he would get a surprise. When he was about 50 yards shy of the convicts, he cut across the opening provided by the wagon track in order to get a better angle.

Almost exactly at the moment that George stepped across to the other side of the thin road, two things happened. Moss Gordon began to ease the wagon, now completely full, out from amongst the stalks, and a bit to his left, farther away from the advancing Purdy, Ed Bertrand's horse, with its rider still in the saddle, stepped from a row into the clear.

Purdy never broke stride. As the others watched him, he stepped back into the head of a row of corn stalks square in front of the wagon driver and lifted his Winchester from beside his right leg. Bertrand and Gordon both stopped where they were. Thirsty Davis' banter tapered off when he realized the other men were quiet. He pivoted on the edge of the wagon and raised his hands even though the gun was clearly pointed at Gordon.

George Purdy's rifle stayed steady. From about 30 paces, it was aimed straight at the man's chest. His gaze was intent on the wagon driver, never varying even as he spoke to someone else.

"I don't want to do it, Mr. Bertrand, but I'll shoot him dead if he moves that mule."

No one even twitched for what seemed an eternity. Moss Gordon's eyes were wide, and it felt like his very breath had stopped. Even with the temperature no more than 70 degrees, a large trickle of sweat fell from the end of the driver's nose.

Ed Bertrand's left hand had loose hold of his reins. He finally lowered his right, slowly, to rest easy atop his lap.

"Moss, I suppose it's a good time to go get dinner."

Chapter 8

Will Ennis scorched the shiplap walls with his response. It started with a lengthy string of curse words and culminated with an empty ink bottle being fired against the wall and a less empty cuspidor being kicked in the same direction.

Ed Bertrand had just explained in detail their failure to pick the Purdy corn. He had the two inmates make their retreat in the empty wagon, leaving the full one, still hitched to the mule, standing on the dirt track. For all of his profane wailing, at least Ennis did not sound inclined to blame Bertrand for not escalating to gunfire under the circumstances.

"He will not make a monkey of me on my own land. God damn it. I say he's running a bluff. We are going to get that corn to-day. To-day, do you hear me?"

While the last of Will Ennis' shout echoed around the room, Ed Bertrand looked on without expression. Faced with momentary silence, he ran his tongue over his front teeth and followed with a sucking noise as if to dislodge a difficult crumb.

Ennis looked back at Bertrand. He was less wild eyed than a minute earlier, but was barely clinging to control. He walked to the office window and scanned the yard. He pointed to the empty wagon where Moss Gordon and Thirsty Davis sat.

"Those two. They look like likely fighters. Wouldn't be here if they weren't, now would they? Get them rifles and bring them along."

"Mr. Ennis, they're convicts. You can't arm convicts with a gun."

Ennis maintained his fiery, glassy stare out the window.

"Yeah. Dismiss them for the rest of the day."

"How about I just send them back to the camp? Camp boss'll give them something else to do. No use just letting them lollygag."

"That's fine."

The only sound in the office was the tick of a Waterbury clock. Suddenly, Ennis turned away from the window and looked directly at Cloyd Moore, the bookkeeper for Sartartia.

"Cloyd, grab yourself a gun. You're coming with us."

Moore was a short, somewhat stooped man of about 50. He was known to sing to himself when he believed no one else could hear him. He swallowed the bite of sandwich he had tried to steal when Ennis had his back turned to the room, then he pushed his spectacles back up his nose. Bertrand suppressed a smile in spite of the tension as Cloyd Moore made first an audible gulp that was followed by a small gurgling cough.

When George Purdy was certain that the wagons and men were gone, he walked back to the house and ate. He failed to realize that he had missed breakfast until the hunger punched him in the gut. Anger had kept his blood pumping out in the corn field, but now he wanted food. He cut off a chunk of cheese and sat down at the table. He also had a nice ripe pear and a handful of Saltines.

He mulled over the past hour or two. There was nothing that he could have done differently. They left him no choice.

Purdy found Charlie Mabin working in his own corn field. He was pulling ears for the corn crib just as George had done two days before.

"Charlie, they showed up an hour or two ago. I run them off with a rifle, but I suspect they'll be back this afternoon."

"Damn. Who was it?"

"Bertrand and two convicts."

"Yeah, I didn't figure Will Ennis would have the guts to come tell you before they started pulling."

George made a single laughing noise. After a moment, Charlie spoke again.

"Let me grab a gun and I'll go with you."

"No. No. I didn't come here to ask for help. I just wanted to see if y'all would catch my kids on their way back from school and keep them away. I don't want them walking into the middle of anything, or even seeing anything, come to that. It ain't your fight, Charlie, and nothing good can come from you getting Ennis all hot under the collar."

Purdy sounded adamant about protecting his friend, but Mabin had his own notions about where he needed to be if the dispute came to trouble. The two talked for ten minutes before George began to waver and admit that Charlie was making good points.

"Like I said, I appreciate you wanting to help. If you can do that without bringing the wrath down on your own head, then I won't stop you."

"Thank you, George. I just reckon that there may be a call for witnesses about who said or done what."

"And your gun stays at home."

"Yes, sir. It's just me providing another body on your side."

George Purdy extended a hand to his friend, then the two of them walked to the Mabin's house to inform Polly.

Cloyd Moore edged over to his desk and quietly took another bite of sandwich. To complete his posse, Will Ennis had summoned Harold Barton from the large warehouse. Barton was his clerk there, keeping meticulous ledgers of merchandise arriving at Sartartia and agricultural product going out on the rails. It was a job vital to the plantation's success, and as such, Barton was confused as to why he had been called away from his work.

Physically, Harold Barton could not have been more different than the fragile-looking Moore. Barton stood about six foot two and weighed north of 240 pounds. He had dealt with a weight problem for most of his 37 years, but above the three chins and slightly pugged nose sat copper-colored eyes that suggested intelligence. He was definitely smart enough to feel a sense of dread as the combative Will Ennis described their impending mission.

"Damn him! I don't know what he thinks he's going to accomplish. I am the last word on this property, and we will show him exactly that!"

The word "we" sent a small chill through Harold Barton's ample backside.

Ennis surveyed the other three men standing in the small Sartartia office. He was reassured to see Cloyd Moore clutching a rifle.

"Harold. Grab one of those shotguns in that rack."

Ennis pointed to three old Parker Brothers bird guns hanging on the wall. The men occasionally took breaks during the fall and winter to shoot some birds, mostly ducks and geese that moved through Fort Bend County by the thousands.

From behind his own desk, Will snatched a fairly new Browning pump action 12 gauge. He already wore a Colt revolver. It was in the same type holster strapped to Ed Bertrand, something Ennis addressed presently.

"Ed, you'll want something more than that won't you?"

"No, sir. The pistol will suit me fine, but I'm not expecting we'll need any of this. George Purdy is not a stupid man, I think he will see reason."

"Well, he's not off to a good start. And I aim to show that son of a bitch who's boss."

At the Purdy place, Charlie Mabin, a normally even-tempered man, tried not to be too upset with his wife.

"Polly, I warned you that there might be trouble. I meant it."

She had lingered over her tasks for another 20 minutes after the two men left for the Purdy house. It took that long for her curiosity to overwhelm the plans she had agreed to. It was not even a half mile walk between the two tenant houses, so she could not imagine that there needed to be a fuss over her change of heart. Her husband quietly reminded her about the reason for their neighbor's visit in the first place.

"George is expecting you to keep an eye on Sarah and Arthur. You can't shirk that."

Purdy reluctantly added his comments.

"I don't want to get in betwixt anything, but that is true. I would really appreciate you intercepting the two young ones. They don't need to be a part of anything ugly."

"I'll run back to stop the kids when the time for letting out arrives, but you need support. You're our friend, George. It's the Christian thing to do."

Describing the intentions of the Good Lord was often the deciding word for Polly in any discussion, and she clearly meant it to be so now. Charlie gritted his teeth and let out a big sigh that was a reprise of thousands just like it. Such was marriage, he figured.

"All right. But if I tell you to git, then you git. I'm not brooking any argument about you being in a safe spot."

Polly Mabin nodded at her husband and did her best at suppressing any trace of a smile.

Will Ennis slowed the mules pulling the buckboard. Ed Bertrand and the wind from the northwest were kicking up too much dust. Harold Barton rode beside Ennis, gaining the wagon's seat by virtue of his size and lack of agility. Cloyd Moore sat in the very uncomfortable bed thinking of his half uneaten lunch.

The anger that Ennis felt in the office had switched from flame to glowing coals, but the heat was just as warm. Barton eyed him surreptitiously and saw a man confident in his own omnipotence. Ennis stared straight ahead as he drove, his tongue prodding one lower tooth and his eyes filled with swash.

They arrived at the top of the turnrow that separated Purdy's land from Ken Harvey's. The back lot of Purdy's plot was 150 yards away, and George Purdy stood just inside the fence next to the corner post. The dirty back wall of his barn stood 20 feet beyond him. Another 40 yards past that, Charlie and Polly Mabin sat on the back stoop of the Purdy cottage.

The corn on the right had been picked two days prior, and many of the stalks were trampled down. Purdy's corn, on the left hand side of the turnrow, was ready for pulling. From the wagon seat, Ennis hollered to Ed Bertrand.

"Go get that loaded wagon you told me about and move it out of there."

Bertrand nodded his acknowledgement and rode into Purdy's field, headed to the dirt track where their earlier confrontation had taken place. Even on horseback, he was quickly out of sight. Ennis, and from a distance, Purdy, watched him go.

For a long moment nobody moved. Moore and Barton were especially unmotivated for matters to proceed, but their boss looked at each in turn and then spoke with the louder than necessary volume that he often used with subordinates.

"Come on boys, we'll settle him. He's not going to do a damn thing."

If George Purdy heard him, he did not respond.

Will Ennis climbed down from the wagon seat, looked up at the blue sky and let go a long even breath. He reached into his pocket and checked his watch. It was almost 1:30 in the afternoon. He fixed a hard stare on his two office employees until they clambered to the ground, then he turned back toward Purdy and started slowly advancing.

Ennis held the shotgun in his left hand, muzzle down, and had his right hand on the butt of his pistol. This time when he spoke to Moore and Barton he did so without looking back.

"Come on, let's fix him."

Chapter 9

Will Ennis may have exhorted his two armed clerks to follow him as a show of force, and in some worlds, their spirits may have even been willing, but on this temperate September Friday their motivation fled. Ennis could sense without looking around that he was slowly striding toward George Purdy alone. He himself was unhurried, and some trepidation could be noted in his steps.

Behind the fence post, Purdy's right hand repeatedly tightened and eased on the stock of his Winchester rifle. In spite of the cool wind, his calloused palm sweated. He swayed his hips slightly, though his scuffed old boots stayed planted in the hen-pecked dirt, about shoulder width apart, the right foot in back of the left.

The gun, an 1873 model, had been Purdy's for a decade. He bought it at a hardware store on the town square in Decatur during flush times. He had shot many a deer with it, but as far as he knew, it had never been pointed at another person.

Ennis kept advancing. He was within 100 yards when Purdy spoke, not shouting, but loud enough to hear.

"Mr. Ennis, I need you to stop right there."

For a few seconds, Ennis did just that. Then he stepped forward again, tentatively and slower. Purdy raised the rifle, fired a shot into the air, and levered another cartridge into the chamber. Some distance behind him, Charlie Mabin sent his wife Polly to hide in the little corn crib. She willingly complied.

"I don't want no trouble. I'm just farming my land like we agreed."

"I want you out of that tenant shack. You forfeited your crops and therefore your right to be there. Now, I want you gone!"

"I've made up my mind, Mr. Ennis. You'll have to shoot me dead."

"That sounds fine."

George Purdy's eyes were feeling gritty. He wondered briefly if he had stopped blinking a few minutes back.

When Will had closed slightly more than half the distance from the wagon, he paused. The octagon barrel of Purdy's rifle was now resting on top of a fence post, chest high. The tenant was not even using the iron sight, but Will felt the gun bearing on him, a physical awareness that he was a target. His heartbeat thrummed in his ears. He took in a breath then quickly brought up the shotgun and slipped his right finger onto the trigger.

To Purdy's ears, the shots came simultaneously. His face stung something terrible. It took a few ticks before he grasped that he had taken buckshot to the face.

Ennis fared much worse. Purdy's rifle, steadied on the fence post, had been true. Two .44 centerfire bullets had passed clean through his body. One tore through his right side under the rib cage and another a little lower, just above his hip. After the second shot ripped through his abdomen, Ennis threw his shotgun to the ground. It was empty of shells. His pistol remained in its holster as he shouted in disbelief.

"Fuck. I'm killed."

He turned and started a slow, weaving jog toward the wagon. Moore and Barton appeared back on the turnrow. From within the fenced lot of the Purdy cottage, George and Charlie watched silently. Neither had moved an inch from the spots they occupied when the shots were fired.

Ennis almost made it to the wagon when he pulled up and stood straight. He cocked his head to one side, and his face wore a quizzical expression as if he was trying hard to recall something important. Slowly he spun to his left and stared back in the direction of George Purdy, then he dropped into the dust.

When Ed Bertrand heard the shots, he was securing his horse's reins to the back of the corn wagon. Though he felt that the safest play was to stay with Will Ennis and mitigate the trouble, he had been told to haul the pulled corn back to Sartartia, so that was what he would do. He had learned years ago that it rarely paid to go against the boss. The sound of shots changed his mindset entirely. He undid the horse, mounted and headed back toward the conflict.

Bertrand emerged from the corn and looked toward the rear of the Purdy lot to his left. George was sitting on the ground just inside his lot fence, leaning against a post with his back to Bertrand. Charlie Mabin squatted in front of him, and Ed recognized Mabin's wife running in their direction from behind the barn.

Looking to his right, he saw Moore and Barton knelt over something at the front of the wagon. He assumed that the lump was Will Ennis. He headed toward them at a trot. Halfway there, he dismounted to pick up Ennis' discarded shotgun then led his horse to the wagon and tied him off. He now saw that the boss was bleeding profusely. Standing over the body, he could hear ragged breaths.

Charlie and Polly tended to George Purdy. Some of the buckshot had gone under his scalp, and the rivulets of blood were flowing down his face and into his shirt. Other pellets pocked his left cheek, and there were some wounds in his neck and one in his shoulder. After just a few minutes of subjecting himself to their fussing, Purdy shook them off and walked to where the others had gathered around Will Ennis. The Mabins followed. Though the looks were far short of welcoming, no further hostilities were forthcoming.

All of the men, including Charlie and George, helped load Will Ennis into the wagon that he had driven out. Polly fetched a horse blanket from George Purdy's shed for a cushion, and Cloyd Moore drove slowly to the store while Harold Barton sat in back and provided awkward words of comfort. Even driving carefully, the ride was rough and interminable. The Mabins and George stayed behind. George had begun to feel queasy.

Ed Bertrand rode ahead as fast as he could to seek help. His first phone call was to summon Dr. J.L. Dillard out from Richmond. Dillard was a taciturn, older man who had practiced in that community for two decades. He was well trusted by the Ennis family.

With that arranged and the sense of great urgency stressed, he called the house. Soon Caswell Ennis and Tom Ward arrived. They left word with Letha to send Emmett and Leigh when they came in from wherever they happened to be.

Cass listened impatiently to the story of the encounter with Purdy, and was ready to ride out and shoot the tenant down. Bertrand calmed him by talking slowly and carefully, at one juncture even taking hold of his arm, and pointing out that his interests lay in avoiding a murder charge of his own. Will had initiated the violence, Bertrand explained, but George Purdy would most assuredly face serious charges. It was also imperative that Cass stay nearby to make decisions while Will was incapacitated. His quiet words did the trick, at least temporarily.

Dr. Dillard rode out from Richmond as soon as he got the phone call. He had saddlebags fitted out as a doctor's kit, and he quickly checked the contents. Once he had clopped across the Brazos bridge, he kept his horse at a trot or canter the whole way, making it in less than an hour.

Will Ennis's body was trembling, and though he could not speak, the presumption was that he was cold. Barton fetched a horse blanket from the stable and covered him. It was the first thing Dr. Dillard removed upon his arrival.

"What the hell is this nasty thing doing on him?"

He flung the blanket to one side and began examining the wounds.

"I thought he was cold. I just..."

Harold Barton's voice trailed off. Dr. Dillard ignored him. He spoke with a determined voice directed to no one in particular.

"I'd like to tie off a couple of those arteries. He's bleeding bad, but I don't have anything to do that. A wagon trip would shake him to pieces, I'm afraid."

Dillard poked and probed at the wounds. Twice he rocked Will's body onto its side so he could look from the back. Blood had soaked the blanket he lay on and the wagon bed beneath it, even dripping through the boards onto the dirt. The doctor was still talking to himself more than any of the bystanders, the number of whom had risen to a dozen. Eventually, he turned and addressed Caswell Ennis.

"This probably calls for cauterizing these wounds. We could heat a piece of iron at your blacksmith forge over there, that is if we can find something the right size. It would need to be a short rod, very thin. The trouble here, and I'm being straight with you, is that I've never done it before. I've treated gunshots in the leg or foot or shoulder, and I've tied off the bleeders with success. But this, this burning him, that's a whole different ball of wax, Cass. Where your brother is shot, well, there are organs."

He paused and let out a breath before continuing.

"Frankly, I'm scared I'd make it worse. It's battlefield medicine, and I just don't know it. I don't want to kill him."

Cass Ennis looked back at the doctor without comment, but his look beseeched Dillard to take heroic action. Instead, Dillard called for as many clean cloths as he could get, and a stack was quickly produced.

"I said clean, damn it. Clean."

He shucked several dirty ones from the pile. Carefully he stuffed the pieces of cotton an inch or so into the holes. When he was done, and had looked them over, he told Harold Barton to hold them in place. Finally, Dillard climbed down from the wagon bed. He absently picked up one of the remaining cloths and wiped his hands vigorously while he spoke to Cass Ennis.

"There's still some life in him, but he is likely to stay unconscious for a time. I'm hoping that the rags I stuck into the wound openings will help that blood congeal. We need to stop the bleeding. He's a lucky man in that there's an eastbound through here soon."

Dillard looked at his watch before continuing.

"Forty-five minutes. If we can get him to the infirmary in Houston, he might stand a chance. Safer to go to Houston than wait for the next train through to Richmond. That's more than three hours from now."

He spoke next to Barton, making eye contact with the shaken big man to stress the importance of his simple instruction.

"Keep holding those rags tight."

Though Ennis family members later argued among themselves that Dr. Dillard's life-saving efforts were overly cautious, there was no denying the outcome. The signal for the afternoon eastbound to stop at Sartartia remained up, but the urgency had vanished. Will Ennis died before he was loaded on the train to be taken into Houston. Instead of the city infirmary on Washington Avenue, his destination was Westheimer's large undertaking operation downtown. The Ennis family would spare no extravagance in selecting a coffin.

The two youngest Ennis brothers did not arrive in time to bid their brother adieu. There were no women on hand, and nary a tear was shed. Those men who were not actively involved in the loading removed their hats. It was a simple and efficient farewell for a man who considered himself a master of business.

Not everyone who had witnessed the demise was still there to see the somber spectacle of the body being placed into the baggage car. As soon as the doctor pronounced Will Ennis dead, Ed Bertrand slipped away from the crowd without saying a word. He chose two horses, rather than mules, from the big stable and hitched them to a buggy. Then he made a beeline for George Purdy's place.

Chapter 10

E d Bertrand had done everything short of slapping George Purdy in his shot damaged face. He had been pleading with the wounded tenant for ten solid minutes and had yet to convince him of the urgency of his situation.

Purdy was not having it. In his view, he had not defended the moral ground only to abandon it now. Blood had been shed on this very dirt in order to protect his family's livelihood. Whether Will Ennis was alive or dead, scurrying off did not feel right. In fact, the notion of it betrayed his original motivation. He sat on the porch edge and listened to what Bertrand was saying, but so far it had not swayed him.

The Purdy children were still at the Mabin house. As soon as the wagon carrying Will Ennis had cleared from view, Polly doctored George's wounds using a kitchen rag and a bottle of Myer's Carbolic Acid. It was the best she could do. Throughout her ministrations, George sat stoically with minimal flinching. By her count, a half dozen or more pellets of number 3 shot were still there, deeper than she could coax out with her fingers.

When she was done, Polly walked back to her own home to intercept the Purdy children as promised. Charlie followed half an hour later. Now Ed Bertrand was sitting on the wagon bench, trying to cajole George into what he saw as the only smart course of action, and the lengthy effort wore on him.

"Look, Purdy, everything changed when you shot Ennis. Whether you were right or wrong makes no difference. You've got to get out of here, or they'll kill you."

"Will Ennis tried that, and I'm still here."

"This time it's revenge, and the people coming won't be shipping clerks. Cass and Emmett will come, and they'll likely round up a couple of working hands who'd just as soon shoot somebody as not. Right this instant their minds are turning from grieving to hate. If they've not mounted up and armed up already, it won't be five minutes from now. I know these people."

For the first time, George's expression softened, and Bertrand felt that he may be getting through.

"And I'll tell you something else. They won't care shit about a fair fight. Cass Ennis would just as soon ambush you. All he cares about at this moment is avenging his dead brother."

George looked off over his fields at the crops that needed to be harvested. Bertrand followed his gaze and then continued his thoughts.

"There is no possibility left where you'll be here to pull that corn or pick that cotton. You'll be dead or in jail. Those are your only two choices."

George examined his feet. Then he spat onto the ground.

"I just wanted to mind my business and to provide for my children."

Bertrand imagined he saw water well up in Purdy's eyes. He eased up his tone.

"George, what happens to those little ones if you stay on this porch to get killed?"

There was a long silence before Bertrand spoke again.

"Come on. Let's go."

George insisted on stopping to talk to his children, and Ed Bertrand did not argue, though he did stress that time was not their ally. Since the Mabin house was the next one to the west, it was not a detour. Everyone was outside when the wagon pulled up and George Purdy jumped down. He nodded his thanks to Charlie and Polly Mabin then squatted and pulled Sarah and Arthur close. Both children stared at their father's scarred face. Some dried blood still matted the hair that extended from under his hat. The little boy nervously placed a finger on one of the pellet wounds.

"Does it hurt, dad?"

"No. Your dad's fine. I just had some trouble, that's all. Now I've got to go take care of it. But y'all are going to stay here with Miz Polly and Mister Charlie."

Realizing that was a big presumption, George looked at the Mabins whose own children were gathered around them.

"For as long as y'all need," answered Polly.

"See there. For as long as we need. I'll try to be back soon, though. Mr. Bertrand and I have to go to Richmond."

Bertrand touched his hat brim at the children.

"Dad, you're coming back, though?" Sarah was fighting back tears. "Not like mama?"

George hugged her a bit tighter.

"No, darling. I'll be back. I just can't rightly say when. But hey, I need y'all to do something for me before it gets dark."

George looked each child in the eye, hoping that a task would ease their worries.

"First thing is I want you to go get Duck, saddle him up if you can manage, but either way, walk him over here and let him stay in the Mabin's barn. That's really important."

George turned back to Charlie who nodded agreement.

"The other thing is to pack up as many clothes and things as you can, and the photos of mama, the good skillet. Just get as many of our things as you can carry. Just our things, though. Don't bring no tools or anything that ain't ours. Maybe y'all can make a game of it and bring some help with you."

Purdy motioned to the Mabin kids and winked. Then his grip on his children's arms tightened.

"But this part is important. Sarah. Arthur. Listen here. If any grown-ups come around there, y'all hightail it back here right away. Run like the wind. Y'all understand?"

Both of the children gave their father a solemn nod, and he hugged them tight. He wanted to linger. He still had nagging doubts about leaving, but they were fewer than before. After a minute, he pushed himself upright and looked at his friend Charlie again.

"Don't you worry, George. We'll see to things. And I'll find time to come see you. This evening if I can, or tomorrow when I can get squared away."

Purdy climbed back onto the wagon seat next to Ed Bertrand. The foreman had stayed silent during the farewell, but he was itching to move. There were several backward glances while George spoke with his children. Bertrand twitched the reins, and the horses stepped off. As they left the yard, George had one last request.

"Charlie, if you go yourself, I'd sure appreciate it if you take that old meat grinder off the wall."

They wound through turnrows and field tracks until they were a mile shy of Sartartia's western edge. Eventually they bumped across the SP rails and turned west onto the Richmond Road. Most of the land around them was that leased to the Ennis family and therefore in cultivation of some sort. A few fields lay fallow, but most were filled with cotton or corn waiting to be picked or the remains of those plants which had just given up their bounty. Dirty cotton lint, bolls that had fallen from the wagons on their way to the gins, littered the ditches like week-old snow.

Most people would judge it to be shaping into an exceptionally pleasant evening. Here and there, closer to the river, were small stands of woods and brush. As they passed the trees, cicadas wailed their vibrous hums. George had loved that sound since childhood, and the bugs calmed him. He had no confidence that things would ever return to normal, but it was something familiar and pleasing.

Heading west on the rutted dirt road, the lowering sun in their faces, both men regularly looked behind them for signs of pursuing riders. After traveling the first mile and a half with not a word exchanged between them, Ed Bertrand finally opened up as if he had been holding back a flood.

"I don't reckon you ever met the old man, but Will was not that. Don't get me wrong, the old man was a right screaming son of a bitch, and a body had best pay heed to his whims. His focus, first and last, was the almighty dollar, but I never saw him act from pure meanness. Least not toward a white man. I can't see him standing on piddling details to throw a man from his home and steal the crop he planted. What Will Ennis done was just low."

George clucked a bitter laugh.

"You'll not get argument here."

"Old man Ennis was smarter, too. He and Ed Cunningham built a fortune around here. But it's that second generation that is spoiled and who you most need to watch out for. Will and his like, they're soft inside. They got to act tough because they're not able to live it, to carry manhood in their bones. They never had to earn a thing, so they never felt another man's shoes. They see the world's transactions through a contract not a handshake, and that is a solid shame."

Bertrand had a distant gaze as he philosophized, and George got the feeling that the foreman was recalling his own slights at Ennis hands, not the troubles that led to the shooting today. When he emerged from his musing, he looked at George, his face clouded over.

"You need to watch yourself, Purdy. You may feel safe enough behind bars, but that don't mean you should take every man at his word even in there. The Ennis clan is one of five or six families who control who lives or dies in the county, at least this side of the river. You think I'm spewing high flung fear, but I'm not. I will explain it like this here - the old man grew to value my opinion at times. He'd ask me what I thought, but young Will knew it all from birth. To him I was no more than the means of carrying out his orders. What his little brothers will be like is anybody's guess, but I see them as still having the power without possessing the morals to wield it. A sharecropper who murdered one of their own, well, they'll pop you like a flea first chance that comes."

In spite of his natural confidence, a small shiver ran up George's back.

"I'll be okay, Mr. Bertrand."

The pair rode on a while without further conversation, not that George felt very chatty. When Bertrand spoke again, his voice was soft.

"We'll be over the bridge in a few minutes, but the river banks here are a tangle. What if you was to overpower me and make good an escape? Just pitching me from the wagon seat is liable to make me muzzy. With that and the waning light, it's unlikely I'd find you."

George's jaw fell slightly open at the suggestion. Bertrand's eyes remained steady on the road before them, and the wagon continued bumping west.

"I don't reckon I'll be escaping Mr. Bertrand."

"Oh, I was just thinking out loud."

"Even if I did believe that was the right thing to do, and I don't, there's my kids. I've got a duty to them."

"Oh, I feel sure that your little ones would find a way to you pretty quick. I think you could count on that."

George took a moment to gather his words.

"Since their mama died, they've moved with me to every job I've had. Scooting across Texas while I built barns or houses for other people. I figured that us settling down and staying in a place was the only way to give them a normal life. They finally have friends in Charlie Mabin's little ones and over at their school. You don't get to be something if you're on the run all the time. Besides that, in my way of thinking, I ain't done nothing wrong."

"That may be," Bertrand say thoughtfully. "That may be."

As they closed in on their destination, Ed Bertrand's backward looks became more frequent. He thought he could make out dust from riders behind them, but he could not be sure. Was it real, or was it the dwindling light playing to his imagined fears? He did not mention it to George.

They were almost to the Brazos bridge before it occurred to Purdy that the entire notion of him escaping might be a ruse. For all of the good nature displayed toward him, Ed Bertrand worked for the Ennis family. Had done for many years.

All of their previous interactions had been pure business as opposed to any friendship. If Bertrand was in cahoots with either side in this mess, there was no logical reason it would be George. The whole idea may have been to drum up an excusable reason to shoot him down.

By the time they rattled into the dirt streets of Richmond, George Purdy was fully invested in whatever trepidation Ed Bertrand had carried throughout their ride. Since the unexpected mention of an escape, he had spent the last mile scanning the horizon to their rear and sneaking sideways glances at his driver. The plantation foreman had been nothing but polite and sympathetic on the face of things, but still, both men were downright happy to pull up in front of the Fort Bend County Jail.

Chapter 11

Mamie Lyons sat alone on the sofa. She had been staring at the wallpaper, peach gladiolas on a seafoam background, for fifteen minutes. She recalled when Amanda ordered that fabric. She had been so proud of bringing a little fresh beauty into her big house on the coastal prairie. The family was very happy then, were they not? Even with her own mother gone and Amanda running the household in her place. The boys had their little clashes with their father, but things were good. She delved deeper into her memory to discern if that notion was really true.

Letha Ward was in the kitchen frosting an orange sponge cake. Her supply of pecans from last fall had dwindled greatly, but this was not the time to be stingy with them. When the icing was smoothed to her satisfaction, she carefully placed half nuts around the top. She had been cooking all morning. With the exception of Mister Marshall, who was seeing to patients in San Antonio, the rest of the remaining Ennises were on hand. That included a smattering of cousins who had probably shown up more out of curiosity that any devotion to Mister Will.

Leigh Ennis, middle teens, was reading in a rocker on the back porch. His brother Emmett, just arrived that morning from Austin, was doing the same next to one of the parlor windows. Two of the cousins, middle-aged females, chatted a touch too loudly on the front porch, their sometimes tacky conversation about the house furnishings easily audible through the open windows. The other cousin, brother to one of the front porch women, was poking around in the stables out back while Tom Ward eyed him with great suspicion.

The family was together to mourn the loss of their oldest sibling who had inherited the role of patriarch, but they were barely talking to one another. That changed soon after the screen door from the back porch slammed closed with a bang.

Cass Ennis swept into the kitchen and plucked a handful of pecans from a bowl while casting a mischievous eye toward Letha. She answered with a ticking noise, and he continued through the dining room and into the parlor. Surveying the room, he went to his younger brother and gave a firm handshake and a hearty grip on the shoulder.

"Welcome home, Emmett. How was the train?"

"Slow and hot. I had to change in San Antonio, and the station was a swelter. Got here a little more than an hour ago. Letha had some cool tea, and I've been navigating an impenetrable volume of Macaulay. Where have you been anyway?"

"Over at the office. There were a slew of telegrams to send about the funeral. Almost as many to answer. My head is swimming, and I am ready for a drink. You visited with Mamie before you dove into your book?"

Emmett lowered his voice, though their sister was but ten feet away.

"Briefly, though she was distantly off in her own thoughts. How about you? Have you seen her?"

"Oh, yes. She left first thing this morning and was here by noon. We had lunch together before I left to deal with all this... claptrap."

Cass added a dismissive wave to his comment.

"She said the funeral is Monday. Don't expect me to be able to stay any longer. The session just started, and I am still scrutinizing my professors," Emmett added.

"More likely scrutinizing the women in your classes, but we shall not detain our important university man."

Mamie had risen from her wallpaper reverie and joined her brothers.

"I was certainly not off in my thoughts. Nor is this the ordinary social occasion you seem to think it is. It's been 24 hours, Cass. Are you finished with your mourning?"

Cass' eyes fluttered at the vehement attack from his half-sister. It was not at all what he expected, and it set him on his heels for a moment or two.

"No, Mamie, I haven't, but I didn't realize I had to sit in the corner and sob, either."

"Well, you sounded awfully glib."

'I've just been dealing with funeral arrangements, responding to well wishers, notifying those who need to be, and mostly trying to dodge reporters and the morbidly curious. I've also been trying to put yesterday's anger behind me. It's all been an unwelcome mess."

"Likely much more unwelcome for dear Will."

Cass and Emmett both looked sufficiently chastened.

"Yes. No doubt."

Cass' response was a near whisper.

"What about the awful man who shot him?" Mamie asked.

"He is in jail as of yesterday. Bertrand coerced him down to Richmond, though I would have preferred to handle it myself. Don't worry. He will get his. One way or another."

"Knowing Will, I'd wager there was a second side to the story."

Emmett followed his remark with a seemingly involuntary sniff.

"He was still your brother, Emmett. He did not deserve to be shot down like some rabid coon," Mamie intoned with an imperious flair.

Caswell answered his brother.

"Yeah. Maybe, but I don't want to talk about it right now."

This in turn brought an answer from Mamie, who evidently had mounted her high horse with plans to stay for a time.

"These are precisely the kinds of things you need to start thinking about, Cass. This type of decision. I know you weren't expecting to be thrust into the fire like this, but it is now down to you to run the family interests."

"Down to me?"

"I didn't mean it like that. Fallen to you. Passed to you. However you phrase it. You have no luxury of time. That is my point."

"Will is not even buried yet."

"And if father were here, he would be the first to tell you that business waits for no one. A single wrong move might resonate for years."

Emmett interrupted on behalf of his suddenly set upon brother.

"It sounds like you're the one with the head for business, Mamie. Not to mention that you have more history at Sartartia than any of us. Why don't you take over? Seeing that father is not here."

He was not serious, but his sister took him as such.

"Please. Marshall has a happy practice, and our home is in San Antonio."
She laughed.

"Can you imagine the gurus of the Cotton Exchange being told they had to deal with a woman. Pardon my indelicacy, but they would soil their trousers."

Letha lit the rest of the lamps after a filling supper that included all of the cousins around the big table. Conversation was superficial and lagged a few times, mostly after Cousin Benny from Navasota opined at length about a hand car accident and the competence of colored railroad workers. Throughout the diatribe, Letha, as invisible to the man as his placemat, maintained a game face.

Caswell Ennis played host in the parlor, serving whiskey and brandy. The two women cousins had small glasses of Madeira. It was too sweet for the Ennis boys' tastes, so Cass was glad to fill their glasses.

There were happy stories of Will as an older child. Stealing a lamb from a neighboring farm so that he and his friends could have a barbecue on the Brazos beach. Being chased from Oyster Creek by an alligator that had grown longer with each retelling. Everyone dutifully laughed in spite of the familiarity of the tales.

Cousin Benny offered an escapade previously unknown. Will had come to Navasota on business once when he was working at the bank in Houston. He awakened Benny in the wee hours of the morning, pounding frantically on the door, convinced that a posse was just around the corner. The housekeeper had presumed their guest had already retired to his room and locked the doors for the night. In reality, Will had been rutting away in a random tool shed with the concupiscent daughter of a local druggist when they accidentally knocked over a wheelbarrow, a shovel and multiple hoes. The crash roused the tool shed's owner who emerged from the back of his house with a shotgun as Will fled, pulling up his trousers in abject panic.

The family's hearty guffaws slowly died away as each one realized that Will did indeed meet his untimely end at the barrel of a gun. No one spoke for an uneasy while until Mamie changed the subject.

"I'm not trying to harp on this, Cass, but everyone is looking to you for leadership now."

Caswell groaned softly before answering.

"I appreciate that, Mamie. I do. It's just that I need a bit of time to let the gravity of the situation settle in. Four years ago, I was at school just like Emmett. I'm sure he will tell you that he'd feel less than competent suddenly running a big plantation."

"Nail on the head, brother," Emmett confirmed.

The others sought to assure. Mamie who had started this, responded first.

"We will all be here to help you, Cass. Any way possible. But the sad fact is that there is no time and you have no choice."

"Absolutely," Benny added. "I've got business experience, and I'm ready to share advice."

Perhaps Mamie was skeptical of her older cousin's qualifications. At any event, she ignored Benny's offer.

"Marshall will be here tomorrow. You should sit down with him for a long talk. Just the two of you. He and Will were very close, as you are aware."

"Look."

Cass stopped himself and cooled the tone he was about to take.

"Thank you very much for the kind encouragement, but I am not looking to run things like Will did. Or our storied father, for that matter. I've had some changes I'm ruminating on. Mostly, I want to stay level headed and not give in to any desires that will make me petty and mean-spirited."

A quiet explosion of shock passed through the older family.

"Mean spirited? Is that what you think of them?"

Caswell raised his palms at his sister in placation.

"We all know that Will was not one to explore all possibilities before diving into something. He got that from Pop. You were the golden girl, Mamie. We boys got a different view of things around here when we were growing up."

"Papa loved you. It would cut him to the bone to hear you call him mean spirited."

"Maybe the war and everything he saw in battle made him into a harder man than he otherwise would have been. We didn't know him before that. I never saw him young and gentle. Was he ever brimming with optimism?"

"Oh, yes," offered the two women cousins in a tipsy Greek chorus.

"He must have been. He took big risks and compiled everything around us."

This from Leigh who had been firmly silent up to then. Cass calmly responded.

"Right. But is our father, as we knew him, really the guide I ought to follow? I would like to start fresh. If those Ennis traits are irrevocably within me, then so be it, but for now, I'm determined to chart a fresh course."

Mamie's condescending look belied her accepting words, though Cass did not notice it.

"We all hope you can, brother. You are very dear to us."

Cousin Benny cleared his throat like a bad thespian.

"Not my business, but it seems to me the time has come for you to take a bride, Caswell. A good woman can do wonders at mitigating a man's responsibilities."

Mamie, not wasting a second, cut off any possible reply.

"I am glad you broached the subject, Benny, instead of me, but it is a capital idea. I'm sure you have prospects, Cass. You should pick one. Time to grow up, little brother."

Chapter 12

Richmond, Texas

The last drop of sunlight was being wrung out of the Richmond sky when Ed Bertrand and George Purdy pulled up in front of the county jail on Preston Street. Bertrand swatted at a mosquito on the back of his hand and flicked the dead bug away, leaving a smear of blood.

As the men climbed down from the wagon, George expected a ball of fear in his chest, but instead he felt tired. His face and neck stung. Dirt from the ride was in his eyes, ears and mouth. He missed his kids. He spat on the sidewalk and followed Bertrand up a few steps and under the right hand archway. An iron gate sat open.

Though Purdy could not discern many details inside the barred and shadowed vestibule, there was no mistaking the solid iron door once Bertrand knocked. A deputy was quick to open it, spilling light into the men's faces. As it squeaked its heavy welcome, the dread Purdy was expecting finally bubbled up. Ed Bertrand was obliged to take hold of his arm to lead him inside.

From the outside, the big jailhouse was impressive. Three tall stories of red brick and white stone, with a turret atop that. It spoke loudly in favor of the forces of law. Inside, however, though the building was only four years old, the smell of sweaty bodies and unemptied slop buckets was unmistakable.

Bertrand did not recognize the deputy, a wiry young man with close set eyes who so far had not inquired into their business. He stated their purpose unbidden.

"I'm the foreman at Sartartia, and we've had a murder. This here is the man who did it. I want to turn him over to the sheriff."

The deputy's left eyebrow shot up at the word murder.

"The sheriff is having his supper and taking a rest. I can get him signed in and write down the details, then I'll throw him in the cells. Sheriff'll see him in the morning."

The deputy made to step around Bertrand and grab George Purdy, but the foreman did not give way.

"If it's all the same to you, I'd like to speak to Sheriff Briscoe directly. It is a murder, after all."

That warranted a blank-faced nod, and the deputy turned and banged on another steel wall that was a few steps behind him. He opened a little pass-through door. In short order, a small panel in the door slid open, and a woman's voice came through.

"Yes?"

"There's been a killing out at Sartartia. Man here wants to talk to the sheriff."

"Tell him the sheriff is resting his eyes."

"I did, ma'am, but he's brought the killer with him. Still wants to talk to the sheriff."

The little panel closed. Three long minutes later, with George's blood rushing loudly in his ears, the front door opened to reveal Sheriff Robert P. Briscoe entering from the outside. The deputy quickly slammed the steel door behind his boss, then pulled a heavy lever that brought a loud clang from somewhere out of sight. Purdy tried to swallow, but could not.

Briscoe was no older than George, mid-thirties, with fine, sandy hair that was mussed on one side. There was an earnest quality about his face which he rubbed at hard. Then a genuine smile broke out and he extended his hand to Bertrand.

"Ed, how've you been. You're looking good."

"Fine, Bob. Fine. How about you?"

"I've been up toward Fulshear for the last day. Somebody run off with three of Buddy Whisenant's cattle. Two cows and a steer. One of the cows had a broken foot from getting hit by a train last year, so I'm not sure how hard a thief could drive her. I just got back an hour ago, so I was catching a little shut eye and a bite to eat."

He smiled sheepishly.

"Mostly shut eye. Anyway, you didn't come here to listen to my escapades. You had a killing?"

"Yep. Will Ennis got shot to death."

"Well, well. That is something."

The sheriff rubbed at his face again while he processed this news.

"Why don't you fill me in?"

"First off, Bob, I want to make clear that I am not an eyewitness. I was a ways away readying a wagon of corn to drive to the crib. But I think the facts of the matter are not in dispute."

With that Bertrand looked at George. Whether he was expecting assent or not, he continued talking without it.

"This here is George Purdy. He is a tenant out at Sartartia. One hundred twenty acres, though I'm not sure that makes any difference. He and Will Ennis had a disagreement, a powerful one, over ownership of the crops."

Briscoe sighed and looked down at his feet. Bertrand paused before going further.

"Yep. The same. Except this ended with Mr. Ennis getting the worst of it. Dead worst."

"Why didn't you telegraph me, Ed? Not that I'd have been here, but still. I'd have liked to look things over."

"Well, given the circumstances, I reckoned it was best to bring George on in myself. No use in delaying things just to see what would happen."

"Fair enough," Briscoe said with a purse of his lips and a small nod. "That does sound like it may have been the thing to do."

George was not quite sure what to make of this talk, and as of yet, nobody had asked him anything. That ended with the sheriff's next question.

"You admit to shooting him, Mr. Purdy?"

"Yes, sir, but he had it coming, and he was fixing to shoot me."

That answer coaxed another brief nod from the lawman. Ed Bertrand spoke again.

"I can make myself available whenever you come out, Bob, so I can walk you over the ground. I'll also point you to the folks you need to talk to."

Sheriff Briscoe turned back to George without responding.

"Have you eaten, Mr. Purdy? That's all right. Trey, fix Mr. Purdy here up with a plate of those red beans and lock him up on the second floor.

George would have sworn he was not sleeping, that is until the night deputy woke him up.

"Purdy, someone's here to see you."

George blinked himself awake. Two lamps in the open area outside the big cellblock offered the dimmest of light. It took hearing his friend's voice before George realized that Charlie Mabin was pulling a chair up on the other side of the iron grate.

"Charlie. What time is it?"

"Almost midnight. Sorry, but it was as soon as I could get here. I had a few things to take care of first."

The two men wordlessly settled on a hole in the thick iron grid that allowed them some eye contact.

"No, that's fine. I won't be going anyplace."

In another time, Charlie might have laughed, but he responded with a simple and serious nod. Facing a ride home of well more than an hour in pitch blackness, he went right to his message.

"Look, George, I know you well enough to suspect that you won't like this, but some of us took up a collection to get you started with a lawyer."

"Oh, come on, Charlie. Y'all shouldn't have done that. I'll figure something out. I'm grateful, but everyone is scraping by enough already without ponying up for my troubles."

"It ain't for no cause. You've helped your neighbors out time and again, so there are people who just want to repay the favors."

"Still, there ain't..."

Charlie cut him off.

"It's already done, George. Everybody knew that you'd wave off our charity, but it truly is not that. We're your friends, that's all. And like I said, it's too late anyhow."

"Too late for what?"

George still felt a touch groggy and confused. It had been a long day, to say the least, and Charlie sounded more than a little keyed up, though he strived to keep his voice low. So far, George's two cellmates had not stirred.

"I've already gone and hired you a lawyer, and a good one, at that. It took me the better part of the last hour to rouse out the telegraph operator over at the Depot. Had to track him down at his house to get him to send off a message to Houston."

The truth was that it took a half dollar tip plus the cost of the telegram by the word, and the expense was making Charlie cringe just to think about it. But he had accomplished his mission. Now it was Purdy's turn to ask questions.

"Who all am I beholden to for this help?"

"Pretty much everybody kicked in a couple dollars. Ken Harvey, Dan Keyser, Paul Lawson, Old Man Hornischer. A few others. You've made a lot of friends around there, George."

"What about Sarah and Arthur? How are they making out?"

"They're scared. I ain't going to lie to you. Polly can work wonders with the little ones, though. I reckon they'll be settled in within a day or two. And they are safe as can be. Don't you worry about that."

George soaked that in before continuing.

"Okay. Tell me about this lawyer that I can't afford."

Charlie proceeded to extol the virtues of J.B. Duckworth, a man he had never met. He had recently read about another Duckworth murder case in the newspaper. Or two, or five, even. The man sounded like an expert at lining out the particulars of a self-defense killing, and that was certainly what was called for here. Matching his fee might be a little bit of a struggle, but they had enough to get started. As George listened, he allowed himself a slight glimmer of hope, though that might have been put down to the late hour.

The Western Union boy knocked on the door of the Waverly Avenue house about 6:30 on Saturday morning. The Duckworth household was not yet functioning. Lola and Katherine were at that moment in the outhouse, and J.B.'s snoring was the only noise to be heard. The third, and loudest round of banging brought the sleepy lawyer to his front door.

He bid the lad wait as he read the telegram, then fetched a coin for the boy, an ambitious nine-year old on a bicycle. Technically, the messengers owed their allegiance to the Western Union Company, but a shiny enough tip might convince a youngster to make a brief detour on his way back to the telegraph office. That's how in just over two hours, John Duckworth boarded the 9:05 westbound from the Grand Central Depot. Ninety minutes later, he stepped off the train in Richmond.

The Duckworths knew little about the case, but the victim's name, from a prominent family like the Ennises, got their attention. J.B. loved few things better than tweaking the noses of the rich. He instructed John, who was the nominal business manager of the law practice, to make the finances work. These prominent cases were always good for bringing in better paying clients later. They became news, not law, and that was precisely what the firm of Duckworth and Fein wanted.

John Duckworth had performed hundreds of potential client meetings. Taking notes and getting the lay of the land did not technically require an attorney. The job often fell to either him or one of the young law clerks. It was a small office, and over the past few years, an efficient rhythm of work had evolved, quickly adjusted for changes in personnel.

John had to admit that none of his previous introductions had opened with quite the same clank. Or perhaps more of a ping. That was the noise John heard as the deputy leading him upstairs to the gray and dingy second floor reached the top of the landing. A smirk graced the policeman's lips as he turned to John and pointed to the little space almost completely walled in by gray steel. The door stood open.

"Doc Dillard is in there with him. We moved him to a small cell to accommodate some privacy."

The doctor was clearly the one with the forceps and rag, leaving the patient to be George Purdy. As John stood there, another pellet came out of Purdy's neck and rattled into a small dish.

"Just stay out of my light, I'm only halfway done," the physician offered brusquely.

"Actually, doctor,..."

John cleared his throat to get the man's attention.

"His lawyer prefers that you leave those shot pellets in there."

That brought the action to an immediate halt out of pure shock on the faces of George Purdy and Doctor Dillard. The doc recovered first.

"What the hell are you talking about? I'm giving medical care to this... man."

When the outraged glare was concluded, Dillard turned to resume his work. George's head was cocked to one side like J.B.'s dog.

"Seriously, doctor. I'd like you to stop until I can talk this over with our client."

As Dillard rose suddenly from his chair, he gave Duckworth a leer.

"There is no 'until.' I would like nothing better than to be removed from the company of this murderer. Yesterday, I had my hands in the wounds of his victim, a fine man who I watched expire. I've satisfied my oath by coming here. When you seek medical help again, and you will, kindly have the jailer call on someone else."

With that Dillard clicked shut his black grip and clattered down the metal stairs. Duckworth and Purdy looked at each other with a shrugging dismay.

"I don't guess that's the worst thing," George told him. "He was pushing and prodding like he was trying to punish me with those little pliers of his, and I'm thinking now it was deliberate. He was not providing any comfort, I'll tell you that."

John Duckworth extended his hand and made a formal introduction before offering his explanation.

"One of the things my brother told me this morning was that if there was any visible wound, he'd just as soon it stay In place. Within the bounds of safety, of course. That sort of thing plays into a jury's sympathy. I've seen it work before."

Purdy pondered that idea.

"We had a dairy cow when I was a boy who lived a good three years with a load of bird shot in her rump. Drunk neighbor shot her. It never bothered her out of giving milk, so I reckon I can handle it."

"We'll get them removed once the trial is over."

George's agreement came quicker and easier than Duckworth anticipated, though newly confined clients facing serious consequences tended to be at their most pliable. The doctor's departure left six pieces of shot in place, including two very visible in his left cheek and one bubbled up at the hairline. John's inexpert opinion was that the angry red swelling would subside, but he advised the client to wash his face every day.

The first question from George involved the law firm's fees.

"I'm sorry you've come to all this trouble without me even knowing that I can see this through. I've got no savings, Mr. Duckworth, and the way Charlie described your brother and all, well, there's just no way I can afford that."

"Not every client pays the same amount, Mr. Purdy. My brother told me to make the cost work for you. Sometimes we collect a pile of money, and sometimes we serve the side of justice. That's how he puts it. And the two don't always coincide."

George considered that statement for a time before responding. In just a few days he had witnessed more mistreatment and more good intentions than over the previous ten years combined.

"I appreciate that very kindly. I'm not much on accepting generosity because I don't like being under obligation. That notion rankles me a good deal. In this situation, though, and I've been thinking on it all morning, I am obliged to accept and not let my stubbornness hurt my chances."

"Other than farming, have you done much else, Mr. Purdy?"

"Yes, sir. I'm a carpenter by trade. I come to Sartartia to build houses, and just took up farming this past season. And I think you can call me George, if you've a mind to."

Purdy followed that invitation by mustering a small smile. John returned a shy grin of his own.

"Thank you, George, and I'm just John. I'm not the important man my brother is."

John Duckworth cast his eyes downward for a second before continuing.

"If it would make you feel any better about things, my brother and I own a couple of properties, and we are always looking for a good carpenter now and again. Knowing we can call on you is worth something. We can count that future work against your bill. Is that okay with you?"

"Yes, sir. That would ease my mind, some.""Good. I'm sure that'll square with J.B., too. All right then, we ought to get started. Why don't you tell me your side of the story, and start as far back as you need to."

It took George Purdy about 40 minutes to recount the bare facts of the shooting and its preceding trouble. Another half hour of questions followed with John scribbling notes onto journal pages in a small, tight hand. When they were finished, Duckworth repositioned himself on the little wood chair.

"There is one other thing, just something to think about until next time. Our firm will be coming up with a witness list, and we need to know from you who is likely to be on our side and who might be against us."

"Well, there were four people there other than me and Will Ennis…"John held up his hand as he cut George off.

"It's not just the eyewitnesses, but which ones will see things in a way that help our case."

George gave a nod and a grunt.

"And then there are the character witnesses, those who will attest that you are a good man. Lawmen, too, if you know any. Those who will be gathering evidence. Any people in authority. We'd like to suss out a little about them. Your thoughts on that would be helpful. To use one of J.B.'s sayings again, we need to know who insists on fighting square, and who will bend with a little wind?"

Purdy's expression was quizzical.

"Like I said. Just think about it, and you can tell whoever comes down next time. That may well be my brother, or it might be someone else."

Their business for the day concluded, John gathered up his papers and spoke his goodbyes. The return train was not until 4:18, leaving him plenty of time for a late lunch in Richmond. He made his standard final enquiry.

"You okay? Do you need anything?"

"Naw. I'm set. The sheriff said I could keep this little cell by myself until they need it. He seems like a decent fellow. Charlie Mabin, the one who sent for you, he'll come back in a couple of days. We talked about getting my kids to visit, but I don't want them to see me caged up."

"Maybe we can work on something in time. The law firm, of course will be working on bail as soon as we can, though I'm supposing you going back home is out of the question."

When the steel door from the confinement areas opened, it was Sheriff R.P. Briscoe on the other side. He extended his hand. John could not decode the feeling behind the level green eyes.

"Mr. Duckworth, I just wanted to introduce myself. I met your brother once when he handled the Hodge case here in the county, and I nodded at him a time or two when he was with Mr. Mitchell, but somehow I never met you. I won't hold you up, but I figured it best to offer you a suggestion to be mindful around here."

John was a bit taken aback, but he recovered.

"Your reputation is for fairness, sheriff."

"Oh, you misunderstand me. It's not my department that should worry y'all. It's just that there are some very volatile folks in Fort Bend County. Your brother, of all people, should be aware of that."

Cryptic message completed, Briscoe open the steel door to the outside and offered John Duckworth a polite good day.

Chapter 13

M arch 1902

The first Sunday in March was chilly and drizzly. The office windows of Duckworth & Fein were open anyway. Two of the men inside were smoking cigars, and the smoke wafted out, but it was the old sweat and past cigars that most contributed to the general fug. In this respect, the law offices were no different than any other business suite in the city.

The criminal district court session opened the following day in several of the state's county seats, and the final preparation for trials was happening this afternoon. Henry Fein was already in Bryan in anticipation of a possible trial, several important motions and one hearing on five cases the firm had on the morning docket there. If timing worked and the man could meet him at the Depot, Henry would also drop a filing with the court clerk in Hempstead on his way home. All other lawyers and employees were expected at the job this Sunday morning.

Though most everyone had arrived almost an hour earlier, J.B. Duckworth was still puttering through papers at his office desk in one of the two private rooms while a bored law clerk stood at the ready. In the larger space that did duty as clerks' office, conference room and waiting area, the cigar smokers killed time until the work started. Sonny Schlottmann, the firm's junior partner whose desk sat in a back corner, and Harris Peterson, present as a strategist at the request of his close friend Duckworth, were each reading copies of that morning's *Post*.

"Looks like they're working on a Jeffries and Fitzsimmons rematch."

Schlottmann offered this conversation even though Peterson held the exact same newspaper.

"That fight'll be moonshine. Fitz is little and decrepit. An old boxer needs to know when to retire."

"He might earn as much as ten thousand for the fight," Sonny countered.

"I got that much for defending Great Northern last year, and nobody punched me in the face."

"It's not cause they didn't want to, Harris."

Duckworth announced his arrival with the joke, but it signaled the start of business.

"I'm off to Wharton tonight for Purdy, and I'll be down there till it's done. Let's go through that one first because I want to hear from Harris, then we can do the rest."

Harris Peterson interrupted before Duckworth could continue.

"J.B., if you don't mind, I'd like to fit in a private word after we talk through your case, then I'll be on my way."

"Of course. I don't want to take advantage."

"Oh, why change things up now?"

Duckworth gave a grin that widened his thick moustache into a line.

"I feel like our case is a pretty clear self-defense, and there are, shall we say... concerns about their witnesses. At least there will be when I get done with them."

There were smiles around the table as J.B. continued.

"I asked you to stop by, Harris, because I wanted to get the lowdown on our judge. You've dealt with him, and this is my first time since criminal work is not his usual bailiwick."

Peterson gave a grunt before starting his assessment.

"Farnham is competent, cranky and, last I heard, still in control of his various faculties. He is older than Methuselah's grandpa, though. He and my old man were friends when we lived in Brazoria. Honestly, my best advice is speak loudly and slowly, and that's not a joke. He gets annoyed as hell when he can't hear."

"Good to know."

"Last time I was before him, which has been a good year and a half, he had a clerk named Cayce. Weasley looking fellow with a big mole on his forehead, but he had Farnham's ear. A little kissing of the devil's ass should go a long way."

"What a lovely picture you paint, Judge," Sonny Schlottmann observed to a general snort of laughter.

J.B. had one more question for his friend, Peterson. It regarded the demographics of the county to which the trial venue had moved. Wharton County, along with Fort Bend, Brazoria and Matagorda, made up a coastal square of what had been Texas sugar growing country. At the time of Emancipation, those counties held populations that were overwhelmingly comprised of recently freed men and women. That made for especially volatile politics ever since.

"Harris, you said in passing the other day that the White Man's Union is strong down there, and it's been fussing at my brain. How is all of that going to affect my jury?"

"Well, I'm only guessing mind you, but it's possible you'll still draw a colored man or two for the jury pool. They outnumber everybody else five to one, for Lord's sake. But Wharton has been prosperous. You've got some Jews and Danes down there. Lot of building going on the last few years. Most of the money is still with the ranchers, of course, but since Shanghai Pierce died, it's spread around some. If you get the chance to shake J.D. Hudgins' hand, he's a good man to know. Really, that's all I can tell you, J.B.. I don't get down there but two or three times a year. Now, if we could please have that private word, ..."

"Gentlemen, if you will excuse Judge Peterson and me for just a few moments, I want to let him be on his way as soon as I can. As opposed to you lot who will be here all day suffering under my tyrant's thumb."

With a genuine smile met with mock groans and grumbles, the two adjourned from the large room and closed the door to J.B.'s office.

Duckworth and Henry Fein each rated private chambers at opposite corners of the rented space. The brick building that held them was nothing remarkable save for its address at 1107 ½ Congress Avenue, directly across the street from the Gothic pile that was the Harris County Courthouse. Each of the firm's second floor offices offered that view through a large window of its own, and like the center window, which opened into the common area, J.B.'s was ajar, but only about four inches. He and Harris perched on the wooden visitor chairs.

"Thanks, Harris. I really appreciate you stopping by. Seriously."

"Glad to take some morning air, and you saved me getting into a dress suit and going to church. Anyway, I wanted to break the news in private. I ran into your close friend the district attorney last night at dinner. I was treating Louise at the Capitol Hotel."

Peterson smiled as he spoke. Duckworth had questions.

"Why are you grinning? I gather you didn't try to lure her into a rented room after the sherry. Or did Lea belch in your phiz again?"

"No. I'm grinning because the gaseous Mr. Lea said that they were going to let your assault charge from last fall drop. The complainant, whatever his name was, is no longer interested in seeing things to completion."

"Hallelujah. That was $50 well spent."

"Oh, and I'll bill you another fifty just to keep you honest. Remind you to stop shoving pistols up people's noses downtown."

"Allegedly."

"Yes, allegedly."

Harris Peterson smiled and clapped his hands in a demonstration of small glee. Not only were the two men fast friends, J.B.'s closest save his brother, but they were also investment partners. Peterson's practice had evolved a specialty of real estate law. He handled legal matters for cattle ranches, railroads, large commercial enterprises and well-off individuals. Frequently, by keepings his ears open to the latest property gossip, he learned of rock bottom deals coming up through probate or foreclosure. The latter avenue had recently led to him and Duckworth acquiring a bowling alley for a song.

"I've got us a tenant for our lanes. German fellow, of course. He said that the Volkesfest and Turnverein are both too crowded these days, and he sees money to be made. He's already put up a deposit, so I'll add it to your ledger. It will help offset my fees for keeping you out of the pokey."

"Much appreciated. I got another couple of thousand that I managed to hide from Lola," Duckworth said with a wink. "What else is coming along the pike?"

"As a matter of fact, there are a couple of houses in the Chapmans that we should try to snap up next week. Good little rentals. That's from a tip I got regarding bickering siblings in probate court. They've decided to liquidate all real property as soon as the settlement ink is dry. I'll count you in."

"Damn, Harris, you've got all my investment money, already, but I always appreciate you asking first before you spend it."

The two friends shared a hearty laugh as they exited Duckworth's office.

Sonny Schlottmann had utilized the time to go over some logistics with the two clerks. Though it was J.B. Duckworth's relentless defense of accused murderers that made the headlines, most of the firm's business was more mundane. Personal injury brought in a good deal of money. Then there was defense work on burglaries, robberies and petty theft. If someone asked, Duckworth & Fein would even do their contract work, though that would undoubtedly fall on a clerk's desk.

Sonny was an eager young man of 24, four years Henry Fein's junior. Like Fein, he earned an L.L.B from the University of Texas Law School. Thanks to his immigrant parents, Schlottmann was fluent in German. It was, in fact, his mother tongue, again like the Alsatian-born Fein. Knowing that language had proven helpful in south and central Texas.

When J.B. Duckworth first met Sonny's parents, he found them to be officious and aloof, precisely what he expected. On the other hand, Sonny, whose real name was Otto Schlottmann, Junior, quickly endeared himself to J.B.. The senior partner saw a good work ethic and efficiency, likely inherited, but it was mixed with ample charm, tolerance and humor. Duckworth & Fein had hired him as a clerk in 1899 and made him a junior partner just 16 months later.

The firm needed the help. Their caseload stretched them to the limits. Even with new additions to the roster, requests for postponement were de rigueur at Duckworth & Fein. It was normal for cases to be pending in over 70 courts spread across at least 30 Texas counties, and that left a paltry five attorneys scrambling, though they learned to flourish amongst organized chaos.

The situation was quickly evident to all outsiders via physical clues. The large common room was as packed as it could be, and when the office was open for business, it often seemed that potential clients must sit on the laps of those who had arrived before them. The precarious towers of paperwork that dotted every open surface no doubt mesmerized the customers in the waiting room like an overlong cigar ash, but so far, they had never fallen.

Harris Peterson slipped unobtrusively out the door while J.B. waited for Schlottmann and the clerks to finish. When they were done, he wasted no time jumping in.

"First bit of good news, Harris is being kind enough to file a motion in limine in Angleton since he is going to be down there on another of his big money land cases. He owes me a couple. So that's one less row to hoe."

Jed Posey, the more outgoing of the two clerks, noted how Duckworth's sentence began.

"You said 'first.' That would mean there is additional good news?"

"Yes, there is, Jed. As soon as my brother gets here, the sandwiches are on me."

John arrived at half past one. Not being a lawyer, his input on Sundays was limited, though the firm usually found myriad ways to use his talents. He unceremoniously set to work reviewing papers, some of which had only arrived on his desk in the last several minutes.

The other four men in the common room had been at it for three hours. They had analyzed more than three dozen cases. Only a few were anything other than standard. The two biggest matters were the murder trials coming up in Wharton and Bryan.

Harris County was a beast of its own. Some of the rural locales might present sleepy court sessions, but in a county that held the city of Houston and several other towns, many people felt that a criminal docket held every other month was highly inadequate. Everything that exceeded the jurisdiction of a Justice of the Peace was saved up.

For Sonny Schlottmann, who would be in the Harris County Criminal Court the next day, that meant motions to postpone four local murder trials and the hope that the lesser trials facing him and the clerks would move along without surprises. He wanted J.B.'s input on one case in particular. Sensing that the next pressing topic would take some time, Duckworth stood up and looked at his brother.

"John, I'm starving. What can we do about that?"

"Charlie Dixon's at the bottom of the stairs. I told him we'd be needing him shortly."

"Then let's get him up here, shall we?"

Charlie Dixon was the firm's errand boy. Nothing official, but he was there most every day, nonetheless. At least, J.B. told himself that it was unofficial. The fact was that his pay had gone from a few odd coins to a de facto salary some months prior. Days when he failed to show up soon became a bit of a hardship.

It was a winter day, colder and wetter than the present one, when a wisp of a boy mounted the stairs, slipped through the waiting clients all the way to Henry Fein's office and asked if there were any jobs open. Replying to Henry's query, the lad assured him he was a full nine years old. He looked younger. As it happened, Henry needed two envelopes couriered to clients. One was going to First National Bank on Franklin at Main Street and another to the Sam Allen Lumber Company nearby. Fein asked the boy if he could handle that task while keeping the envelopes dry.

"Yes, sir," was the immediate answer accompanied by a smile. "I can slip them right inside my coat here."

He then demonstrated the suggested location with his hand.

"It'll cost you two nickels."

Henry suppressed a smile. It was risky to rely on a total stranger, a random Black kid, less than four feet tall, who wandered in off the street. But there was an earnestness in his young eyes, and the paperwork was nothing that could not be replaced.

"All right. Two nickels it is."

Henry handed the boy the envelopes, but the youth did not move.

"Begging your pardon, sir, but I'm going to need one of them nickels up front."

This time Henry laughed, but he produced a Liberty head nickel from his pocket.

The youngster not only returned for his other nickel, but brought a response from Sam Allen, a task which he pointed out to Henry should earn him a third coin.

"What's your name?" Fein asked the boy.

"Charlie Dixon, sir."

"Well, Charlie, I think..."

Henry was cut off in mid-sentence.

"It's Charlie Dixon, sir."

Over the intervening year, some of the law office personnel, most notably J.B. Duckworth, had graduated to calling their new co-worker Charlie, but more often he was referred to by his full moniker of Charlie Dixon.

Duckworth encouraged the young man to go to school, and told him not to show up at the office until after two. To prove his compliance, Charlie Dixon would sometimes offer the lawyers a brief, unbidden recitation of that day's lessons at the grammar school rooms of Colored High. It was very close to Charlie Dixon's home on Robin Street near Heiner in the Castanie Addition of Fourth Ward.

As they came to learn more about their youngest employee, the lawyers found that Dixon's mother ran a home laundry. Charlie was the oldest of four children. His father, who had been a brakeman for the Houston & Texas Central, was dead, crushed while coupling freight cars that suddenly moved. There was no settlement to speak of, and almost needless to say, the family's lawyer in that matter had not been Duckworth & Fein.

In the present day, Charlie Dixon awaited his instructions from J.B. Duckworth for the shortest errand imaginable. He was being sent to Yadon's Saloon almost directly below the firm's offices.

"Run downstairs and bring us a dozen sandwiches, whatever's fresh, and a gallon of beer," J.B. requested. "On my tab, of course."

"Do you want whiskey, too, Mr. D.?"

"No, just beer, Charlie. We're not drinking today. Too much work to do."

"Yes, sir."

"And that'll be it for today. Once you've brought those up, get out of here and go play. Have some fun for Christ's sake."

Charlie started to go, then made one last look around the room, even leaning over to peer into J.B.'s office.

"Where's Maizy?"

"I have to catch a train this afternoon, so Maizy stayed home. She'll be back at work next week."

Once half the sandwiches were consumed, ham and cheddar on somewhat stale rye bread, Sonny Schlottmann brought up a robbery case that was expected to be called for trial on Tuesday. The firm's client, Ed Underwood, was a repeat offender, but they had worked acquittals for him twice before.

"It's as if he gets more stupid with each case he brings us," Sonny opined.

Jed Posey answered and drew a laugh.

"There's nothing that says thieves need to be good at their jobs."

"This time the store owner picked him out of the police mug book. I'm already planning to offer up two flimsy alibis, but those are from known criminals. The D.A. will pick away at it. And I'll hammer the unreliability of eye witnesses till the cows come home, but I was hoping you'd have other suggestions."

J.B. brushed a bread crumb from his shirt and raked his moustache with his bottom lip.

"Lighting. This was the little store on Sampson Street in Second Ward, yes? There's not a streetlight to be seen within ten blocks of that place. So, he had only a kerosene light or whatever's in there. John, you'll already be out that way on the Swearingen goose chase, go around that store tomorrow night to scout out how many lamps there are. And if there's one on the counter, suggest that the flame had temporarily burned his vision, rendering his eyesight suspect."

"Hang on."

Sonny shook his fountain pen a few times then held it back over his pad.

"Sorry. I liked that last part very much. Burned his vision? How did you phrase that?"

Even though the steady stream of case review slogged forward like trained soldiers on the march, the senior partner had been watching the wall clock for the last hour. At precisely 4:10, he offered low-key admonitions of good luck as he picked up a small stack of paperwork and folded them into an already bulging grip by the outer door. They barely noticed him walking out. The remaining three lawyers had more to go over while J.B. left for Wharton on the last decent train tonight.

Chapter 14

J.B. Duckworth nodded hellos to a few people he did not know as he walked up the gleaming wood stairs. When he got to the landing, and faced a choice, he took the stairs to his left, just to be contrarian. The double doors to the district court room stood open. Streams of sunlight and the glow of the gas lamps lit the scene.

The pews for the general public were mostly filled, and there was a low hum of conversation as he strode up the center aisle to the defense table. When he entered the Houston courts, where he had a name, the talk would at least dip in volume, but here, nobody paid him heed. Just as it was a rare appearance for him inside the Wharton County Courthouse, it would be most spectators' first time seeing Duckworth spin a defense.

Like most every trial attorney on Earth, J.B. dearly loved courthouses. The touches of grandeur, the details of brass, and the smell of wood polish and law books. He treasured it all, and took the time to walk completely around the square and admire the Wharton Courthouse this morning before heading inside. This tall Empire design was the creation of his late acquaintance Eugene Heiner, an architect who had made his living through public commissions for courthouses and jails. Duckworth made a mental note to raise a glass to Eugene when he got a chance this evening.

He was in Wharton because the District Attorney had asked for a change of venue. It baffled J.B. at first. Moving the trial out of town was one of his most frequent tactics, so to have a prosecutor request it was rare indeed. He opposed it on reflexive principle. If the prosecution wanted it, he should damn well be against it.

On the day of the hearing in Richmond, J.B. had been deep in another murder trial in Beaumont, a hundred miles away, and could not appear personally. Since the Fort Bend criminal court met only twice a year, he was not disposed to postpone just for a venue hearing. Instead, he sent Sonny Schlottmann, his newly promoted junior partner, to argue against the move. He lost.

Since that hearing in late October, Duckworth had begun to understand two things that might have been the motivation behind the venue change. First, the Ennis Family was not universally loved. They had made a few enemies in the area, though J.B. assumed much of it could be attributed to sour grapes. They were, after all, a wealthy bunch. Second, many of the Richmond folk believed the East Fort Bend crowd was too beholden to Houston interests. The Ennis family had lived in the county for more than 30 years, but they were still not local enough for some people. Though there was nothing he could gain from that second perspective, the enemies angle was intriguing. He filed it away as a potential avenue to exploit.

Jury selection was from a special venire. Being a murder trial with an expectation of multiple days, the court summoned a panel of 70 men. Prosecutor Samuel Styles, the District Attorney for Fort Bend, Matagorda, and Wharton Counties was running the show. Styles was a young man on the come. He had family ties in Bay City and Brenham, and already sported a reputation as a political dealmaker. He wanted men from town, not farmers who carried memories of hard work in their hands. J.B. wanted as many working men as he could get.

There was no consultation for the defense. Only Duckworth and George Purdy sat at the defense table. George, in a suit J.B. had paid to have cleaned, looked very ill at ease. The Mabins and three other friends from Sartartia sat in the gallery behind him. Sarah and Arthur did not attend.

While George carefully examined the wood grain on the table top, J.B. squiggled and doodled on his pad. His thoughts on the potential jurors were securely in his head, but he hoped that with each scratch of his pencil, D.A. Styles would imagine mental gears grinding.

Harris Peterson's surmise had been correct. Four Black men were among the pool of 70, all property owners with small farms. A handful of the men wore bib overalls, but most had come to court in trousers and a rough jacket. Perhaps a third had neckties. Duckworth counted eight of the 70 sporting what he considered proper suits.

They ended up with an even split. Six farmers and ranchers from the rural stretches of the county, and six men from towns, five from Wharton and one storekeeper from the hamlet of Egypt. Styles dismissed all four of the Blacks.

Brief opening statements made, the prosecution set forth their case. The crux of their approach was that Will Ennis was justified and exercising his rights as Sartartia's managing owner. George Purdy killed him to prevent a perfectly rightful eviction.

The first witness was Francis Marion Otis Fenn, a Richmond lawyer well known to J.B.. He was currently serving as Fort Bend County Attorney, but more to the point in this matter, he had authored, or cribbed, the tenant farming agreements in use on the Ennis Plantation. The fact that he was now a prosecutor did not erase his past work or even prevent him from performing other legal tasks.

Duckworth had long since formed the opinion that the slender, wavy-haired Fenn was uppity. Though he grew up near the East Fort Bend County town of Stafford, Fenn's father shipped him off to Roanoke College in Virginia, an ancestral home, and then paid his way through the University of Virginia Law School. He practiced in Houston before J.B. arrived, and had just returned home as Duckworth himself showed up on the Richmond legal scene. Fenn did not have time to waste acknowledging a junior clerk with no formal legal training, and Duckworth never forgot it.

Styles led Fenn through the ins and outs of the contract, something which half of the jury might already know. To his credit, Fenn's oratorical skills kept most of the jurors from the land of nod. He smoothly assured them that the concept of evicting a farmer for abandonment of their fields was standard practice. He then followed that up by very calmly outlining that a hypothetical tenant who left for more than two weeks, even to visit a dying parent, would be in clear violation of the terms. By the time Fenn was done, Duckworth wanted to slap the smug velvet from his mouth.

J.B. rose from his chair slowly, wearing a confused expression.

"Mr. Fenn, did you ever have a mother?"

The laughter caused Judge Farnham to slap his desk top with a block of wood.

"Yes, Mr. Duckworth. I do."

"That's good to hear. And is she living?"

"Yes, sir. She is, and in good health. Thank you for inquiring after her."

With that Fenn gave a toothy smile to the jury.

"Glad to hear it. I hate to be the bearer of sad tidings, but your mother will pass on some day."

Fenn quickly dropped his smile and adopted a suitably sad face.

"Let's hope it's not too soon."

"Indeed. But when it does happen, do you intend to go to her funeral?"

Fenn was ready with his response and delivered it with taciturn sincerity.

"I would certainly hope so if my responsibilities allowed, but as you well know, not every man is afforded that luxury."

"So, attending your mother's funeral is a luxury, a frivolity?"

"Only in the sense that it must be weighed against one's responsibilities. While it is important to pay respects, many people believe that nothing is more important than a man's word."

Over a dozen people on the spectator pews nodded, but Duckworth did not see them.

"I'm sure your intact integrity will be a comfort to your dear mother as she takes her final breath alone. Nothing further."

A few small gasps accompanied J.B. back to the defense table.

Sam Styles had an assured bearing as he went through his witnesses, and he frequently made eye contact with the Ennis family members seated two rows behind him. With a businesslike manner that underscored his business oriented case, he used other witnesses to build up Ennis' right to expel Purdy because of the contract violation.

Next, he set out to establish Purdy's great anger. It was easy to do. The first called on this topic was Emmett Ennis, who was a witness by the window to Purdy's outburst on the family's back porch. He recounted his oldest brother stepping outside to deal with a livid George Purdy. Emmett was clear that tenants did not come to their home to conduct business, nor were they welcome there.

When Styles asked if Purdy made a direct threat, Emmett answered without hesitation.

"Definitely. He said that he would kill my brother before he gave up the crops. I heard him plain as day."

In his cross examination, Duckworth tried his best to create leeway in relation to any threat of killing, but Emmett Ennis was a rock. In the end, J.B. took his lumps on the matter and sat down.

Ed Bertrand followed Emmett to the stand, and his testimony was equivocal from the outset. Styles repeatedly led with talk of George Purdy's anger, but shortly into the questioning, Bertrand set him straight with a correction.

"I'd call it more frustration, honestly," the overseer told him.

At the defense table, J.B. Duckworth felt like clapping. Behind the prosecution, the three surviving Ennis brothers glared.

Though prosecutor Styles clearly knew that Bertrand was not a witness to the shooting, he had him line out the confrontation up until Will Ennis ordered him to tend to the wagon of corn. When J.B. got his turn, he spent a solid fifteen minutes having Bertrand detail the specifics of the dispute between the principle players in the fatal drama. The lawyer hoped that the jury noted a sympathetic tone.

If there was momentum for the defense, it reined to a halt with Duckworth's next line of questioning.

"This was not the first time that Will Ennis used the fine print of a contract to evict a lawful tenant, was it, Mr. Bertrand."

Before he could even enunciate Bertrand's name, the prosecutor was on his feet, objecting for relevance. Thrice more in succession, J.B. broached Will Ennis' treatment of his sharecroppers, but the questions were shot down by the bench before responses could be given by Bertrand. Finally Judge Farnham rapped his block of wood.

"Mr. Duckworth, you need to hurry along to your next item. I have made clear that William Ennis is not the defendant here, and I would hate to hold you in contempt for your insouciance toward my rulings."

"Yes, your honor. In light of the exclusion of Mr. Ennis' lengthy record of evicting poor tenant farmers without due cause, I have nothing further for Mr. Bertrand."

Half of the courtroom sniggered, including some in the jury box. Farnham gave a single rap of the block as J.B. took his seat.

After a leisurely, and somewhat tardy, lunch break, Prosecutor Styles summoned the first of his two ace witnesses. Cloyd Moore adjusted his glasses and placed his hand on the Bible. Once seated, he scratched lightly at his scalp and adjusted the specs again, with a hand at each temple.

Prosecutor Styles began with the wagon's arrival at the Purdy lease. The bookkeeper injected a surprising amount of drama into his recounting of the scene. He placed George Purdy ominously holding the Winchester at the corner post. He built the tension, as Will Ennis advanced with a steely eye, ignoring Purdy's shouted warning. He had the men facing each other like gunslingers in a dime western. In Moore's telling, it was the tenant who raised his rifle and shot first.

"So, it was William Ennis who was defending himself and his property, not the defendant, wouldn't you say then, Mr. Moore?"

"Definitely, sir."

With jurors physically leaning into the tale, Styles next had Moore recount Ennis' stagger back toward the wagon and his fall into the dirt. That was followed by the story of Ed Bertrand's return, the moving of Ennis to the Sartartia rail stop and his eventual demise. As he concluded and took his seat at the prosecution table, Sam Styles' eyes sparkled with smugness.

J.B. Duckworth was in no hurry to get to his feet. He made a small show of consulting with his client. One skinny juror shifted on his hard seat as if his rear was troubling him. With every second of delay, Cloyd Moore added another nervous tick. Finally, J.B. approached the witness.

"Mr. Moore, please tell us precisely when during these events you jumped into the ditch."

The bookkeeper's head snapped back a good three inches, and his eyes blinked hard. The reaction was evident to every single spectator in the courtroom. Finally, the slight man recovered himself.

"I don't know what you mean."

"You were in the ditch. You jumped in the ditch. When you thought the threat of violence was imminent, you dove headlong into the ditch. I'm merely trying to determine exactly when that was."

Duckworth had phrased the entire exchange as a series of statements, not questions.

"Well, taking cover from flying bullets is just common sense, sir. Only a fool would stand and be shot at."

"Oh, I'm not denying that notion, Mr. Moore. I'm not a man for flying bullets myself. But I would like to know further details about your view of events during the time your face was pressed into the dirt at the bottom of the ditch."

That drew a loud laugh from almost all assembled. With a wind now at his back, J.B. kept the state's witness unnerved for another eighteen minutes. He managed to insert the word ditch a dozen more times. He also attempted, without success to have Moore confirm that Ennis used phrases such as "Let's fix him." Moore's denials were plainly given with an averted eye and tremulous voice.

At that juncture, Duckworth paused and walked back to the defense table. He looked down silently at his client. As he turned back toward the jury, he scraped a thick law book, the only one on the table, off the front edge. It hit the floor squarely on its back with an echoing bang.

Cloyd Moore jumped like a touched frog.

Still facing the jurors, his face impassive, Duckworth smoothed the corners of his big moustache.

"That's all, your honor."

Judge Farnham did not even bother to use his wood block.

Harold Barton's testimony and Duckworth's cross examination went much the same as Cloyd Moore's. When J.B. inquired repeatedly into Barton's own hiding place behind the wagon, the big man maintained himself better than his cohort, but the rising blush in his pale cheeks gave him away.

Styles did score when Barton carefully described holding Will Ennis' head with one hand and pressing a rag to his gaping wound with the other while his boss breathed his last. Jurors watched Barton's face closely for a wayward tear.

The state's final witness was Dr. J. L. Dillard who, to Duckworth's eye, was every inch as disagreeable as his brother had described. His testimony remained heavily scientific, though J.B. could plainly see that Styles was angling for the old gentleman to offer a few traces of humanity.

As Dillard stepped from the witness chair, Judge Farnham consulted his pocket watch.

"My wife will be waiting supper. That's enough for today. We are adjourned until 9:00 A.M. tomorrow. Good evening, gentlemen."

With that and a single rap of his treasured wood block, the first day of the trial was done.

Chapter 15

Since childhood, J.B. Duckworth had liked his eggs sunny side up. There was something immensely satisfying about sopping up the bright, runny yolk with a biscuit, and he had to admit that the City Café, two doors down from the Nation Hotel where he was staying, made a pretty good biscuit. He dabbed and swiped at his plate and silently observed the scene on courthouse square.

A wagon fairly full of sawn lumber stood catty-cornered in front of a dry goods store, and a sullen boy sat on its bench. To Duckworth's eye, the store had undergone recent repairs, most likely hurricane damage mended. Halfway down that block, a man was trying on new boots. The stiffness was evident since he had stepped onto the sidewalk and was staring at them while stomping his feet. With a mostly satisfied look, the gent turned and went back into the shop. Four farmers visited at the corner of the courthouse lawn opposite. One of them got off a real knee-slapper, and the men threw back their heads and howled.

It was not that J.B. was dwelling on the sights. The mindless observation of the action allowed his brain to process other thoughts. It unbuttoned some mental chamber, that quiet perusal of his surroundings did. His best thinking often came while he saw, but ignored, what was happening around him. A good walk through town worked wonders, a ride, a beer on his front porch, or a solitary breakfast by a plate glass window.

The waitress asked about his tea for the third time.

"Oh, yes. Please."

The young lady rolled her eyes as she walked back toward the counter. J.B. daubed at his moustache. Between the runny eggs, the flaky biscuits and the hot tea, his napkin was getting quite the working over.

Specifically, he was thinking through last night's conversation with George Purdy at the jail around the corner. Though he was in the Wharton Jail only for the duration of the trial, the accommodations were not as hospitable as what Sheriff Briscoe had provided at Richmond. Here George was stuffed into a cell with six other men, and they were all parties to the attorney-client consultation. Two drunks actively so.

George had recited the events of his deadly encounter with Will Ennis yet again. When he told of pumping two rounds straight through Will's gut, the drunks shut their gobs and resumed the opposite end of the cell.

As much as mental quickness and a smart-mouth were natural attributes for J.B. Duckworth, none of his casework was done by improvisation. He had tried that approach a few times upon his late arrival to the legal profession, and it had not worked well. Defeat was a very personal humiliation for Duckworth in spite of any cavalier lip service to the contrary. Since those early times, he, his clerks, and partners strived for meticulous preparation. Even more importantly, J.B. seemed to have intuitively scripted out most possible twists and forks of every trial before the first remarks were ever made. Those mysterious notes remained solely in his head and were sometimes a bafflement for those who knew him best.

Some of his talk with George Purdy was replowing familiar ground, but there was a sprinkling of new questions. When the attorney finally said good night and walked around the corner to the squarish three-story building on Burleson Street where he was lodging, he felt slightly energized. It would take a few shots of Old Taylor and an hour with a Rudyard Kipling novel before he would attempt sleep. From his side of things, the client was exhausted.

The defense of George Purdy began with the tearing down of Will Ennis' reputation. J.B. called a total of eleven men who claimed to have known Ennis well. Some had socialized with him. Some knew him through business. Duckworth paid their expenses to ride the train from Fort Bend County and back. District Attorney Styles voiced frequent objections about the relevance of the testimony, but Duckworth's march of attrition against the Ennis character lasted the entire morning.

Farnham's obstinance about admitting mention of previous disputes over the tenant contracts mostly continued, but the point eluded no one. Though Purdy's neighbor Polly Mabin acknowledged that she was hiding in the corn crib during the shooting, J.B. called her to reinforce the negative view of Will Ennis. She called the man unpleasant. Other adjectives offered by the witnesses were swaggering, boisterous and erratic.

The statement that earned the most vicious looks from the Ennis family came from a stubble-faced storekeeper from Sugar Land.

"It ain't unanimous," he said. "But I'd reckon that the killing of Will Ennis brought a happy holler and a tipping of the jug in most houses around there."

J.B. also managed to get in three references to the fact that the prosecution had called no witnesses whatsoever to attest to any positive attributes of Will Ennis' character.

After lunch, Charlie Mabin took the stand. As he swore in, Duckworth considered the look in his light brown eyes. It was the same one George Purdy carried in his better moments, when fear had not taken precedence. J.B. speculated that it was virtually universal among small farmers the world over, even sharecroppers. It was a look that J.B. first clocked in his boyhood in Georgia. Tired but defiant. It showed a man who had taken nature's best punch, suffered through drought and plague, frost and fire, but knew that he could coax something important from the dirt. J.B. counted on that palpable defiance to be in Charlie's words.

Mabin had arrived at court with a jacket, worn but still serviceable. The attorney asked him to leave it with his wife in the pews when he rose to testify. Polly had no doubt boiled his pale green shirt to within an inch of its life, but there was no hiding the threadbare fabric on the linene collar at which Charlie Mabin now tugged. When he sat, he looked every bit the sinewy Texas farmer.

After thanking him for appearing, Duckworth wanted to talk about the friendship between Mabin and Purdy. Charlie gave concise answers in a low and apologetic drawl.

"My family has been at Sartartia for five years now. I've known George since he moved down from North Texas."

Purdy himself had thus far been a cigar store Indian at the defense table, but as his friend Charlie Mabin told of their swapping favors, the obvious affection for his children, the gifts of handmade chairs and the general good feelings that existed among the croppers on their section of Sartartia, George fidgeted a bit.

Duckworth made frequent looks at the jury and hoped that he saw some softening of their expressions. When he was satisfied with Charlie's painting of that image, he moved to life on the plantation for a tenant.

"I never had too much trouble with Mr. Ennis myself, but I knew those that did."

"Some who were run off with crops in the ground?"

Judge Farnham banged his wood block, just as expected. D.A. Styles, who had not even risen to full height, sat back down. Duckworth continued.

"Why would you say you fared so well with Will Ennis."

"Can't rightly speculate. But out of better than 30 tenants, only one has been there longer. I do reckon that I am overly careful in my dealings, though. My wife complains about it."

Though far from a brilliant joke, it garnered a large laugh from the courtroom.

"Let's go a different direction, Mr. Mabin. Keep the district attorney in a gleeful mood. What is your assessment of George Purdy? Is he a good man?"

"Good as they come."

At the defense table, George returned an ever so slight smile and nod back towards his friend Charlie.

"Does anybody ever get away from tenancy, from sharecropping?" Duckworth asked next. "By that I mean does anyone ever rise above the system?"

Charlie Mabin gave a rueful laugh.

"Nobody I've ever known. They say you can buy your own plot of ground someday, but that's just a ... a mirage. Like in the Arabian Nights. Especially when you're dealing with bad faith."

The inevitable bang from the block came again. J.B. nodded slightly but did not break his rhythm.

"What about George? Was he ever going to get out?"

Charlie considered his answer carefully before verbalizing it.

"Well, I'd hate to lose him as a friend, but I hope he'll go back to carpenter work."

Duckworth then led Mabin through the deadly day of the previous September, several times calling back to that "good man George Purdy's" actions. When he reached the shooting in the chronology of events, J.B. slowed his pace. He knew that he was moving toward his most important point of the entire trial.

"When Mr. Ennis stepped down from the wagon with Mr. Moore and Mr. Barton, did you hear him say 'Let's fix him' or 'Let's get him?'"

"No, sir. I was too far away to hear anything clearly.

"Did Mr. Ennis say something to the others?"

"It looked that way. Yes."

"So, he could have said that."

It was intended to sound almost under his breath, but it was audible to the front half of the courtroom. J.B. hurried to his next question before anyone could slow his rhythm with an objection.

"Were you armed at this time, Charlie?"

"No, sir."

"And why was that, suspecting there was going to be shooting trouble and all?"

"George made me promise to leave my gun at home."

"Why on Earth would he ask that?"

Charlie paused and stared down at his lap for a moment, then he looked Duckworth dead in the eye as he answered.

"Well, I reckon he didn't want me getting my tail in a crack on account of his troubles."

Fully half the jury nodded silently to themselves. Three or four of the empaneled Wharton businessmen maintained their stony gaze.

It took fifteen or more minutes for J.B. to walk Mabin through the story of Will Ennis' advance toward George Purdy and his fence post. When Charlie matter of factly told of Moore and Barton diving for cover, a titter of derision rippled through the courtroom. Neither man was back in court that day to see it.

Finally, the defense attorney and his witness arrived at the salient point.

"The two men were about forty yards apart, you said?"

"Yes, sir. That's what it looked like."

"And you could see both men well?"

"Oh, yes, sir. Clear as the nose on your face."

"This is very important, Charlie. Who fired first?"

"Will, that is Mr. Ennis, raised his gun. It had been down by his leg, but he raised it as quick as he stopped walking forward. Then they fired at the same time."

"You're absolutely certain of that?"

"Yes, sir. They fired at the same time."

J.B. turned directly to the jurymen sitting in two rows of chairs. He tried to make eye contact with each, reading their faces as he went.

"Thank you, Mr. Mabin."

Duckworth sat down at his table and gave his client a solid slap on the back.

Sam Styles asked Charlie several questions about Purdy's trip to Montague County, with each one underscoring that George was in clear violation of the tenant agreement, but the prosecutor got less satisfaction from his questions about George Purdy's building hatred of Will Ennis. He sat down with dignity intact, but the smug look of the previous day had waned a touch.

When Styles' cross-examination ended at near four in the afternoon, the court adjourned. Only the calling of Purdy himself was left for the following day.

Chapter 16

J .B. Duckworth could think of nothing that brought him more enjoyment than the final day of a murder trial. He looked out his second floor window at the Nation Hotel and took a deep lungful of the crisp morning air. It had dropped down to 40 degrees just a few hours before, and J.B. had generously cracked the window and used all the blankets supplied by the hostelry. He had even liberated one worn quilt from an open room down the hall. He was certain the maid could sort it out. The important thing was that he slept like a sawn log until the sunrise came through the lace curtains.

Looking at the courthouse where he would soon go to work, J.B. could not say that the air wafting up from Wharton's streets smelled especially pleasant, but it was energizing nonetheless. On the eve of a competition, all results were possible. For this trial in particular, he felt that things were going well. The six working men should be sewed up, and he sensed a sympathetic eye in the Egypt storekeeper and the dentist from Wharton. That left four worrisome jurors to target today. He took another deep breath and clapped once, all to himself.

In his corner of the big cell inside the Wharton County Jail, George Purdy tried not to inhale. He knew that the stench of overflowing slop buckets was likely to stay in his nostrils for days, intruding at unexpected times, but it was far from his biggest worry. Twelve men, strangers to whom he had never spoken, would decide, perhaps by days end, whether he could rejoin his family and start life someplace else. If they failed to see things his way, his kids would be hauled off to Lord knows where. Maybe to strangers. Maybe a county home. Maybe even split apart from each other. The worry tore at his gut.

"Your honor, I'll call George Purdy."

"Mr. Purdy, step forward and be sworn."

George brought outward calm to the stand, but there was an occasional chink in the armor that came in the form of an errant heavy breath or the loud growl of his stomach. He had been too nervous to eat the jailhouse porridge.

Just as instructed, at intervals throughout his two and a half hours on the stand, George rubbed a bit at the large black spots on his face, the shotgun pellets that he was requested to leave in place. The defense intended the gesture to be a clear reminder that Will Ennis was not the only person shot that afternoon.

Purdy recounted the trip to see his dying mother, and he solemnly detailed arriving to find that he was too late to bid her adieu. He told how he heard about his potential eviction, third hand from his neighbor. He used the term "not man enough" when stating his wish that the plantation owner had spoken to him directly. It was a seminal insult in rural Texas.

The need to know the true status of his tenancy brought George to the back porch of the big white house, and nothing more sinister was behind it. Purdy adamantly denied making any sort of threat while he was at the Ennis home, or anywhere else, for that matter.

His lawyer asked George to recount his fear as he realized that the plantation owner was likely to come after him with multiple armed men, and Purdy tersely described his thoughts and preparations for trouble. That led to the next big point that Duckworth wanted to underline - one about the weaponry at this particular gunfight. He flowed into it with a smoothing stroke of his moustache and a knitted brow.

"Now, as Mr. Ennis approached you, he was clearly armed, was he not?"

"Yes, sir, he had a shotgun in one hand and a pistol in the other."

"And Mr. Barton and Mr. Moore, what about them?"

"Well, they each were carrying a long gun when they stepped down from the wagon. Neither of them ever got close enough for me to tell much else about it."

"So, George, that's three armed men coming after you, but you still told your friend Charlie Mabin to leave his gun at home. Why did you do that?"

Purdy did not hesitate one whit in responding.

"You can see where standing up for myself has landed me, Mr. Duckworth. I sure didn't cotton to throwing Charlie in the soup."

"But that left you at a great disadvantage, didn't it?"

"Yes, sir. If you're counting firearms, I was outnumbered four to one."

Duckworth paused dramatically to let that scenario sink in with the jurors, though he kept his gaze firmly on George.

"As you stood there, watching Mr. Ennis and his hired guns ..."

Styles started an objection, but J.B. raised his voice to drown him out as he raised a supplicating hand.

"All right. Apologies. Mr. Ennis and his hired hands were advancing toward your leased yard. Did you say anything to ease the situation?"

"Yes, sir. Most surely I did. I warned Mr. Ennis to stop coming at me. Twice. I told him I didn't want to shoot."

"But he kept coming?"

Purdy answered with a grunt, and Duckworth took one step closer to the stand.

"George, as Mr. Ennis approached you with a gun in each hand, as your life was in mortal danger, do you recollect what you were thinking at that exact time?"

"Yes, sir. I was just looking to live out the harvest there with my family. Would've been on my way once the crops were turned in, given the trouble. I ain't so stupid as to stand in the way of danger, but I ... I can't be robbed neither. I was only wanting what was rightfully ours. I did the work, me and my own kids. For someone else to get the money, well, that's no different than if they walked through my front door and absconded with all my cash."

"I suspect it isn't."

The remark was another sotto voce commentary, and though, both the prosecutor and the judge wore disapproving looks, nothing was said. Duckworth walked close enough to touch the first row of jurors, then looked back to his witness.

"George, I've been watching you fuss at the wounds on your cheek. You were shot, too, weren't you?"

"Yes, sir."

"And do you think Mr. Ennis was aiming to do you serious harm?"

George Purdy's right hand reached for the embedded pellets, but he stopped himself halfway and lowered it to his lap.

"I took a pretty good shotgun blast to my face and head. Yes, sir, I did. I do reckon that Mr. Ennis was sure enough trying to kill me dead."

Duckworth turned to the jury box and nodded. He took two steps toward the defense table then turned back toward the witness with a last question.

"Do you have any second thoughts about killing a man, even in self-defense?"

"Like I said, I was just trying to protect what's mine. Feed my family through my own work. Taking a life to do that, well, yes, sir. I feel bad about that every day, but the fact is that if I hadn't fired my rifle when I did, if Mr. Ennis had even a second to aim, I'd be rotting in the cold ground today."

Behind the prosecution table, Emmett Ennis stared daggers. His older brother, Caswell, scrunched his mouth and took in a deep, loud breath.

J.B. had purposely timed the end of his examination of George Purdy to leave little license in the court's schedule. George's heartfelt sorrow came at precisely two minutes before noon. The luncheon adjournment gave jurors more than an hour to dwell on those words.

Upon returning to court, Sam Styles took up his cross of the defendant, and surprisingly, he was briefer than he could have been. He tried to get Purdy to waver on the subject of any threats made either directly to Will Ennis or even in the course of blowing off steam to his neighbors. Though he spent only ten minutes on the subject, he was no doubt frustrated.

The D.A. concluded with three direct questions, getting the defendant to admit clearly that he had signed the agreement to farm the land at Sartartia and that he knew what was in it. The final query was answered with a simple yes. He had broken his contract.

J.B. Duckworth had been known to stretch a closing argument for hours, though his partners excoriated him for it. No one wants to listen to even a good storyteller for that long. J.B.'s logic was that when there was not much evidence to make a case, spin a great yarn.

Today, though, he used less than an hour. After summarizing the case he had built, Duckworth trowled the emotions on thick. A good man and his dying mother. A family man providing for his children. A real man dutifully standing up for himself against injustice.

"Gentlemen," he said to the jurors. "I believe each one of you would have acted the same. And that means that George Purdy is not guilty."

With a final iron-eyed look at the jurors, J.B. sat down next to his client.

The prosecution, carrying the burden of proof in an American court of law, got a second chance at the last word. In his rebuttal to Duckworth's closing statement, Sam Styles harped some more on Ennis' right to evict Purdy. It was the only solid card he had. There was no disputing that the deceased had gone to Purdy's allotment armed and expecting a confrontation. Styles was simply saying that under the law, Will Ennis had every right to do just that, and George Purdy had no right to resist.

As he looked the jurors in their eyes, he calmly spun an example of a businessman with a customer not upholding his end of a bargain. What if a man walked into your store, signed an order to purchase a piano, then had his friends load the piano onto his wagon and drive away without paying? A deal was a deal, and a signed deal even more so. That shopkeeper had every right to reclaim his property, and the man who failed to honor the signed agreement could not stop him. The jurors were compelled to follow the law.

J.B. and his client carefully watched the faces of those jurors, and George felt a chill as several of the men nodded in agreement.

It was too early for decent people to enjoy another meal so quickly after a large lunch, but J.B. was willing to give it a try. His client was shuffled back to his cell to await the jury's deliberations, and there was time to kill. An old friend, Captain J.C. Mitchell, a leading lawyer from Richmond, was in Wharton on business and had stepped into the courtroom to watch the closing arguments. The two were closely involved in a case in Houston that was both high profile and very personal, but Mitchell's business in Wharton was unrelated. When matters went to the jury earlier than expected, Captain Mitchell agreed to join Duckworth at the Nation Hotel Café. For good measure, Mitchell's client, a rancher named McMurdy, came along.

When the waiter left to fetch their order of a pint of beer for Duckworth and whiskeys for the other men, McMurdy posed a question.

"Only beer in case you get called back to court tonight?"

"I'll switch to whiskey as soon as I've quenched my thirst from talking so much. If there are any objections, I'll remind them that beer is safer than the water."

The other two men laughed. Duckworth puffed a bit and continued.

"Look, there is nothing I can do to change things now. Consider it an early celebration. On the other hand, if for some reason the jury is just too ignorant to understand the sterling case that has been laid before them, then I might not have the stomach to dine well, as I will be overwhelmed with pity for the newly convicted."

"You really get that emotionally invested in these cases?" McMurdy asked.

"Naw. A man's got to eat."

Full-throated laughter followed, and then Mitchell added a small brag.

"I taught him well."

The other two men contented themselves with plates of ham, cheese and a boiled egg. J.B. opted for a roasted half chicken, herbed potatoes, sauteed carrots and green beans.

Before the check could even be settled, the bailiff from the court was there to summon Duckworth back across the street. Mitchell, with much more legal experience than Duckworth, look surprised, and the defense lawyer himself cocked his head to one side expectantly.

"Yes," the hangdog bailiff said. "There is a verdict."

Welcome though it may be, a fast verdict always felt like an anticlimax. It spared a trial attorney the foreboding and disquietude, the endless replaying of the arguments and answers, yet it somehow left J.B. feeling a mite cheated.

There was little time for tension inside the court either. By the time Duckworth entered, his client was in his chair and Judge Farnham was on the bench. The old man gave one disdainful stare at the defense table and requested the verdict. It was simple. George Purdy was acquitted.

Duckworth had felt it time and time before. A great and palpable sigh of relief from the man seated next to him when they heard the words "Not guilty." It sounds like a complete deflation of the body, and he always expected to look to his side and see the skin of his client collapsed like a spent balloon.

He slapped George on the back. Loud conversation filled the courtroom. The ambient noise masked the hard slap that Emmett Ennis gave to the oak railing in front of him. The other two brothers hung their heads. Duckworth pulled out his watch. He had plenty of time to pack up his belongings and have a few drinks before catching the late train home.

Chapter 17

Near Richmond, Texas

April 1903

George Purdy enjoyed the birds. The fields of Sartartia were so vast, so open and devoid of trees that songbirds never brought their music. When the corn got high, crows and ravens were a nuisance. Occasionally jays, quail or chachalacas came to eat and be shooed away. So today, George sat on the back step of his tenant house and watched chickadees with their wavy flights, flitting from tree to tree in the woods down toward the river. He listened to the chattering of the barn swallows, scouring the late afternoon air for their flying meals.

His kids had gone down to the river to bathe with the usual admonition to be careful and never let go of a sturdy limb. He was alone with his thoughts and the birds. Work for today was done.

It was a fine time of year. His young cotton plants were poking up nicely from the soil, but it was not yet time to start chopping. His corn was in the ground just over three weeks. The vegetable patch was weeded and looking good, but not yet producing. Spring rains had been more than generous.

After the trial, George had fallen into the fluff. He found a wood shop in Richmond that gave him work, maybe out of sympathy, but it was enough money to get through the whole year and into the winter. It was not the carpentry wages he would earn on his own, but it was heaven sent. The shop was small, and the owner pleasant enough. George's skills were appreciated, and the deal was that he could continue to put in as many hours as he wished.

There was a fifteen dollar bonus when George built them a treadle lathe like the one that had been confiscated when he fled Sartartia. It allowed the shop to turn more legs, spindles and balusters. Purdy even fashioned Arthur a child-sized baseball bat out of a discarded piece of hickory. It had quickly become the boy's prize possession.

In December, the week before Christmas, George negotiated a sharecropping deal with an old man named Lane Smither. He would take on 62 acres in the old Jane Long League just a mile west of downtown Richmond. It was flood prone land in a northward bulge of the Brazos. There was a comfortable enough tenant shack raised up on tall piers, and Smither agreed to count any improvements on the little house to Purdy's credit. The family could move in immediately.

Terms were fifty-fifty unless the river completely flooded his crops, in which case, Smither told him, they would call things even and share in the misfortune. Either way, the place was Purdy's to live in through the last day of the year. Smither told him that the family would be his first white tenants in years, and the generous terms reflected that fact. When George gingerly asked about a written contract, the old man scoffed.

"I know all about your legal troubles, son. I do my business with a handshake. Always have. I hope that's good enough for you."

The house sat on the flattest of bottom land. Two horseshoe lakes on the opposite side were evidence of the perpetual whims of a big river. The main channel itself was about a half mile away from the shack's back door, reachable in two directions on the bend. On a still day or with a south or east wind, every scent the river had to offer was laid on the Purdy's steps.

The Brazos, in its lower reaches, is easily the muddiest river in Texas. It is constantly agitated like a teenager in love. Mountains of dirt and silt wash southward toward the Gulf, suspended so tightly that the raw umber water looks thick enough to chew. One story is that if not for a Spanish map maker's error, this great river would rightfully bear the name of Colorado, or red, instead of its clearer, placid neighbor to the west.

When the heavy rains come, the Brazos is a coppery torrent. There is no true whitewater, only lighter shades of sienna or foamy creamed coffee atop the waves. Loose logs and other detritus sails along toward Velasco, and fishermen know better than to test it.

Arthur Purdy, already looking forward to his eighth birthday, was bathing in the lukewarm shallow water. His clothes were tossed in a very untidy bundle in some weeds. He held to the branch of a willow with one hand while he splashed and rubbed with the other. In the Brazos, as much dirt went onto a body as came off, but the notion was that it helped. The water was barely over his knees, and his feet stood on one of the soft beaches that formed easily on the inside of the great bends in the watercourse.

His older sister, Sarah, sat a good eight feet higher up the steep bank, her bath completed and her muslin dress drying in the warm sunshine. She was turned sideways to catch the rays of light while still keeping an eye on her little brother.

He may have been reaching for a fish, or a floating geegaw may have caught his eye. It may be that the hanging willow branch broke or pulled free, but when Sarah heard his little cry, Arthur was already neck deep in the murky rush. Neither of the Purdy children had ever learned to swim. The best that George could do was dog paddle, and there had never been a press to teach that ungainly skill to his little ones.

In spite of her complete lack of knowledge, Sarah slid down to the river and hurriedly waded out to Arthur. By now he was pulled farther into the current, and Sarah got a mouthful of nasty water as she felt her feet unexpectedly fall away beneath her. She coughed and spat, but never stopped splashing in the direction of her brother who was screaming and calling for her and his dad.

Arthur's little head was bobbing like a fishing cork, but she thought she was getting closer. She started to yell to him, but her words were cut short by another gagging mouthful of river. She could reach him and then push toward the bank, even though it looked so far away, when she could see it at all. Something hard brushed against her bare leg. Another scream, and another unwanted swallow of dirty water. Her stomach was queasy, and her thin arms had begun to ache.

Finally, against all Earthly odds, Sarah grabbed at her brother's arm. There was no holler left in him, and as she spun him around, she saw that his eyes were closed tight against the spray. She pulled him close, hugging Arthur and willing him to look at her. Still holding him with both arms she intuitively kicked her legs, but she was getting no closer to the bank from which they had come. Her strength was sapped. Refusing to let go, Sarah tried to pull herself up straight and see where they were. But there was no shoreline in her view, nothing but the speeding torrent of mud. With his little body in her embrace, they slipped below the swirling red current.

Chapter 18

Houston, Texas

John Duckworth walked into his brother's private office and closed the door behind him. He held a copy of the *Houston Chronicle* folded open to an inside page.

"I think you need to see this, Jamie."

J.B. read through the article that recounted the drowning of George Purdy's children. He handed the newspaper back to John.

"That is truly a shame."

It was a rare moment when John lost patience with his little brother, but he did so now. He did not raise his voice, there were people in the outer office, after all, but to someone who knew him, there was no mistaking his tension.

"It's more than a shame. It's a tragedy. Those kids were all that man was living for, now they're taken from him? How can you not care about that?"

J.B. bristled, taken off guard by the harshness.

"I kept George Purdy out of prison. If it wasn't for me, he would never have gotten the last few months in the first damn place. I gave him a gift. The gift of more time."

John Duckworth offered a hollow smile and a few quick shakes of his head, as if trying to rid himself of a bad thought.

"That's it. You did your job and that absolves you from all compassion."

They were statements, not questions, but J.B. answered anyway.

"Yeah. Pretty much. You can't let yourself get involved, John. I've told you that a thousand times."

John, who had still not taken a chair, was silent for a long time. J.B. was about to give up and resume his work when his older brother finally spoke.

"Jamie, of all people, you ought to understand George Purdy's situation. Our family was taken from us when we were just boys, too young to do anything about it. After a time, it came down to just you and me. All we had were each other."

J.B. felt like nodding at the sentiment, but he did not. John continued.

"We flicked from place to place, scheme to scheme, searching for something that would bring us success. Or I should say bring you success. Still, I was willing to follow you. You were the one with the brains. It was easy to see that. You finally found it in the law, a place where your wits would give you the victories and recognition you needed so badly. But here's the thing, Jamie. Those clients of yours, they're vulnerable, too. At one of the lowest points in their whole lives, most likely. Sure, they need you to win, but they also need you to care."

"I act like I care. That should be enough. I do my job."

John Duckworth turned around and left his brother to his work. On his way out, he slammed the door. Waiting room be damned.

Part Two

Cass

Chapter 19

Sartartia, Texas

M ay 1905

Caswell Ennis held his crying four month old daughter and wondered for the third or fourth time today just what his life had become. His wife, Nelly, was trying to comfort their older daughter who had fallen and scraped her chin against a plant stand. Just the luck that Letha was out picking and cutting vegetables for supper. Comforting children should be her job, after all. To make matters worse, every time Cass vainly yelled Letha's name toward the distant garden plot, it just made the baby cry more. Though his voice was lost on the wind, the baby's was full throated and right in his ear.

By the time Letha ascended the back step with two heavy baskets full of fresh produce, Nelly had already taken the baby back. She was holding one child on each knee, patting their backs and trying to lower the cacophonous din. None of that stopped Cass from shooting Letha an exasperated look.

"Great Jesus, Letha…"

She cut him off mid-sentence with a withering stare that could only be delivered by someone who had known her boss since he was still occasionally wetting his britches.

Though she was not in a comfortable position to say anything, it was possible that no one in the Ennis household had noticed the change in Cass more than

Letha Ward. Just a few short years earlier, he had been a carefree boy getting into boy trouble. He had been rusticated from the University in Austin near the start of his third year for reasons that were unclear, and the family discussions wavered as to whether or when he might return. For his part, Caswell took it all in stride.

When it came to the deep political arguments and fraternal jockeying between Will and Cass, Letha almost always sided with the carefree Cass. In her stewardship of the four Ennis boys, Will, perhaps guided by the unseen hand of his late mother, was ambitious, unpredictable and often disagreeable. Emmett had shown a mean streak since the time he could walk. Letha had mental pictures of that boy beating everything and everyone around him with a scavenged stick. Leigh, the baby, had his nose buried in a book for what seemed to be all his waking hours. He often shirked chores to read.

Then there was happy Cass. He was bestowed with a certain human curiosity, as least compared to the others. Whatever life threw at him was shed like water off a duck. If anything, that blindness to consequences was his biggest fault. Though their father had passed on, Will continued Caswell's allowance at the same level that he was getting at college. Back at Sartartia, however, his social spending was non-existent. What was not provided from the larders, cupboards and spirits cabinets of the big white house, the boys freely took from the family's store. It was merchandise recorded with no inkling that it would ever be repaid.

That path ensured that a good portion of the allowance ended up at the bawdy houses along Railroad Street in Richmond. It was Fort Bend County's den of iniquity. Three or so blocks just over the train bridge that was cheek by jowl with bars and bagnios. Tom Ward had told her of one drinking establishment called the Horse Saloon. It certainly was ill fitted for men, he said. The short alleys and back buildings promised even worse. Across the tracks to the north, Mud Alley provided the same services to the town's Black residents, but in the squeaky, busy beds, the color line was sometimes blurred, at least in one direction. The Wards secretly laughed about it from the safety of their home at Sartartia, and Letha despaired of Caswell's proclivity to patronize it.

Her fears were redoubled when she heard about the boy's relationship with Naomi Walker, a mulatto harlot at one of the red door houses. Throwing one's money down for a fifteen minute liaison was distasteful enough. It was certainly not to be countenanced by good people. But a White man entering a relationship with a colored woman, strumpet or no, was nothing but trouble. Letha knew it, and so did Tom.

When mixed with a little drink, violence was liable to come from any side, Tom told his wife. One evening, when Cass and Tom were alone, talking quietly about a horse out at the stables, the Black man had gingerly broached the subject with his boss. The comment was oblique and had been prefaced by multiple disqualifiers. As soon as Cass sussed what Tom was getting at, however, he laughed heartily and slapped the older man on the back like a mate.

"Thank you, Tom, but that most definitely falls in the category of my concern alone."

That brief comment forever concluded the matter between the two.

What Letha did not know because her husband thought it best not to tell her, was that Cass and his dusky girlfriend may have a child. At least that was what Naomi had made known among the other fallen women of Railroad Street. The gossip spread like greased lightning amongst the Negro population of Richmond.

Tom Ward understood exactly how fondly his wife looked at Caswell, and he chose never to burst that balloon. Still, he was a proud man. He recalled the years of the 1870s and early 80s when there was promise of a better life for the Negro in America. He kept the thoughts deep within himself, but knowing his newly married employer had rather openly fathered a colored baby brought a certain shame to his race.

The best guess was that Nelly knew nothing about her husband's paramour. She was mostly happy with her marriage and her life in the big white house. The two of them had dated at college, and she liked Cass very much. He was roguish with his crooked, ready smile and his unruly shock of hair. They had a great deal of fun together and things had gotten rather intimate one or two evenings along Shoal Creek in the wilds of Pease Park.

Still, Nelly did not consider him a solid marriage prospect, that is until Caswell's brother had been killed. Though he was taking a semester off from school, he began to write her not long after the tragic event. He had begun to examine his life, he told her. Though she was, of course, sad for the family, she saw this occurrence as a bit of a romantic windfall. Cass was now firmly and forever tied to Sartartia. Knowing that he would have to settle down, and certainly not minding the Ennis family wealth, she had accepted his subsequent proposal. A less than gentle nudge from her parents in Granbury helped her decide.

Their engagement was quite brief, though the bride's family put together a lovely wedding in their hometown. Well over a hundred guests were in attendance including old cousin Benny who had come up from Navasota. He could not resist giving Caswell a lewd wink and a hard elbow to the ribs. It was almost as if he knew of the young man's quiet nocturnal forays down the hallway at the Granbury house every time he came courting.

Daily married life for Nelly at first was spent trying to change the entrenched bachelor culture of her new home. She also felt like she had been heavily pregnant almost from her arrival. She was certain that those blessed with the skills of addition were wagging their tongues, but it did not bother her even a whit.

They named their first daughter Mary, after Nelly's mother. The second one, following fewer than fourteen months after her sister, was Amanda in honor of Caswell's mother, Littleberry Ennis' second wife. During the few months in between babies, Nelly spruced up the rose garden beds next to the house and added a handful of new plants that she ordered from a nursery in North Texas. She also improved the needlepoint skills that she had learned from her grandmother.

Raising two tiny, fussy girls was exhausting, but Nelly also found tremendous gratification in it. She had found her place in life, safe and living in a marvelous home with no wants in the world. Cass was not one to take a major part in raising the girls, but that was just as her older relatives had warned her about the ways of husbands. After all, he had been so busy the last three years instituting major changes at Sartartia and providing for their growing young family.

It was, in fact, three and a half years since Cass Ennis was thrust into the role of plantation manager. Once the shock wore off, he almost embraced it for a year or so. Though he was very young when his father oversaw the largest convict lease program in Texas, his early memories were filled with awe at the work gangs in their dirty stripes cutting sugar cane. The hum of that season when men worked around the clock to process the fresh cut cane through the mills before it dried out. There was an efficiency to it. A power. He may not have pressed the issue too hard with Will, but he was smart enough to see that the tenant farming system lacked that. There was too much leeway for problems to arise, and some of that trouble had finally put his brother six feet in the ground.

Cass resolved to reinstitute the convict lease system that built Sartartia in the first place. He talked to veterans of the state prisons, and though they stressed that times had changed since the 1880s heyday, he became convinced that his change to the old ways marked the family path to the future.

Finally, Ennis journeyed to San Antonio to consult with his father's former partner, Ed Cunningham. Those two men took over the entire Texas prison system, and when the state officials, steeped in their greed, refused to renew the deal, Ennis and Cunningham simply leased convicts. L.A. Ennis had some 400 of them at one time. Cunningham built a railroad down to the plantations at Arcola and connected their shipments to Galveston and the sea, all with convict labor. Those two men returned from the war with a financial hunger and determination. Caswell smelled the same glory and profit. Even if his taskmaster of a father was not alive to see his second son succeed, he would show him nonetheless.

Ed Cunningham was a tough old bastard. He had come to Bexar County well prior to the War, dealt in land and ranched it all. He would happily tell of roping and branding right alongside his Mexican hands. He was another veteran officer of Hood's Brigade - lost an arm at Sharpsburg, lost a brother at Gaines Mill and gained a friend, Littleberry Ennis, in a campaign command tent. Together they later grew rich.

Cass rode up the long drive from Grayson Street on the north side of San Antonio to find an imposing stone mansion. He had not seen Cunningham for more than a decade. The dissolution of the partnership between Cunningham and his father happened before Caswell was even born. That separation was lukewarm, no acrimony, no backslapping farewells. He did not know what to expect.

A Mexican woman of indeterminate age admitted Cass to the house, and left him standing in the foyer. Cass heard a few muted words of Spanish being exchanged in another part of the house. Momentarily, the old man appeared. It was clear from his gravelly eye that there was no spark of recognition.

"I'm Caswell Ennis, Mr. Cunningham."

"Well, I'll be goddamned."

Seated in Cunningham's office, drink in hand once the old man had decided Cass was of age, the two talked. More accurately, Ennis asked a single question, and then listened.

"You're half right, boy. Sharecroppers have the wanderlust. They're always looking to move on. They want a better deal. It's like I told those braying jackasses who wanted us to use free labor instead of slaves. They'd only be there until they could afford their own place. Not that these croppers will ever have that kind of money, but ..."

Cunningham waved his hand in disgust. He then used it to pound his desk as he made a point.

"You make money with a steady supply of labor. Constant. The convicts were that. It wasn't that they were cheaper, son, it's that they can't quit on you. Sure, they come and go with their sentences, but there was an endless supply of what we needed. Three hundred, 400. They were interchangeable. As long as the good Lord keeps making poor people, there will be criminals. Feed them enough to stand upright for 12, 13 hours, and the profits will flow. They worked hard with the guards standing over them. Damned hard."

The old man took a sip of his drink and resumed his diatribe.

"You thinking about it's okay, but you're missing the lifeblood of the thing. Times are different. Progressives. It's horseshit. Steaming horseshit. That bespectacled ape in the White House and his reforming ain't no different. He may not be spouting equality of the races, but some are. There are White men in this country today, some right here in Texas, shit stirrers in the press who would tell you that it is unfair to make money off the work of an imprisoned darkie. Can you believe that? Unfair."

The outburst had fatigued Ed Cunningham, and he stopped for a breath and a sip of his drink. Cass took the opportunity to ask a second question.

"Do you think I'm doing the right thing, to go back to the leasing?"

"I think you should find something you can control. Did you not hear what I told you? Within the next few growing seasons, the leases will float away like trail dust on the wind. They won't last."

Another flap of his age-spotted hand.

"Too many people think we're dealing with the Devil."

He paused to look at his slippers, footwear that Caswell had not even made note of until then. Ed Cunningham had always been a man with fine tall boots. Soft slippers or no, the old man had more to say. He now spoke about his own situation.

"Sugar Land has been losing money for years. The whole business has changed, though it's not mine anymore. It went to a receiver in ought two. You know that. We couldn't grow enough cane to keep the mills running like we should. I ran up too much debt, and that's on my shoulders. I didn't have it in me any longer to stay vigilant."

Cunningham's voice had fallen to a hoarse croak, and for the first time during his lengthy tirade, Cass glimpsed in the old man the health concerns and the decline that he had been hearing about for the past few years. Still Cunningham kept talking.

"It's a shame. The whole lot of it will be sold in the wink of an eye as soon as the right buyer comes along. Everything I built. Your old daddy was part of that, of course. I'd advise you to sell, too. You're in debt, just like me, son."

Caswell stuttered some prideful noises.

"Don't bullshit me, boy. I'm not over there like I used to be, but that don't mean I lack scuttlebutt. Your brother was in financial trouble, and I can see it in your face. You'll not right the ship."

With that, Ed Cunningham turned in his chair and offered only a profile of disgust, not so much at Caswell, but at the modern world.

The two men, of very different generations, exchanged some pleasantries about families and common friends, but Cass was gone within half an hour. He returned his rented mount and caught the next train home to Sartartia. In spite of the unequivocal warnings, he would increase his convict leases. Grumpy old naysayers be damned.

The State of Texas had some 4,000 men in its prison system. Half of them were confined at Huntsville or Rusk, but the other half were available to be leased to a private enterprise. The great railroads of Texas found the notion to be hot stuff. There were 10,000 miles of track in the state, and Caswell reckoned that a good three quarters of it had been laid by convicts or slaves.

For decades, though, the biggest customers for the state were the planters of the four sugar counties, and none came within a country mile of using the system to the extent of Ennis and Cunningham. Perhaps that was it. Maybe old Cunningham wanted to cozen him. Lower the demand and therefore the price. Was the old man act just a way that Cunningham could have the whole caboodle? Cass made up his mind. He would follow his instinct.

Cass Ennis' decision was now three years behind him. Once his changes were instituted, his interest had begun to decline within a matter of weeks. Running

Sartartia was not a grand adventure or a game of strategy. It was a job, a day to day slog through the administrative mire. He was forced to deal with people he disliked, and he had almost no social outlets to ease his burden.

Ennis still considered himself a young man destined for swashbuckling fun and worldly exploits. He was a second son, and that meant that he should be kicking up his heels. Yet here he was with a young family and a raft of responsibilities that left him feeling as confined as a penned rooster.

Even after he married, Cass continued the relationship with Naomi with barely a hesitation. Frankly, it was easy. They were business trips into Richmond, and his wife never raised an eyebrow. Since the easing of his infatuation with running Sartartia, the trips had become more frequent.

In truth, though, that exchange had drawbacks, as well. It was no longer the simple transaction that had led to a genuine fondness on both their parts. If she was to be believed, and that meant things were by no means a certainty, Naomi had borne his first child, and likely aborted another.

The boy did look like Cass, though, at least to his eye. A khaki colored little Ennis. Cass could not stop himself from roughing the little scamp's hair when he went to lay with Naomi. Once or twice, he brought a toy that his daughters had failed to cotton to. They were overflowing with playthings, after all. It was not as if he loved the boy equally with his girls, but it was nice having a son. As he got older, he could teach the boy a thing or two.

When he made his inspection rounds of Sartartia and looked at the various Negro convicts, Caswell Ennis found no irony.

Chapter 20

Houston, Texas

"That was a strike, Ed! You're blinking too long!"

J.B. was already screaming at the umpire from his seat In the boxes between home plate and first base, and the tilt was less than a half inning old. The Duckworth family was enjoying a beautiful spring Saturday together. They had a late lunch downtown, then took a San Felipe line streetcar out to the brand new ballpark. Husband, wife, daughter and Maisy. Young Katherine said she loved the grandstand's "shiny green color."

The lawyer slipped a dollar to an usher named Dan to get around the prohibition against dogs in the ballpark. Dan had been his mark at the old Fairgrounds, and luckily for Maisy, who always welcomed a plain hot dog of her own, the management had retained him at the new place. Much like the law itself, policies pertaining to well-behaved dogs were never evenly enforced in Houston.

The local nine were taking on the Beaumont Drillers in the very early days of the South Texas League season. The old Texas League had fractured in two some years prior, and the Houstons were one of four teams that battled for the south crown. Also officially gone was the moniker Buffaloes that had graced the team for the better part of a decade. In 1904, the team wanted to be called the Lambs, and in the weeks before this current campaign kicked off, a newspaper contest slapped them with the name Marvels. Duckworth hated it. He and many other rooters still stubbornly called them the Buffs.

Like most fans, J.B.'s favorite was the player/manager Wade Moore, a college man from Kansas who was nearing his 40th birthday. Moore used Duckworth & Fein to do a little contract work. Though the two had not met, J.B. still considered it a personal connection.

Lola remarked that the boys looked spanking in their white home uniforms, and she liked the blue trim. Her husband answered that they were less dingy than normal since the team, for the first time ever, was wearing road grays when out of town. He appreciated that his wife was enjoying the baseball, and his daughter was content splitting her attention between the field and the grandstands. Maisy dozed at their feet.

As he watched the onfield contest, Duckworth also waved to several prominent Houstonians who luxuriated in other parts of the stands. For all of its growth, Houston was still a small town when it came to running into the same people. A quick hello to remind the potential client base of his presence was never a bad thing for a hungry lawyer.

There was only the slightest tinge of guilt or restlessness in J.B.'s mind about not working today. Others at the firm were no doubt out finding fun for themselves somewhere, Henry and his kosher ways excepted. Though Duckworth briefly considered that the dutiful observation of religious tradition might be enjoyable to some, he quickly dismissed the notion as ludicrous.

The practice of Duckworth and Fein was busier than ever. In addition to the steady stream of high profile criminal cases, the income from handling delicate legal matters in front of the appeals court had become significant. Contracts and injury cases were still another source of bread and butter. They took over a dentist's space across the hall in the building on Congress, and two new clerks worked there, alongside a bona fide file room. As Duckworth himself joked, he kept them all busier than Bob Cratchit.

J.B. and Lola had bought a new house less than six months ago. It was an eight-room beauty that sat across six lots on Whitty Avenue. John had moved in with them which should provide a healthier lifestyle for him than a seedy boarding hotel. Katherine was also thrilled since the big lot in Fifth Ward provided room for her long desired pony. They also had a place for their milk cow.

This sunny Saturday was J.B.'s second time at the West End Park on Andrews Street in the Fourth Ward, but his first with the family. It was comfortable and modern. There were graveled walkways to the steps that led into the seats, and the streetcar company had even popped for planked sidewalks from the car stops. Unlike the old Fairgrounds Park, there were no chiselers watching from the limbs of a tree, though the knothole gang of youngsters had already riddled the outfield walls with holes. The paper said it looked like a Russian battleship after a Jap torpedo boat attack.

Only a year before, the site was the Fourth Ward Grounds, a glorified open lot near Cash's Grocery where semi-pro and amateur teams toiled. In spite of torrential downpours in February, hard work created a yard with 3000 seats, another 1500 in the white bleachers on the left field line and 500 more in the colored section down toward right, benches that were often filled to the guards.

By five o'clock, an hour into the contest, the Drillers held the slimmest 1 to 0 edge. Clarence Nelson, another crowd favorite and native of the Duckworth's own Fifth Ward, was spinning a dandy. Two errant pitches in the fourth, one off the Beaumont third sacker's toe followed by a double to the wall by their shortstop Fred Tullar, made the only difference. Tullar was hardly a swat artist, but such was the beauty of baseball.

The trouble was that Ewing Harris, a spare, lanky righthander from Tennessee, was pitching rings around Moore's Marvels, an appellation that flashed through J.B.'s mind with a large dollop of sarcasm. The local lads were hitless through five frames, whiffing at Harris' offerings like tired hounds.

The large crowd was trying their damnedest to will their team on. Many, especially in the bleachers, rang cowbells and shouted through megaphones. One enterprising soul had brought a marine foghorn and was enjoying it unsparingly. The cheers were encouraging pitcher Nelson.

As he admired the shoots and slants being offered by the Fifth Ward Peach, J.B. felt a large hand on his shoulder from the seat behind him.

"How are you, J.B.?"

It was his friend Orren Holt, a round, walrus-faced man who just completed a term as Houston mayor. They had worked a handful of cases together and frequently recommended one another's services. Holt was popular with his fellow lawyers, much more than could be said about his standing with the voting public.

"Some duel," Holt said, nodding his chins in the general direction of the pitcher's mound.

"It sure is. Clarence is sharp."

"I suspect you've been following the train wreck?"

Everyone in town had. A Galveston, Houston & Northern passenger train left its track at the big curve near Harrisburg the night before last. The locomotive rolled onto its side and burned, dooming the two men inside. The tender and other cars piled into a jumble. Fortunately for those traveling, it was but minor bumps and scrapes from hitting the walls. A rescue special sent out from downtown Houston found pleasantly few casualties.

Holt lit into an explanation.

"I'm handling the claim for the engineer, but I've got the solid angle on the fireman's family, too. Pete Donovan. Wife's at a boarding house over on Odin. I figure I shouldn't do both of them, and I saw you sitting over here. What do you think? Your firm interested? Your neck of the woods anyway."

"I suspect we are. Yes, and much obliged."

J.B. offered his friend a smile, and Holt slapped him on the thigh.

"Good, good. You'd want to nail it down tonight or tomorrow, but it ought to be duck soup."

Suing railroads on behalf of maimed or killed workers was a lucrative blood sport for attorneys in Southeast Texas.

"I've got a few murders cooking, but this would be right up the old alley for one of the new clerks. Doesn't sound like it would see a courtroom, but Henry or I would be ready, if it does. I'll send my boy around..."

Lola gave J.B.'s right hand a squeeze and reproved him in the most sweet and gentle of voices.

"Jamie, it is family time."

"I know precious."

He sounded suspiciously as if a but was about to follow. Instead, his wife stopped him short.

"You'll be back in the office on Monday, and I imagine for a few hours tomorrow, too. Surely that's soon enough. Then you'll burn the late oil, and we won't see you until 10:30 every night."

She threaded her arm through her husband's, and he could not help but offer up a smile that turned into a laugh.

"You're right, sweetie."

Duckworth patted her hand warmly, and shrugged at Orren Holt, then he turned back toward the field and cupped his hands around his mouth.

"You're blind! I've seen potatoes with better eyes!"

Chapter 21

Sartartia, Texas

Harry Duplantis was listening to the bullfrogs down at Oyster Creek and thinking of poor choices he had made. A soaking rain was falling. His crew had worked in it for eleven hours, and still it came on. Steady. Tomorrow the mud would be six or eight inches deep between the rows, and that was when it would be dangerous. Loose footing with a sharp hoe or cane knife. Varmints after bugs, and big snakes after varmints. Blankets of young and hungry spring mosquitoes covering the back of your neck where you couldn't even swat at them in those close rows. Until then, he relived his mistakes and the many warnings he had ignored. This was his nightly ritual. Not counting sheep, but counting the errors that led him here.

The life story of convict Harry Duplantis was not a happy one. A simple reading of the prison intake ledger showed that he was serving a two year stretch for petty burglary in Cuero. That might be all his keepers knew, but there was more to him.

He grew up at Hopkinsville, a Freedom Colony in DeWitt County. Harry was too old to take advantage of the school there by the time it came along. They were teaching just across the pasture at the Antioch Church. It was a chance to better yourself, his elders told him. He guessed he might have attended, but as the oldest and biggest boy, he would have brought on daily ridicule. He decided that learning was not worth that price. Then he had gone bad with drink.

His story was very much like every other man sleeping in these bunks, Harry reckoned. No good options on offer. Mama died giving birth to the child that followed him. The baby had died, too. The boy left to scramble for food and guidance.

A lucky case, Harry was. His grandfather was right there in the community and already taking care of his cousins. Next to the preacher, his grandpa was one of the wise men of Hopkinsville. He was a church deacon. People listened to him. He was changeless, a reliable hand reaching out. Young Harry had only to take it.

Harry's paternal grandfather was a very dark-skinned man named Cicero. Grandpa always described his name as some White man's joke. He was brought from Louisiana to South Texas in 1862 by a man from Franklin, Louisiana who was determined to retain every being of his property. Harry's father, four years old, came along, as well. Each Black man in Texas knew that his people were brought here by somebody. No one arrived of his own accord.

After Emancipation, with hard work and saved earnings, Cicero Duplantis invested in a plot of ground. Even after two decades of ownership, that land defined the man. It was the highest accomplishment worth striving for, and it still burst his buttons. He was quick to remind his grandson of that.

"The fruits of your own labor. That's what can happen when no White man is trying to rob you."

Since he arrived at Sartartia some eighteen months ago, past conversations with his grandfather, unheeded lessons more likely, gnawed at him. They were rarely far from the surface. They bubbled up in his head while he was cutting cane, or when he was alone at night, lying on his back on a hard wood bunk. Bunk six, Barracks one, Camp three. The old man's ghost gave him little peace.

This was his third stint in the Texas prison system, and all three times he was leased out for farming. He had talked before with men who had spent their time inside the Walls up at Huntsville. It was hard time there, too, and it might not come with the chance to breathe the open air every day. The worst that Harry had heard tell about was from a con who had spent 20 months leased in a Georgia coal mine for stealing a turkey. In just that time, the man had acquired a phlegmy cough and said he was happy to have it when he thought of the panicky fits some got in the dank, dark hole. He called it torture. Of course, if you drew bad guards, it did not matter where you were.

Harry had turned 34 years old this past February. Same birthday as Lincoln, a fact that often made him laugh. Him and the Great Emancipator, and here he was all bung up in some convict camp. It was just like his grandpa had prophesized.

The convicts at Sartartia were divided up into three camps in different parts of the plantation. Each camp had multiple frame buildings that served as barracks for prisoners. A dining shack and outdoor kitchen, partially open at the sides, sat just beyond. There were also quarters for the bachelor guards, two small cabins for married guards, and a barn for their horses, all of which were located outside the wire. A couple of stinking privies served each barrack. Where Harry bunked, that meant 56 men leaving every kind of vileness imaginable in and around a hole that could now only be sufficiently cleansed by fire.

The first thing a person noticed on the inside, where the convicts lived, was the smell. Though the men themselves were permitted to jump in the creek from time to time, scheduled boiling of their uniforms was once every week, maybe two. It was the sweat of those bodies that could slap a first timer in the phiz. Thankfully, everyone became fast immune.

Along each wall were triple stacked wood bunks with thin straw mattresses and a little walkway in between. There was supposed to be a low bench in front of each set of bunks, but wear, neglect and occasional flares of rambunctiousness had ended the lives of most of them, leaving the sides of the bed as gapped as an old woman's smile.

A mishmash of personal items populated the spaces under the beds, something that Sergeant Pryor groused about most every day. Sunday pay bought smoking tobacco, papers, magazines and what have you. The state issued chaw, and that had to go someplace. Other inmates might get something mailed to them, and if it was not worth confiscating for the guards, they might even get to keep it. Harry had scrounged a broken cigar box one day when his gang was leveling ground in preparation for a new shed going up near the little depot. It only had half a lid, but it did a decent enough job of holding his odds and ends. Every inmate had something they valued.

Ty Pritchard had a beat-to-shit guitar. The guards allowed it because Ty could play. Herman Moore and Willie Clay were sanctioned for harmonicas for the same reason. The three of them and a few of the inmates with a sense of key provided the nightly entertainment. When Alvin Robinson's folks mailed a mouth harp to him, it lasted less than two weeks before Officer Shaw snatched it up one night saying it was out of mercy to the other convicts. Though Shaw had a snarl and a strong smell of whiskey at the time, none amongst the inmates could say they disagreed with the sentiment.

The back of the barracks, which ended just four beds past Harry's, was the worst place to be. At night, it was the darkest, and that meant it was the spot for beatings to get doled out when one con had riled another. Sometimes that back corner saw and heard even worse. Harry did not want to think about the buggery. If your bunk was there, you turned toward the wall and did not see a thing.

Maybe it was the barracks themselves that brought his grandfather's voice to mind. Maybe it just plain galled him that the man had been so right in sizing him up.

The conversation he relived most often was the one haunting him now. The crucial one looking back on it. The greatest of his miscalculations. Lying here now in the dark, a single lantern glowing at the night guard's table at the far end of the barracks, Harry heard his old grandfather asking, "When will you own up to your mistakes? You're at a juncture when you're either fixing to make your mark on the world or you'll drink it away. Which will it be?"

The morning of that harangue, Harry, with his hangover already brewing amid his drunkenness, had waved the admonition off with a scowl, a grunt and a stumble.

"You're going to wind up right back at that lease farm. Third time. You won't be coming out. Once you're in that system, well, it ain't much different than slavery. A way to make money off the back of the colored man without paying that poor bastard a dime. State's making money. Plantation's making money. Guard's making money. Whole passel of folks making money. Poor dumb darkie's doing the work. And that's you!"

Harry could hear the man's voice as if he was sitting at the foot of grandpa's rocker even then.

"Is that all you want to be, boy? Poor and dumb? If so, you're sure doing the job."

"I'm doing fine, old man. Better than you. Mind your business."

Harry pictured Cicero Duplantis squinting at him in the dim lantern light of the pre-dawn.

"Are you? Then I don't reckon you need to be here eating my beans no more. Get on out."

Harry had stared at his grandfather, open mouthed.

"I mean it, boy. Get on out of my house. I have a son-in-law, four or five other men better than you who can and do help me take care of this old place. I can't afford to carry you."

That was the end of hope, though he had failed to understand it until it was too late. Harry Duplantis lived rough much of the time after that. Sleeping behind some country joint or out back of where he was doing odd jobs. From time to time, he managed a girlfriend. More like a today woman, most likely. They all quickly tired of a no account who would rather lay about in self-pity and hooch than seek out and hold a paying job. They were not stupid. There were much better pastures to graze than Harry Duplantis.

He had tried to find good work, of course. He did not always shirk away from hard labor. He was not born lazy, but there were few decent jobs to be had, and almost none if a man cared about how he was treated. After a while, he could not tell if it was pride or drink that kept him from gainful employment. What difference did it make? It was easier to drink, and he liked the way it made him feel.

He saw his grandfather a few times, but it was just watching the house from the mesquite scrub. He had never summoned the courage to face the man again. His beloved grandpa may have caught his gaze a time or two, but that was the sum of it. Being evicted from his caretaker's life was the final time they spoke.

Another memory came now, two years and then some before his grandfather had kicked him from the house. Harry, who had been catting about for the better part of a week, was hungry, powerfully so, and he had robbed a man riding alone out toward Reed's Branch. There was not but a sliver of moon. Harry stepped out of a little wash and blocked the man's path. The fellow did not even see him at first, but the horse did. The poor, scared animal reared a little and stopped cold.

Harry was unarmed, but he had whittled a piece of scrub cedar into what he guessed was the rough shape of a pistol, at least enough to hold a man up on a pitch black night. The rider was as drunk as Harry, and he handed down a barely jingling tobacco pouch that had been emptied for use as a coin purse. It held two pennies and a five cent token for Kahn & Stanzel's Hardware Store in Hallettsville. Harry was so mad that he grabbed the mounted man by the ankle and yanked him down into the dirt. As his victim mumbled an apology, Harry stumbled off in the general direction of home.

He was not worried. Lawmen would not stand a wisp of a chance of finding an outlaw from a night so impenetrably dark, Harry told himself. Nevertheless, a little after dinner the next day, a small posse of four men, two with badges pinned to them, was riding house to house in Hopkinsville, and it did not take them long to select Harry as the culprit.

He thought later that any young Negro man would do, and perhaps it was blind fortune that they found the right one. His fate was sealed at the DeWitt

County Jail when the sheriff's deputy had charged him with armed robbery to which Harry replied that he had not even had a gun.

The last time Harry Duplantis was caught was after he had burgled the house in Cuero. His grandfather had been gone for a couple of years, three maybe. He lost count. He stayed numb to such memories in those days.

Harry fenced his haul and had been living for almost a week at a lean to over halfway to Terryville. Middle of nowhere and a good place to hide. That is until they brought the hounds. He heard them a mile or more off, and he immediately lit out to the south. Harry ran until his breath left him. Lungs on fire, legs betraying him, he flopped down in a big patch of bluestem that was plenty high enough to cover him.

As he was resigning himself for the inevitable, the sky sprung a glorious rain, a soaking rain just like tonight. As the heavens opened that afternoon, Harry stole a glance and saw that the sudden downpour was even blurring his view of a sugarberry tree that could not be more than a hundred years distant. He almost cried out his thanks to the Lord. A torrent like this was bound to wash away his tracking scent.

Somewhere in the warm country rain, with the dogs baying, Harry, on his hard upper bunk in the convict barracks, drifted off to sleep.

Chapter 22

Most of the guards at Sartartia Convict Camp #3 liked their job well enough. They got a place to live and rock bottom state pay. If you were a man who could get along, there was a camaraderie to be had. It was not unlike some of the stories their granddaddies had told about being in the army, wallowing in shared misery, but without the long marches and getting shot. Still, they got halfway edible food most days, and their beds had fewer bugs than the men they oversaw.

This was a newer generation of Texas prison guards. They were men who had always worked for the state, and they took a bit of pride in having good employment when they gave it any thought. Back when Cunningham and Ennis operated the system, control was entirely local save a stray state inspector who stumbled into town looking to sign a report, get a few free drinks and a lay, and then head back to Austin.

Everybody working for Texas prisons knew the old stories from those years. Unruly inmates made to lie down in an anthill. Dragging them behind a horse. The guards who staged weekly fistfights between the inmates were mostly on to other pursuits now. Time was that some of those mossbacks would force men to beat each other half to death. Those days were mostly gone. Of course, if two prisoners really had a beef, there was no harm in a few bits changing hands on the outcome.

There were supposed to be at least six of them guarding Camp #3 at all times. Billy Pryor, Burt Smith, Fred Shaw, Chick Tenney, Joe Conner and Chappie Dineen. Pryor was a longtime sergeant, and Burt Smith had recently been promoted to that rank himself. The last several months, Sgt. Pryor had been working at

Camp #1 most of the time, but he was still living in the guardhouse at #3. That made Burt Smith the boss of the yard. It also generally left him a man short.

Captain John Veale was the head state man at Sartartia. He lived with his wife and four children over at Number 1, in the nicest little house at the largest of the camps. Veale was a Texas prison veteran. Most of the guards were in their twenties or early thirties, and they would have been shocked to learn that Veale was but thirty-eight, a number he never shared with anyone aside from his wife. His skin, dark as wine-tanned leather, was creased with valleys and scars. His hair had receded to mid-forehead and was showing gray. Though he was quick to laugh at a joke among the guards, he was just as fast when flashing temper at a slow moving con.

The longer a man worked as a prison guard, the more legends sprang up behind his back. New guards at Sartartia were always cautioned not to get hurt, and the warning was invariably accompanied by a tale about Veale when he was sergeant at a camp down toward the coast. One of his guards got thrown from the saddle and busted his head open. When the man came to, after a dram of whiskey had been poured on his wound, the other guards convinced Veale that medical care was needed. Finally, the sergeant relented. He agreed to let the wounded guard seek some bandages as long as he returned immediately. Veale rode with him, since he figured the ride was about ten miles, up to the store in town, and the fellow was still losing blood by the pint full. Riding along would also nip any malingering in the bud.

They arrived at the store with the fellow's eyes all rolled back and him barely clutching the reins. Veale related the story of the accident to the man behind the counter.

"Don't y'all have medical supplies at the camp?" the store owner asked.

"I suspect we've been out for the better part of a year."

The storekeeper pulled a horrified look.

"Good Lord. What if one of the prisoners cuts his foot off with a cane knife or something?

Veale winked at the boss man.

"Doctor comes first of every month."

How much truth lay in tales like this was difficult to say.

The community of prison guards was insulated. Law enforcement did not encroach unless one guard killed another as happened a few years ago at a railroad convict camp up in Falls County. They lived at the camps, so there was minimal contact in the towns save a trip into Richmond now and again. With the small salaries they received, they could not afford much town fun anyway. Instead, they talked and drank with each other. Complained about the convicts, the weather and the food.

Guards at Camp #3 ate the same things as the prisoners. Fried pork and bacon. Boiled vegetables from a big kettle. They did tend to get better cuts of hog, though that did not stop someone, usually Dineen, from opining that it was not a fit cut for a White man. Cracklins were a favorite with everyone, and several of the guards kept a pouch of them tied to their saddle in the field.

Burt Smith was in his seventh month as sergeant and camp boss. He had served ten years with the Prison System, and the last four were at Sartartia. He hailed from Brazoria County, near Oakland, and his first guard job came at the spanking new Clemens Farm when he was but twenty years old.

He was steady and well-liked among the guards, and it was probable that he was better known in Richmond that most of the others. It was where he met his wife, a mousy blonde woman who had moved to Camp #3 in November. As one of two wives at Number 3, her adjustment was steep, especially since she found Joe Conner's wife deplorable.

Guards do not form attachments to prisoners. If they were trustworthy men, they would not be inside the wire. What they do construct is a dislike for problems, a view fashioned after as little as a single interaction that tells them a given convict has forfeited his chance for consideration.

The perception of any specific inmate was not necessarily universal. One guard might tolerate a guy while another guard hated to see him walking. Making a guard laugh bought appreciation from some. Others could not care less. What was undisputed was that every guard at every prison prefers a con who keeps his mouth shut and does what he is told.

From the inmate's view, humanity equals respect. Not too much, or a guard could be labeled as an easy mark, but a small acknowledgement that the convict is also a man is noted, and word spreads. Such sentiment was sporadic in Texas prisons, particularly with poor White men watching over Black cons.

One morning, soon after Burt Smith's transfer to Sartartia, Charlie Barnes failed to roll out for work. Normally such a lapse brought a few pokes from a billy club, or a whipping or time in the tin sweat box.

That morning, after hearing that Barnes was claiming to be sick, Burt Smith went inside the barracks to investigate. The other inmates were mustered in the yard, so it was only the two of them. Smith was free to inflict whatever punishment suited.

What he did was give the bunk a hard kick then step back to a safe distance.

"Get up."

"I'm sick, boss. Bad sick."

Even in the odiferous barracks, Smith could not fail to notice a pool of yellow vomit on the floor and more drying at the edge of Barnes' straw tick. He tried to not inhale too deeply, afraid of what other smell might come next.

"Got to go work. Rows to be hoed. Sick or no. We ain't leaving you here."

The answer came back in a convincingly hoarse croak.

"I can't do it, boss. My belly is churning something awful. Like a knife stabbing at my gut. Came on during the night. I can't straighten up."

Barnes had not moved other than to half lift his head while speaking to Smith. His knees were drawn up towards his waist.

Smith looked him over for a solid minute or more. A growing squadron of flies provided the only sound in the stagnant room. If it was a troublemaking convict, he was dragged out of his bunk and all the way to the fields. Let him sweat out whatever malingering complaint he had. They were guards, not nursemaids.

Finally, Smith spoke softly.

"You know I got to chain you to your bunk, Charlie."

"I know, boss."

It was a small gesture. It was rendered almost meaningless when Charlie Barnes died from his burst appendix just over two days later, but word got around that Boss Smith was all right.

Escapes from the convict camps happened often enough. The inmates knew how to count, and part of the guards' gruffness, and even the calculated part of any cruelty, was to maintain the veneer that a single man with a gun could control five or ten others who were muscled from the hard field work that filled the daylight hours six days out of seven. If a convict got a mind to rabbit, he could. As one guard phrased it, "They're held here by bleached planks, a few strands of wire and a shit load of fear."

The general belief was that the dogs were what inmates feared the most. The best were a mix between bloodhounds and plain old pot-lickers. A good pack of those mongrels could perform magic tricks. They could get a nose full from a con's blanket and track him for miles.

The guards would tell you that when a young con jumped, he could make as much as twelve miles in the first day, and you needed dogs who could keep up. Every convict camp had them. The baying and howling they put up was deafening for their handler, and was the very sound of biblical doom for a man hiding in the brush. A trained hound dog would not hurt his prey, at least not much, but the inmates had seen enough mean house dogs that their fear outweighed any trust in that notion. Just to remind them, the camp sergeants ran a few dogs after an inmate trusty almost every day.

In the end, the convicts scarpered, but their vacation almost always ended up back in the tin sweat box.

Captain Veale stopped in at Number 3 on most days. He normally made the rounds of the camps unless special attention was required at one place or another. Most of the guards figured that they could have a worse boss. Veale did not tend to ride them too hard.

He was always there on those Sundays, generally once a month, when the preacher came around. He would stand with the others, hat in pious hand for the sermon. The inmates had no choice in attending, but Burt Smith, Fred Shaw and Chappie Dineen would find something else to do during these services. Usually that meant retiring to the stables to brush their horses and swap tall tales.

Fred Shaw summed up their feelings well one Sunday when he was quietly gazing across the yard at the church gathering.

"Veale laps that gospel shit up with a spoon, don't he?"

With a social circle of only six or seven, there was a very high repetition rate when it came time to swap stories of an evening. The relish became the embellishments, the refining of a story into a work of art. A favorite was one recounted by Captain Veale in the guardhouse yard one night. Like his daytime rounds, he often dropped in at another camp once the inmates were locked in for the night. The guards noted that such visits kept him away from his wife and kids.

"Smith, Tenney, this was before you boys got here. You too, Neenie. We had this one old coon who would whine and carry on about lice. He couldn't stand lice. He'd pantomime them crawling on him. It was comical. Well, one morning, we get out to the field where we was cutting, and there was this big old bull gator. Eleven foot, if he was an inch. Our horses was shying, so we had to get that son of a bitch moved. So, I motion at the Liceman, that's what we called him. I said, you jump in there and haul that gator back to his house in the creek."

The newer men were tittering by now. Joe Conner was laughing at the memory of a tale he had heard countless times.

"Well, he goes to crying and saying how he can't do that. He's just sure that gator done gonna eat him up. Finally, this one big buck, we called him Tiny, and Lord above he was a big one. Six foot six, I reckon. Don't you think, Shaw?"

Fred spat a stream of tobacco juice before he answered.

"Easy six six, captain. Arms this big around."

He held his hands almost a foot apart. Veale nodded appreciation before continuing.

"So, Tiny walks around the gator's head and says, 'I'll do it captain.' I tell him that Liceman has to help him. Liceman's wailing gets even louder. I ease my horse a step closer and look right into his eyes. 'There's two of y'all, boy, and only one of him. What are you worried about?' I tell him. Liceman went all herky-jerky, but Shaw held a rifle on him. He made a few stabs at grabbing that big tail, but still shit himself."

Captain Veale paused to laugh at his own story.

"That tail thrashing about. Like would have killed him if he'd stepped close. When Shaw finally shot the gator in the head, Tiny looked goddamned disappointed. Genuinely let down that he'd missed out on a chance to gator wrestle. I let him drag the carcass back to the creek, and he did it by hisself. Easy 900 pounds. And he dragged that fucking thing 80 yards."

Veale paused and let out a sigh.

"He died of some fever, old Tiny. It was a shame. Hard worker. Quiet fellow."

Billy Pryor, a somber look on his face, made a motion with his chin.

"He's buried out in that graveyard yonder."

Chapter 23

It was a beautiful, bright morning, but it would be a hot one later. As he lay in bed, enjoying the early sunlight streaming through Nelly's lace curtains, Cass Ennis listened to a white wing coo and let his mind wander. The doves had been finding grain again. He'd seen some fat ones. Time to pull out the bird shot and show those birds who was eating who.

The last few weeks, he had been mulling about renting a place for Naomi and the boy. Get her to stop banging other men for a living. As much as his head told him it did not matter, his heart and stomach told him otherwise. Some days the idea of her rutting with a stream of strangers was a great hollow in his gut. Getting her a room across the tracks past Mud Alley would be a pittance, pocket change, and nobody would ever be the wiser.

Oatmeal, fresh sausage, biscuits and three eggs up. Letha had started the skillet as soon as she heard Cass stirring about upstairs. Nelly and Mary had eaten an hour earlier and were playing with the baby on the sun porch. As he tucked into his fourth biscuit, half drowned in honey, Letha made a quiet joke about Caswell's waistline. Rather than retort with a joke, he shot her a look and put on a sullen expression. It annoyed him. She thought to herself that she must not be the first person to broach the subject.

Tom had Cass' horse saddled and ready, efficient as always. He offered a kindly morning greeting. Caswell answered with a curt nod and a grunt. Earlier, while considering the options with Naomi's lodging, he was reminded of Tom's vague admonition given weeks earlier. Cass had laughed it off at the time, but this morning, it struck him as presumptuous.

If he stopped for any inward reflection, which he did not, Cass Ennis might term his thoughts as restless, but he failed to connect that to his overall mood. He sloughed off any distant concerns and pointedly told himself to focus on the day's tasks. A choice about Naomi and the boy could come later.

He decided to loop out by Camp #3 first thing then come back to the office. Most of his work was in the cluster of buildings that constituted Sartartia town, but he enjoyed his inspection rides around the property much more. He tried to vary his route every day. He needed to look through the books at the store, a task which bored him silly, so hopefully he could soothe his mind watching the inmates work.

Harry Duplantis was chopping and burning corn stalks at a field that was scheduled to be fallow this year. A dozen or so striped inmates stretched more than a quarter mile, all doing the same work. Boss Tenney and Sarge Smith were watching them all from horseback, that is when they were not larking and chewing the fat. Harry had been assigned the pile nearest the Sartartia depot, so anyone riding out from there would reach him first. It was a spot that raised his hackles. Cons knew instinctively that the safest place in a work gang was the middle. If trouble was to approach, it came from the edge.

That was his first thought when he saw Caswell Ennis, the plantation owner, riding along the turn row in his direction. Harry could tell even from a fair distance that Ennis looked confused, dumbfounded. As the rider got closer, the emotion on his face turned to anger. He was shouting at Harry before he even reined to a halt.

"Boy! Stop burning that fodder."

"Yes, sir, boss, but this here's how the state boss showed us to do it."

Caswell Ennis exploded.

"Goddamn you, boy. I'm not asking for an opinion. We can run barbed wire and graze cattle on this."

Harry looked straight down at the well-trod dirt of the turn row. The last thing he intended to do now was speak, but Ennis was having none of it. His voice got even louder, as if Harry was hard of hearing.

"Boy! I told you to stop. Throw dirt on that fire! Douse that!"

After absorbing another half of minute of invective, all while examining a dung beetle near his feet, Harry heard Caswell Ennis spur away. He let out a heavy sigh and shifted his gaze toward the heavens.

Ennis rode down the line at a trot to where two guards, mounted on horseback next to one another, had just turned to see the hubbub. As he got closer, he identified one of the men as Sergeant Burt Smith. At least something was going right. Smith was just the man he needed in this situation. He pulled to a stop.

"Burt, we've got ourselves two problems, and I need them fixed. I've decided that we can use those stalks as fodder. This burning needs to stop. It's a waste."

To Burt Smith's eye, Cass Ennis was as agitated as he'd ever seen him, though the man had been edging that way of late. When Cass took control, he was undemanding, sometimes to the point of indifference. It was a welcome shift from his mercurial brother.

Burt responded with his languid drawl.

"Morning to you, too, Cass. First I've heard of it, but it's sure something we could look at."

"Just get it done. Now."

Before Burt could reply, the plantation owner was pointing down the row of working convicts, and his anger ratcheted up another notch.

"The big thing is that boy on the end down there sassed me. Halfwit or whatever is wrong with him, I will not abide insubordination. I want him whipped."

"He's doing what I told him to do."

"That is not the issue. He backtalked me."

"Cass, I didn't hear you..."

Ennis cut him off.

"When I'm ordering you to do my bidding, like I pay for, you can call me Mr. Ennis."

Smith sat his mount a little straighter before he replied.

"The Texas Prison System pays me."

"Well, I pay for these convicts, and I want that mouthy boy whipped."

Cass was pointing down the line at Harry Duplantis who had resumed his work and was no doubt willing himself to be invisible.

"Look, he's still at it. Disobeying my orders. They all are. You stop this destruction, then bring him up here and give him a licking!"

Ennis' voice was loud enough to be heard at a distance, and several of the convicts slowed their labor to listen. Chick Tenney eased his mount around to his left, creating a slight angle on Cass Ennis. Smith, fighting hard to maintain his composure, gave him a slight shake of the head.

"Whipping is a last resort. You know that," Smith offered.

"They understand the bullwhip."

A half dozen of the convicts had now stopped working entirely and were looking sullenly toward the three mounted White men. The thought of potential trouble nudged Burt Smith to the very limit of his patience. Still, he kept his tone even.

"We use a strap, not a bullwhip. And furthermore, as you also already know, I'd have to call to Huntsville to get authorized for a whipping."

"That's bullshit, Burt. With my own eyes, I've seen y'all strap some of these boys."

"Even if I wanted to, and I don't, it's not my choice alone. And I'll tell you again that that man over yonder was just following my orders. He is under my charge. Clearing and burning a field has always been the way of doing things since I got here... Mr. Ennis."

The sergeant's disdain was as tangible as Caswell's balled up fist. Instead of acting out on his anger, Ennis wheeled his chestnut horse and headed back toward the plantation office in a hurry.

Smoldering all day long, Cass Ennis was too mad to even go home for dinner. The very first thing he did when he reached the town was to telephone the prison up at Huntsville. The four or five minutes it took for the clodpoll of an operator to connect his call did nothing to soothe his mood, but he would be damned if he was just going to give up and let this lie. The Ennis family had been keeping Texas prisons solvent for nigh on thirty years. If he could not get satisfaction on his own farm, he would go to the top brass, men who knew how to read a ledger.

The regional captain of Texas prisons was Cliff Adams, a tough man 25 years his senior. Cass had met him several times in person, and knew him to carry a domineering air. Still, he was not feeling particularly deferential today. As soon as he heard Adams' voice snap and frizzle through the heavy earpiece, he jumped into his grievances.

"Cliff, I've got a few bones to pick. I've got an inmate down here burning fodder after I told him to stop, and the uppity bastard backtalked me. I told Burt Smith to whip him, and he refused. We've got inmates slacking and others running off. It's a mess, and I need something done."

Adams' shouted reply crackled over the long distance line.

"Cass, I can barely hear you. I'll tell you what. I can come down there day after tomorrow. I'll send you a wire, and we can talk over supper. Got that? Day after tomorrow."

The line went dead, though there was no telling if it was deliberate or just a whim of the wires. Cass Ennis would have to wait.

In Huntsville, Cliff Adams, who had just cut the line on the state's biggest convict leaseholder, knew that Ennis would also have to either cool or simmer. He hoped for the former.

True to his word, Adams wired Ennis to meet him for a nice evening meal at the Adams Brothers Saloon in Richmond. The owners were not related to the prison man, but he got a kick out of patronizing them all the same. His train trip had been uneventful, and he dropped his grip in a room at the Exchange Hotel before ambling toward the saloon. With his perfect posture and close cropped peppery hair, he looked to an outsider like a successful businessman, unless they noticed that the quality of his suit cloth was slightly below average. Still, Adams was much too assured to let the prospect of some civilian's harangue spoil his evening, whether it was coming from an Ennis or not.

Chasing a predictable goal, Cass arrived in Richmond a full hour before the appointment. His first destination was the familiar bordello just a block north. He strolled in like the cock of the roost only to find Naomi occupied and a square-headed ranch boss waiting ahead of him. Daisy, the decidedly unfresh woman who ran the house, explained that one of her other girls was unavailable after a rough set-to with a besotted railroad man. Until that one was healed up enough to entertain, Naomi was in high demand. She staked Cass to his first drink, and he proceeded to toss back four more in quick succession before he stalked around the block to the restaurant with his true thirst unquenched.

For all of Cliff Adams' calm determination, he read the storm on Caswell Ennis' face the moment the man pushed through the saloon doors. Though Ennis seemed steady enough on his feet, a budding drunkenness was evident. Adams steeled himself for the worst.

A round of drinks were ordered along with two beefsteaks and trimmings. They each also opted for bowls of the tomato soup. General pleasantries, slightly strained, lasted until their whiskeys were half gone before Ennis mounted his list of grievances.

"I want you to do something about the situation at Sartartia. For the last week or so, I've been unhappy. Longer than that really."

Adams had held a position of power over other men for many years. From humble beginnings, he worked himself up with his wits and resolve. Maybe that was why he kept a strong distaste for anyone who tried to circumvent the chain of command.

"You should have worked this out with Burt Smith or with Captain Veale."

"I did not get any satisfaction there."

Cass raised his chin in what Adams viewed as a cartoonish display of childlike impudence. The captain suppressed his rising bile and nodded impassively.

"Go on."

"I've had hands running off. Two went rabbit in the last month and a half. Thirty-five dollar reward each, and they were still missing for weeks. There was another one who run off during the cover from the great storm and was gone almost two years, and now he ain't the worker he used to be. He's not Class A. He's bound to be nearing 40, if not more. You can't ever tell with these people. He ought to be swapped out for somebody fit."

"Yep, and Officer Stone was discharged for that escape. If you're dissatisfied over that one, you could've brought it up before now, Cass. He's been back at your place nigh on three years, for Christ's sake. Look, we're pegging away to keep the best inmates down here, but you have to let us know."

"Maybe we deserve more guards. If the cons can't stay put, maybe there's not enough supervision."

"You've got a full complement of guards. Maximum number of anyplace in the state of Texas."

"Then why do I keep losing workers for weeks at a time?"

"When they jump, they head for the railroad, and at Sartartia, they don't have far to run. With a head start like that, it takes a little time to get them back, and we adjust your account sheet accordingly."

"What is sticking hardest in my craw is that Burt Smith won't issue licks when I tell him to. I've got an insubordinate inmate on my hands, and that has always warranted hard punishment."

"I talked to Burt earlier this afternoon, Cass. He said the inmate was following the orders that he gave him."

Ennis sat back in his chair as he accepted a fresh drink from the waiter. He sat it down untouched for the moment and looked at Adams with condescension.

"Cliff, you know how much money the Ennis family sends to the state coffers. Has done since my daddy ran the whole goddamn system."

This was the dropping of the other shoe Adams anticipated.

"I'm well aware of the history and the numbers. I've been here, remember."

"Then you can understand why I'm irked!"

Cass' voice was loud enough that two suited men at another table paused their own conversation to look over. Adams kept his own tone steady.

"The system has not changed for years. The instructions and the discipline come from the guards."

Ennis slammed back his whiskey and motioned toward the waiter for another. When he got his focus back on Adams, his eyes were dark like thunderclouds. His volume was lower, but his voice had taken on a gritted tooth growl.

"I want the boy whipped."

Cliff Adams paused to consider his response. He decided to diffuse things by trying a different angle.

"Many people nowadays are of a mind that whipping and beating inmates is not the best way to run a penal system."

Cass raised his voice yet again.

"Well, I'm damn sure not one of those people."

Adams took a moment to run his tongue against the inside of his top teeth while he took in a deep breath.

"If those were White men on your work gang, I think you might better understand the state's position here."

"That's why we have it in our contract with the state that we only take class A colored convicts. Goddamn it, Cliff, we pay extra on account of we know we're gonna work them harder and longer. It's thirty goddamned bucks a month for a first class colored hand. You can send the White men and Mexicans to the railroads all day long. Let them lay track. That's what they want. But me? In my cane field, I want a big strong buck that I can push as hard as I damn well need. Ain't it enough that you got prisoners all over the state, White and colored, who'll cut off their own goddamned toe to get out of an honest day's work? You want to carry on like you're worried about the welfare of some no account jigaboo? Me and everybody else in Texas can see right through that shit. Yet here you are with the gall to talk to me about whipping like it concerns you. You are goddamned straight I expect the cons on my farm to be whipped. I'd keep beating those sons of bitches until they follow my orders! I'm paying for just that!"

With that, Cass slammed his open palm on the table hard enough to make a soup spoon jump from his saucer to the tile floor. By the end of his diatribe, the voice of Cass Ennis was reverberating off the walls, and the Adams Brothers Saloon was at a stop.

Chapter 24

The frustration overwhelming Cass Ennis had not waned overnight. If anything, it had grown hotter. The morning after his public outburst toward Cliff Adams did not bring a change to his run of luck. It merely saw another dry log added to the fire.

He snapped at Nelly when he arrived back at the big white house after midnight. Her horrible feelings of isolation bubbled up, and she briefly overstepped her upbringing. She dared question her husband's time away from his young family. In a calmer moment, Cass may have countenanced such questions, but instead he lashed out, stridently reminding her of her place. When she had the temerity to suggest that their marriage should contain reciprocity, he told her, in acerbic tones, that she should be happy that he provided for them so well.

When the sun rose on Friday, she was still not speaking to him. Their daughter, Mary, sensed the bitterness between her parents, and was giving her daddy the cold shoulder, as well. His attempt at a morning hug was soundly rebuffed. His wife and children quite literally turned their backs and huddled on the sun porch.

In response, Cass grew very angry, first with himself, then with anyone dim enough to engage in conversation. His outbursts felt totally out of his control, yet at the same exact moment that harsh words left his lips, he fully understood that his behavior was inexcusable.

Now here he was arguing with Burt Smith, the man whose inaction had started this downturn in the first place. The two men sat on horseback, their mounts beside one another at the far end of the guard lot at Camp #3. He did not come seeking trouble, but he was demanding dominance.

The morning was already steamy when Ennis arrived at the yard about ten. Heavy rain overnight had cleared, but humidity under overcast skies was relentless. Cass was already down to sleeves with his coat strapped to the back of his saddle, and the shirt clung to him like a coat of paint.

Inmates were gathered in the camp yard, waiting to be led to their next task by Bosses Conner and Dineen. Most of the cons at Camp #3 were already scattered about their portion of Sartartia, hoeing weeds from fields that were well established. This squad had spent the first few hours of daylight working the hogs and mules. There were more than 35 of each at the camp, and they required constant attention.

Sergeant Billy Pryor unexpectedly showed up from Camp #1, arriving with Cass Ennis. Burt Smith, who knew from his superiors that the Tuesday tantrum was not yet quashed, assumed Pryor was there for Ennis' moral support, and not as his fellow guard. He also cynically wondered if this was an opportunity for his recent superior to crow a little. Either way, he made sure that Pryor saw and understood his scowl.

The three of them exchanged greetings then got right to business. Ennis requested that Smith ride out with him to inspect the work over past the old Field's Gin. To Smith's relief, Pryor made no attempt to join them. They had barely started their tour before Cass lit into his complaints. As soon as Burt Smith grasped the extent of the new items, he reined his tall dun to a stop.

The list of grievances had grown since their previous encounter. Cass Ennis now wanted three men whipped. He wanted to revisit the issue of the burned fodder. He wanted his pound of flesh over escapes that had taken place as far back as his brother's death and even before. Mostly, he felt like excoriating Sergeant Burt Smith.

Smith felt that he parried the first two items rather deftly. He would make the change to running cattle over the cut fields before they burned them off. Happy to oblige. As for requesting more guards, he assured Ennis that they were on the same side. More hands were always welcome. He would add his voice to the request and pass it up the chain. When Cass Ennis turned to the subject of corporal punishment against convicts who personally offended him, Smith cut him off mid-sentence.

"You can stop right there. I've talked to Captain Veale and Captain Adams about that inmate, and there ain't going to be any whipping. He was following the orders I gave him, and my word is law at Camp Three."

"We'll see about that. I also want to talk about that boy who run off during the big storm."

"Happened before my time, but Captain Adams told me you'd brought that up with him. I know that an officer lost his post over it, and the convict, Andy Hall is his name if you're interested, got two more years added to his stretch."

"Then you can take my word for it," Cass told him. "When they fetched him back after him gadding about the countryside for two years, they never laid a whip on him. I'm demanding now that he get some stripes on his back. Might put some pep in his step."

"That won't be taking place."

The civility dropped from Smith's tone like an anvil. In response, Cass Ennis raised his voice to a near shout.

"He doesn't pull his weight around here. You may think I'm stupid, but I've been watching. I'm fed up, and I'm not going to let the state keep fleecing me thirty bucks a month for that boy. He's a no good old jig who ought to be sitting on a porch someplace."

"He does his work just fine. Sometimes in the field, and sometimes he works tasks here in the yard. I can vouch for him personally."

"You're a liar."

"What did you call me?" Smith bristled.

"A lying son of a bitch."

Sixteen convicts, three other guards and the sergeant's wife were all between 100 and 150 yards away. The blacksmith from the Sartartia shops was making a new pair of strap hinges at the camp's small forge, as well. At first, none of them paid the pair the slightest heed. The few who casually glanced over at the stopped riders might have seen Caswell Ennis grab Burt Smith by the shirtfront. None of them could hear the conversation on a windless morning, but they could have guessed the gist of it. A few folks may have noticed the two men struggle, pulling at each other, angling for position, but if so, none remarked on it.

Even from their great distance, the people in the yard could hear the two horses whinny, and that is the first thing that called attention to the arguing men. The sharpest eyed observers could see when the horses' eyes grew wide with fear. No one was close enough to notice Ennis' chestnut chew his bit, but they could see that the steeds were dancing, necks pulled back and nostrils flared.

When four gunshots popped off, everyone in the yard turned toward the noise. The two horses stepped a few feet apart, as if moved back by the recoil. It became clear that Burt Smith was holding a pistol. Though several jaws dropped back in the camp yard, no one spoke at first. No one moved. They only watched in silent shock.

Cass Ennis bent forward slightly and dropped something in the dirt, then he rode off toward the guard house. Burt Smith's wife ran toward her husband, and Cass Ennis, still slumped over his horse's neck, passed her as he headed toward the main camp yard. If he saw the frantic woman, he did not acknowledge her.

Burt Smith slowly eased his horse over to meet his wife halfway. He stepped down and called loudly to Chappie Dineen to not let Ennis have a gun. His subordinate answered with a wave. After a short exchange of words and a tight hug to his wife, Smith climbed back on the dun and rode out to the west, in the direction of Richmond.

Caswell Ennis continued slowly to the shop where Billy Pryor had been idling with the blacksmith. Ennis dismounted by sliding off the chestnut horse, but holding tight to the stirrup, he managed to stay upright. He briefly said something to the blacksmith and Sergeant Pryor, then he staggered back into the yard, doubled over and laid down in the dirt. In an eerie reprise of September 1902, a rider galloped to Sartartia where they telephoned the sheriff.

Chapter 25

Caswell was brought back to his house in a buckboard. Four men carried him, moaning in agony, up the staircase and placed him on his own bed. Nelly had a fleeting objection about her best sheets, a wedding present from her favorite aunt, but it was never voiced. For the second time in three years, a doctor was called out to Sartartia to see to a gunshot victim.

The doctor examined the wounds, three entry holes. One had gone wide, even at that point blank distance, but the others took devastating effect. There was one in his chest and two in his belly. The suggestion was made to call Dr. Robert Morris out from Houston. Morris was a top surgeon, and if anyone could save Cass Ennis, he was the man.

Morris' probes brought considerable gasps of pain. The determination was that a .38 slug had entered between ribs 8 and 9 on the right side. Two others had severely perforated the intestines, and as Morris put it, "all sorts of unwanted effluvia were leaking out." After a thorough examination, Morris believed Cass was far too weak to survive surgery. He suggested they wait and hope that their patient regained some strength.

Nelly Ennis was beside herself with grief. It was heavily tinged with guilt knowing that she and her husband were not on speaking terms when he rode out that morning. For the most part, people were successful at keeping young Mary occupied, but the baby, Amanda, wailed and screamed, possibly sensing the great agitation of her mother.

The two younger Ennis brothers, Emmett and Leigh, sat on cushioned chairs to the left of the bed, staring at their prone and bloody sibling. Neither offered much in the way of conversation.

A few close friends assembled, hearing that the end was imminent. J.C. Sullivan, an Irishman who had taken the plantation foreman's job, was on hand. The loyal bookkeeper at Sartartia, Cloyd Moore, noted instructions in a bound ledger. Albert Russell, a paper-pushing lawyer who recently began attending to the Ennis family's business, was summoned from Richmond when it dawned that young Caswell, still in his twenties, had no will and testament.

It was Russell who suggested that Cass make a formal declaration of the events which had put him in this painful position. Cloyd Moore dutifully transcribed the words of Russell and Ennis in a perfect Spencerian hand.

"I realize that I am at the point of death and wish to make a statement of all the facts surrounding the shooting of myself by B.C Smith. This statement I desire to make before the world ere I go to meet my God.

Smith engaged me in a controversy. I told him to cut it out and started away. We were both on horseback. I told him I was not armed and that he was. He called me a no good son of a bitch. I explained that I wanted to cut those things out. He said he would not, that he had a notion to fix me right then. He drew his revolver and said he had a good notion to kill me.

'Don't do it. Don't kill me,' I exclaimed.

Just then he fired on me and the bullet struck me here.

Almost instantly thereafter, he shot me in quick succession three or four times, and I rode away as best I could.

He hit me every time he fired except the last, and I begged him not to kill me, and told him before he began shooting that I was not armed.

I seldom carry a pistol. I never advanced on Smith and I endeavored to get away from him. He just felt in his belt for more cartridges. He said something, but I could not understand. That is all."

At times, there were as many as fifteen people in Cass and Nelly's bedroom. The air got so close that, even with the windows thrown open wide and the curtains tied back, some folks leaned against walls in the upstairs hallway. Others milled about downstairs.

When Caswell's statement was finished, all of the White adults who were then present in the big house, eleven of them, attested to it as witnesses. It was an ironclad indictment of Burt Smith's guilt.

Of course, Letha and Tom Ward were constantly in and out of the sick room, performing various tasks for everyone present. It was particularly difficult for Letha who could not fully express her feelings to the family. Still, she did all that was asked of her.

Cass Ennis lingered for twelve hours. When he breathed his last, about half past ten that night, the visiting traffic had long departed. The children were in bed, and Nelly was having a lie down after the most draining day of her life. Emmett was brooding on the back porch, listening to frogs and crickets and drinking brandy. Doctor Morris had taken the train back to Houston hours before with a promise to return the following morning. Only two people shared Cass' final moments. Leigh Ennis sat by the bedside reading *Cabbages and Kings*, a gift for his 18th birthday the previous month.

Most people would hardly have remarked on the other person who witnessed Caswell's Earthly departure, but heavy tears cascaded from Letha Ward's eyes. When she could no longer choke back her sobs, she went out of the room. She found her husband lingering silently on the porch of their little cottage.

"It feels so wrong to make the grief about me," she managed to choke out. "But I can't help it. I will miss so many things about him. He was like my own boy."

Emmett stepped outside five minutes later and hollered for Letha to make them some food.

Grief hung heavy around the Ennis house again, but there was there was little of the coping normality and occasional laughter that appeared at the previous occasion. This time, the surviving family could put forth nothing but a dull, organic ache. Few words were exchanged. Unlike with the shooting of Will, Mamie Lyons did not rush from San Antonio. She arrived at her old home about midnight, almost two hours after her half-brother Cass was gone.

Burt Smith met Sheriff E.A. Hickley on the road, headed toward Sartartia. Without saying much of anything, the sheriff wheeled his mount around and the two men rode back toward town.

Though he had been elected county sheriff in the fall of 1902, half the people in Richmond still referred to Ed Hickley as Major. He was a solidly built 38-year old veteran of the First Texas Cavalry in the recent war against Spain, though he had spent the brief hostilities stationed in San Antonio. Prior to that, Hickley spent some years in the Texas Guard. The military formed his adult life, and he was not apt to let anyone forget it.

With the right people, Hickley was known as a hail fellow well met and often showed an open sense of humor. He asked a few questions of Burt Smith as the two men rode side by side, slowly heading toward the county jail. His tone was pleasant as he tried to get some basic information about the shooting.

The camp sergeant was sullen. He supplied only the barest of answers, and the sheriff mostly nodded or offered a simple, upbeat noise to show that he registered the information. There would be time enough for more in depth questions, no point in stepping off on the wrong foot, Hickley figured. He did not even mention the spreading bloodstain on Burt Smith's shirt sleeve.

The two crossed the bridge and turned right to zig and zag toward the imposing jail. There was but a single entrance for prisoners, up the same front steps and through the same portal that the man who had shot the eldest Ennis brother traversed in the fairly recent past. As a precaution and without comment, Sheriff Hickley closed the iron bars to the outside vestibule behind them and, upon entering, instructed the duty deputy to get the proper key and lock it. To lessen the chance for escape, every key inside the Fort Bend County Jail was different and secured in a safe.

If Hickley ever feared trouble from the guard turned prisoner, he gave no indication. His first words to Smith, after giving brief booking instructions to the deputy, were about food.

"I reckon you missed dinner. I can get you fed. There should be some ham and beans left in the pot, and it's pretty damn tasty. Made yesterday, so it's had time to season. We'll get you settled upstairs, and then after you've ate, you and I can have our chat. I'll get hold of somebody first thing tomorrow to let them know you're in here, though your guard buddies are most likely way ahead of me on that, ain't they?"

Smith shrugged a reply. Hickley continued as if he was engaged in the liveliest of conversations.

"No idea how long you'll be here, but if I had to put a bet down, my money would be on a long spell. But no need to make things unpleasant. Because you're almost law enforcement, I suspect we can cut a corner here and there and keep you comfortable, can't we? Prison guard, that's like a kissing cousin to wearing a badge, ain't it?"

Hickley let go a big, hearty guffaw at his own joke and slapped Burt Smith on the back.

The deputy who led Smith upstairs was not as talkative as the sheriff. He seemed more inclined to pointing and apish grunts. On the other hand, Smith noted that he was not manhandled or even prodded in the manner that often happened at Camp #3, though the deputy held tight to a short wooden truncheon.

A key unlocked a formidable padlock, and a hasp was pulled back to open a heavy door. It was an individual space, about six by eight feet, enclosed with the same steel plating cut with square holes that surrounded the large common prisoner tank. A narrow cot was attached to the left wall and a dented but empty slop bucket rested in the opposite corner. Smith sat down on the rock hard bed and looked at his surroundings. After fifteen seconds, the view was committed to memory.

The same taciturn, rat-faced deputy opened the door a few minutes later with a wet rag and an amber bottle.

"Roll up your sleeve," he drawled.

Burt Smith looked at him through narrowed eyes. The deputy pointed down at him on the cot.

"Your arm is bleeding like a pig come to slaughter."

Smith nodded understanding and rolled up his left sleeve. The gray shirt had soaked through and then dried with a dark stain of blood and grime that ran from elbow to cuff.

The deputy tossed Smith the rag, instructing him to scrub off the mess. When things looked sufficiently clean, and the cut had started oozing again, the lawman grabbed Burt's wrist, held the arm out straight and poured the dark liquid over the cut. As he tried not to yelp from the sting, Smith made note of the skull and crossbones on the iodine bottle.

Before the pain had subsided, the deputy handed Smith a large tinware mug of ham and beans then locked the door behind him.

Since his lunch had been a late one, it was barely three hours before Sheriff Hickley himself brought more ham and beans, this time with a slice of skillet cornbread. Even though the meal was room temperature, the flavors were fully melded. It was decent eating, better than most meals at the prison camp. In coming days, the deputies even supplied Smith with leftovers from the Sheriff's own table.

Hickley left the heavy cell door ajar and produced a small wooden chair that he dragged inside and plopped down on. He motioned with his hand for Smith to start eating.

"So, why'd you shoot Ennis?"

Burt looked at the sheriff long and hard before answering. When he finally spoke, the tone was matter of fact.

"He pulled a knife on me and threatened to kill me."

"You shot him four times. Just how big was the knife?"

Hickley grinned amiably, but got stone faced silence in return.

"Is that how you got the cut on your arm?" the sheriff asked.

Smith repositioned his left hand closer to his leg without thinking. He looked Hickley in the eyes and nodded.

"Well, I'm going to head out there in the morning. Second thing."

He smiled and continued.

"If there's a knife, I reckon they're holding it for me."

He went on to establish the physical layout of the incident and a basic timeline, at least as much detail as Smith was willing to give. When the sheriff felt that his prisoner was done talking, he bid him good night and, crossing the small open space, let himself into the large common cell on the same floor. Four White prisoners lounged in there. The Black county inmates were locked in a different communal pen.

Hickley used his night stick to point to the far side of the cell, and the four prisoners duly moved there.

"Evening, gents," he said with a closed mouth smile.

He then bent and picked up the empty tin mugs from supper. As he turned to go, one of the men spoke.

"Hey, sheriff, I had a big old hunk of gristle in mine. I want to complain to the cook."

As the man laughed, Hickley dropped the cups to the floor with a clang. In four strides he was across the room. Like the flash of a viper, his cocked right arm uncoiled, and the backhanded billy club slammed into the prisoner's mouth.

"Problem solved. You won't be eating for few days anyhow."

While the man, doubled over and moaning, spit blood and teeth onto the floor, the sheriff picked up the cups a second time without further comment. He pulled the steel double door closed and turned the key in the heavy locks. It was hard to be certain in the evening gloom of the cells, but Burt could swear he saw the sheriff wink at him as he closed the door at the top of the stairs.

Burt Smith told the sheriff that he would not be making any statement to press, but that did not stop Hickley from sending a local man into the cells about nine that first night. J.C. Florea, a school teacher from Missouri City and Houston who had just bought the *Texas Coaster*, wanted to get the exclusive.

Florea was a bulldog. He had read the law with a local attorney, but with the Fort Bend Bar already chock full of barristers, he felt that the newspaper business offered the surest path forward. He found the murder suspect with his back to the door, staring at a shaft of moonlight that streamed through the narrow window.

"Mr. Smith?"

Burt turned expecting a deputy.

"I'm John Florea with the Richmond newspaper."

"Not interested."

Smith resumed his contemplation of the sunbeam, but Florea kept talking, hope building in each phrase.

"I met you once. You were sparking your girl, your wife, I mean. It was last summer. My wife and I were at Augie Meyers Grocery when y'all came in shopping for supper."

Smith glanced up but said nothing.

"Your Ivy knew my missus."

The sergeant walked slowly toward the latticed steel that separated them. Florea had one final reminiscence.

"I recall that you were in town for a meal with your betrothed's folks."

Burt Smith put his face very close to the three inch square that allowed him to make eye contact with the slightly taller Florea. His voice was a low rumble off the hard cell walls.

"I told the sheriff that I have nothing to say to reporters, and if you have any goddamn sense at all, you'll keep my wife's name out of this. One of these days, I just might get out of here."

The sheriff was true to his word about another item. Not long after the day had dawned, Hickley had a long distance call placed to Smith's brother in Houston. The sheriff then rode out to Sartartia. Well before noon, J.B. Duckworth himself was on a train down to Richmond.

Chapter 26

Richmond, Texas

The longer the young man waited on the train platform, the more difficult it was to suppress his anger. The first morning that ever dawned on this Earth with him in charge of anything, and he was staring at empty railroad tracks. The boy who was quite used to feeling alone, now felt more isolated than ever.

It was not the railroad's fault that he had now been there for over half an hour, stewing alone on a baggage cart. The train from Houston was right on time, at least as far as he knew. He looked over his right shoulder at the depot clock. The locomotive will have lumbered through his tiny home town without even slowing to a stop and will be chugging over the bridge any second. In truth the time mattered little. He was not taking the train anyway. He was waiting to spring himself at an arriving passenger.

Emmett Ennis' first business of the morning was a stop at the solid, stone-fronted bank at Third and Morton in downtown Richmond. There he presented a hastily drawn paper from Attorney Russell attesting to the death of Caswell Ennis and the assumption of managerial duties at Sartartia by his 24-year old brother. It should have been a routine change of information on one of the plantation's main operating accounts. His brother had not been dead twelve hours, but the business of change and enterprise would not be slowed.

Instead of an unremarkable but sad formality, the whole thing became a stinging embarrassment. First Judge Davis himself was reported to be unavailable on short notice. That in spite of the fact that Emmett arrived barely ten minutes after the bank unlocked its big corner doors. He was taken to the desk of Bob Wessendorf, a clerk. Once condolences were solemnly offered, Ennis felt that he might as well have been some laborer off the street. A form had to be filled out, and notes had to be entered in multiple ledgers while he waited.

When that business was complete, and after Wessendorf had spent copious time in a back office, the banker informed Emmett that the line of credit which the Davis & Company Bank held for Sartartia was fully extended. The judge was happy to discuss raising the limits under a change of terms, but that discussion would require an appointment. The toady Wessendorf again offered sympathy on behalf of everyone at the bank, and then Emmett was unceremoniously bid adieu.

As he walked west toward the passenger depot, Emmett's face burned with rage. He was certain that people passing him on Morton Street could see him lit up as red as a fireman's suspenders. It took him all of two blocks to come to the sad realization that it was not the bank that should be the target of his wrath. At least not entirely. Though they were unconscionably rude to a newly important customer, and he resolved to consider making them pay for that. Momentarily, he stopped walking and leaned his back against the iron fence that surrounded the court house block.

The epiphany was that he was livid with Cass. His brother and best friend, and he had died and evidently tossed Emmett into a deep pond of unperfumed financial shit. He was only four years younger than Cass. It was not as if he was a child who needed to be protected from the bogey man. Sartartia was his, too, and though neither brother had ever stopped for a solitary second to consider that Emmett was a mere heartbeat from having to run the entire operation, he had been kept completely in the dark. Emmett started walking again, wondering if the overall financial outlook was even bleaker.

He turned north on Fifth Street and west again at Railroad. Across the tracks from the freight depot was an open saloon, and he fully considered diving into a bottle of whiskey until he could not touch bottom. Ultimately, he continued the last block and plopped himself down on the empty baggage cart at the back side of the depot. Drinking could wait. Right now, he needed to ensure vengeance and justice.

Almost instantly, Emmett's new found resolve ran smack into the news he had gotten at the bank. Could the Ennis Family even afford the offer he was ready to make?

He sat staring across tracks at the empty cotton platform and the big Richmond cotton gin beyond that. For now, the platforms and warehouses and seed houses sat empty, but they would be filling soon enough. Sartartia would have crops to sell. That income could right the foundering ship. He knew it. He could hear the hum of machinery since the gin also housed an electric light plant that operated day and night. The future was literally bright. Bob Wessendorf and Judge Davis could go straight to hell. Sartartia was not broke.

The last westbound of the morning huffed to a stop right as Emmett made his decision, and a dozen passengers were disgorged. Emmett looked them over and hoped that his tipoff was sound.

He spotted the man with the big moustache stepping down from the rear of the passenger car. Medium build. Hair line receding. Nicely dressed in a light gray suit and a fresh collar.

"Mr. Duckworth?"

The lawyer turned to appraise the young stranger. Emmett extended his hand with slight trepidation.

"I'm Emmett Ennis."

J.B. shook his hand but still said nothing, so Emmett continued.

"I hear that you're thinking about defending Burt Smith in the killing of my brother."

"That's right," Duckworth said with a curt nod.

"What's your fee?"

The youngster's bluntness did not seem to surprise the lawyer.

"That's between me and my client, Mr. Ennis."

Now it was Emmett's turn to nod. For good measure, he thoughtfully pursed his lips.

"I was told it was fifteen hundred dollars. If that's the case, I'd like to offer you triple that amount to join the prosecution. Our family lawyer says that the county attorney is out of his depth, and I believe you are the man for the job."

J.B. cocked his head slightly to the right and thoughtfully smoothed his moustache.

"I've given my word to the defense."

Emmett gulped slightly before speaking, but he managed not to choke.

"Mr. Duckworth, you've let the murderer of one of my brothers walk free. My family does not intend to see that happen again."

"A jury determined that verdict, Mr. Ennis. I just try to put forth a compelling case."

He did not intend to appear threatening, but with his heart racing, Emmett Ennis took a half step forward. If the attorney found the distance between them too close, Duckworth did not betray that feeling with even a flinch.

"How about this, then," Emmett posited. "We'll give you six thousand dollars to do nothing. Don't even take a side. Just pocket the money and sit in your office back in Houston. What could be more fair than that?"

Tough as it was to tell behind the face whiskers, the left corner of Duckworth's mouth rose a little before he answered. His tone was soft, almost like he was speaking to a dull child.

"I can't do that, Mr. Ennis. I've given my word."

The pique that Emmett had successfully tapped down shot to the surface. His right hand grabbed a tight handful of Duckworth's gray sleeve. His next words were loud enough to make the porter and two lingering passengers spin toward them.

"Six thousand dollars? Your word means that much, or is it pure cussedness. Or do you just crave the battle, Mr. Duckworth?"

"Yes," J.B. answered as he pulled his sleeve free and walked west toward the jail.

Emmett Ennis watched him go then threw a hateful scowl at the curious passengers, forcing them to quickly turn away. Finally, he wiped an eye and headed down Railroad toward that saloon. His second class train was not due for over an hour. He might as well start drinking.

J.B. Duckworth had come to Richmond personally because of the importance of this case. Yes, he had plenty of other things piled on his desk, but this was of the highest profile. Newspapers all over Southeast Texas would be writing this one up. The testimony would appear in their pages almost verbatim, or at least verbatim with a heavy gobbet of sensationalism.

Certainly, John could have traveled to Richmond and done his usual fine job of conducting an initial client interview, but J.B. felt like doing this rare one in person. His successful defense of George Purdy would be breathlessly recalled, and numerous other victories along with it. The murder of a second Ennis had just pushed its way past every other case in the queue.

Duckworth took a deep breath of late spring air, horse manure and train smoke and smiled to himself about having just turned down six thousand greenbacks. No, Mr. Ennis, he thought to himself, acquittals make headlines, and this good publicity cannot be bought.

J.B. had left home that morning in a hurry, heading out the front door shortly after getting the telegram during breakfast. There was no packing to do, but he had to swing by the office and give instructions. Henry Fein had not yet arrived, so he asked Sonny Schlottmann to step in on an armed robbery case that was coming up across the street. Everything else should take care of itself. The attorneys of Duckworth & Fein were hard workers.

J.B. did turn and offer one last thought as he headed out the office door to the Grand Central Depot.

"I won't be back in time to go Liberty, so have Posey run up there and get us another continuance. Whatever you do, don't let Henry go. That judge is a Jew baiting old bastard. If you don't stop him, Henry'll go just to tweak the son of a bitch on the nose."

The morning in Richmond was definitely sultry as Duckworth crossed the tracks and ambled past a big lumber yard on his way to the jail. He shucked his jacket and thought about how much he enjoyed the smell of fresh cut wood. A few deep breaths, and he imagined he could identify pine and oak. Maybe ash, too.

At the jailhouse, J.B. banged on the front door and was admitted to the front room. He signed a visiting ledger, and then he was escorted through a steel door and up ringing stairs by a rat-faced deputy that Duckworth had seen on several previous visits to the Fort Bend hoosegow.

With different sheriffs, it was doubtful that anyone even paid heed to the fact that Burt Smith occupied the same jail cell as had George Purdy, the other man who had shot a son of Littleberry Ennis. Though his trial time meetings with Purdy were in Wharton, J.B. had sat in this dank cubby with Purdy once while he was in Richmond seeing another murder case client.

The deputy opened the heavy door, stuck a plain chair inside and locked the cell behind the lawyer.

"If he starts killing you, yell."

With that bit of glibness, he disappeared to an unseen niche of his own.

Duckworth broke the ice by inquiring after Burt Smith's lodgings and well being.

"They're treating me okay. Better than most in here," Smith answered. "But the scenery don't do much to inspire carefree singing or dancing."

He pointed to the holes in the steel wall. The hanging scaffold loomed a few feet outside the door and up a half flight of stairs. The death cell was poised just above that. Smith was right. It did not make for a comforting backdrop to contemplate one's murder charge.

In representing more than two hundred accused murderers, J.B. Duckworth had seen all sorts of reactions from the men, and three women, who sat in the cells. Some were argumentative, even aggressive to the edge of further violence. Some whimpered. Others became sullen shells, physically withdrawing within themselves. Then there were the men, usually from families of the merchant class or better, who truly failed to grasp why they were being held in a jail house.

Burt Smith was none of these. He sat in the Fort Bend calaboose wearing an almost businesslike acceptance. He exuded calm pragmatism, not desperation or anger at his plight. He had indeed killed a man, and now he wanted to pay the smallest penance possible.

The lawyer leaned back a little in the wooden chair and asked Smith to explain what happened. The prison guard's response was to the point.

"Ennis pulled a knife and tried to stab me."

He held out his tattered and darkly disgusting sleeve. The bandage, which would probably welcome a changing, showed underneath. J.B. promised to buy Smith a new shirt before he caught the train back to Houston. Then he requested more details, and Smith obliged.

"Ennis said 'I will cut your goddamned throat.' If you'd looked into the man's eyes, you'd have taken him at his word just like I did. So, I shot him, and I shot him enough to make him stop."

Duckworth thought to himself, calm or not, he had never had a murder client recount their killing in a pure chronology. He nodded and redirected the conversation a little.

"All right. Let's back up a little bit. How did you come to the trouble in the first place?"

From then on, Smith was more than creditable in unfolding the events. He even took a few minutes to theorize on Caswell Ennis' overall change in demeanor the last half year or so. Finally, he got to the shifting list of demands on the morning of the shooting. Smith paused and shook his head. It was impossible to fathom that being only yesterday.

"I know I've got a temper," Burt told his lawyer. "But I swear on my own mama that I tried to keep away from trouble with the man. I know he pays the bills for those camps out there. I didn't make sergeant for being a village idiot."

With the particulars of the killing itself laid out, the two men talked about witnesses for close to half an hour. It was a satisfying first meeting, and after he hollered for the deputy, J.B. reassured Burt Smith.

"Don't worry. We'll get you out of this."

Duckworth had to walk all the way to Morton Street to make good on his promise to get Burt Smith a new shirt, but he finally found a tailor shop midway down the block on Third. He fished a dollar out of his vest pocket and put it down for a soft shirt in blue. Plain front. He decided to forego the collar until the first court appearance loomed. No use having a new collar get ruined for no reason. He did add a dime to his purchase and took joy in watching the Mexican tailor Mr. Bravo's eyebrows arch when he asked that the package be delivered to a prisoner at the jail. With that business done, J.B. sought a beer and a sandwich before he caught the next eastbound train.

Unlike his older brother, J.B. Duckworth took very few notes during an initial interview for a murder case. He jotted down small action items that he did not want to forget, but when it came to the details of the incident itself, he wanted the story to simmer in his brain for an hour or two. He believed that the ingredients for a defense must find their proper place. Once the story for a jury began to coalesce, J.B. would find a quiet place where he could put his thoughts to paper. As he saw it, his job was to craft a great narrative, not a thorough history. A cool beer was just the thing.

A few blocks east of the jail, Naomi Walker wiped tears from her face. She had sobbed half the night and had been crying since she woke up. After the last customers of the night before had left, one of the other girls padded down to

Naomi's little room, sat on the bed and shared a hug. Then she quietly passed along the news casually given by some john. Cass Ennis had been shot out at Sartartia and would not survive.

It was opening time, and Naomi gathered herself. She heard footsteps in the hall, and then the door knob turned. It was the short, fat Polander from Needville. She sighed and summoned a warm smile. He was a harmless man, and at least it would be quick.

Chapter 27

Houston, Texas

October 1905

Across the street, things around the courthouse were quiet on this final Sunday in October. Temperatures had not yet rallied above the mid-sixties, and broken clouds skated over impossibly blue skies. A Bohemian looking group, possibly touring players, milled on the sidewalk in front of the Opera House. A hack driver flicked his reins and pulled away from the curb to head south on Fannin. The whine of an electric motor wafted over from the glass works on San Jacinto.

The lawyers of Duckworth & Fein were gathered for their pre-court session. While their leader and his dog reviewed paperwork in his private office, the rest of the staff traded tales of their exploits on Saturday. Henry Fein, for whom Saturday before sundown was counted as the Sabbath, leafed quietly through the morning paper and puffed on his pipe.

Sonny Schlottmann had wanted to take the train up to Dallas for the opening day at the state fair, but a painfully slow court clerk on Friday afternoon held him up until the entire enterprise would have been unrewarding. Henry Albrecht was clerk to three of Harris County's four district courts, and on the Friday before a session started, things were hopelessly backlogged. Sonny should have known better. Instead, he settled for a last minute date with a young lady who was ever-so-grateful for an excursion at Highland Park.

Jed Posey turned away from his reveries out the open window and interjected.

"I was there, too. I had a date with the mercurial Miss Howze, step-niece of my boarding house owner."

"One of the Quality Hill Howzes, no doubt," Walt Dawson offered with an exaggerated nobility.

Dawson was a newly added clerk who had already endeared himself through his retinue of jokes and mimicry. Jed Posey, who sometimes missed humor from others, responded in all seriousness.

"No. Her father is a merchandise dealer, and they live on Smith."

Amid the ensuing groans and hoots, Henry Fein looked over the top of the *Post* to make a bad pun.

"As long as she's not as big as a house."

That only brought more groans.

J.B. Duckworth strode in from his room and seamlessly hijacked the conversation. He recounted how the Duckworth brothers had slipped away yesterday afternoon to watch horse racing out Harrisburg Road at the Driving Park. J.B. even returned home twenty-two dollars to the good.

"I took Lola for dinner last night, and am flush for lunches for the rest of the month."

He ruffled his dog's head as she lay down next to his chair.

"And Maisy will get a raise in her treat allowance, won't you sweet girl?"

Duckworth then grinned mischievously at his brother.

"Tight John here was not so fortunate."

John Duckworth responded with a grimace and a dismissive wave of the hand.

In Judge Charles Ashe's absence from town, Duckworth's pal Norman Kittrell was hearing twice the number of District Court pleadings and motions in the big courtroom across the street tomorrow. That meant the firm had plenty to occupy them during the Sunday session. J.B. would want to know that his brother had returns for all subpoenas issued and that his legal associates were confident in the lines of questioning that needed to be hammered home.

It was the Fort Bend court that was the first center of attention, however. Criminal cases only came up there twice a year, and the eighth Monday after the first Monday in September had finally arrived.

J.B. had consulted his primary partner, Henry Fein, weeks ago and they decided that they did not want delays or a move. The latter was based jointly on their knowledge of the general opinion of the Ennis family in Fort Bend County and the fact that the district court judge, Wells Thompson, had twice denied bail.

Normally, continuances and venue changes were important pieces in the Duckworth & Fein tool bag. By postponing a trial for years, chances increased that key witnesses drifted away to regions unknown. As long as bail could be procured, the weight of the docket was heavier on the state. In this case, with the prisoner remanded in the county jail for five months, that notion was turned on its head.

The two times J.B. had dispatched attorneys to Bay City, the judge's home town, to request bail, they had been sent home with scorched trousers. The judge was offended that they had even asked, though he told Jed Posey that he was not surprised to see such impertinence from Houston lawyers. This was the murder of a prominent citizen whose family had experienced tragedy only a few years before. This killer could not be at large.

Sadly, the state prison system bosses were in no rush to come to the aid of their ten year employee, either. The Ennis family had been the largest lessor of Texas convicts for much longer than a decade. The prison superintendent and commissioners understood that their bread was not buttered by Burt Smith.

Likewise, delaying for witnesses made no sense in the B.C. Smith case. The closest people at the time of the killing were at least 100 yards distant. Their recollections and eyesight could be attacked. Moreover, most of the witnesses were Negroes, and that was not worth the time of putting them on the stand. That was the exact point that J.B. had just made, but Henry Fein disagreed.

"Just hear me out. Remember, they put the colored maid on the stand in the Rice trial a few years back. She was the best defense witness they had."

"And nobody paid one iota of attention to what she said. She may have been the most believable person up there, but she was colored. If the jury had noticed her at all, Albert Patrick wouldn't be rotting in Sing Sing."

Sonny's answer brought nods from all the clerks. When J.B. spoke, he was more conciliatory.

"That was in New York City, Henry. You really think putting colored witnesses on the stand in Richmond, Texas would play to our advantage?"

The room sat silent while Fein rubbed his glasses on his tie. Finally, he gave in with a wave of the hand.

"Yeah, forget I said anything."

Charlie Dixon never looked up from the copy of *American Boy* magazine that he was reading in the corner. If he heard his employers' dismissal of his entire race, he did not betray his thoughts in the slightest. He sat on the floor, leaning against the wall, not demonstrating a care in the world.

The next brief question was simply a reassurance that they call Burt Smith himself. It was still an unequivocal yes. The other guards from Sartartia Camp #3 were another story. John Brockman broached the subject.

"My man down there says that he thinks most of them are still with us, but one or two may be hedging on their story. He's heard rumors. If he's right, they may do us more harm than help, and the trouble is it's tough to pin down who's who."

J.B. was exasperated.

"Well, that's a fine time for this shit to surface. We can't win without them. They're the only reliable witnesses we have. God damn it!"

J.B. gathered himself before continuing.

"His wife saw it, but that's his wife. She won't carry much water. It's those guards. We need them."

The moustachioed lawyer shook his head as he looked around the room.

"We've got a stack of shit against us on this one, boys. Yes, sir. Shit piled high as the outhouse door."

Next, Duckworth proceeded to lay out his plans to contest Caswell Ennis' death bed statement on grounds of impaired mental faculty. Jed Posey sought to encourage that strategy.

"The poor man..."

J.B. Duckworth interrupted, using his cigar as a pointer.

"Never the 'poor man.' He was the evil belligerent who intended our client deadly harm."

Posey smiled ever so slightly, then continued.

"That hideous individual had three bullets festering in his chest and belly. He was fevered and slipping in and out of consciousness. No reasonable person would fail to see that, would they?"

This time it was Henry Fein who was the voice of negativity.

"Yet all the witnesses to that statement are Ennis family and their close friends. That's what? ..."

Henry checked his notes.

"...Eleven people who will solemnly swear that the man was so coherent he could write out the entirety of King Lear from memory."

John Duckworth offered another idea.

"I'll see if we can get to Doc Morris. They called him down from here in town, and he's a reasonable man who has seen things our way in the past."

J.B. and Henry both voiced support. The younger Duckworth added a soft word in his brother's ear.

"Whatever we need to do."

The team moved on to the next major cases. There was an important evidentiary hearing in the Starky Collins case that Henry was handling. It was judged to be in hand.

Walt Dawson was to go with Sonny and enter a not-guilty plea in a shotgun killing that happened the previous week in a totally ungovernable gin joint up at the Humble oil field. Their new client shot a man in the back through an open window. If they were going to get him bail, they needed a very clever twist on the story. Schemes and proposals were floated and debated for the best part of an hour.

About one o'clock, Charlie Dixon, who had been dispatched on a sandwich run only minutes before, raced breathlessly up the stairs to tell them the bayou was on fire. His enthusiasm immediately grabbed everyone's attention.

"What? What building?" Sonny asked.

"No building, Mr. Sonny. The water is on fire. Down across from the golf club. They say it's burning bright from bank to bank. Come see. The whole city is a-buzzing."

Sure enough, from the far sidewalk on Congress, the entire firm saw thick black smoke that was blotting out much of the early afternoon sun. Crowds were gathered everywhere that offered a clear sight line, and many people walked in the direction of the mystery conflagration. Charlie Dixon had already scampered off to the west in search of better views and potentially grisly stories.

Henry Fein spotted Gussie Riemann watching the smoke from farther down the sidewalk and went over. Riemann was a fellow Alsatian, a watchmaker who owned a nice jewelry store a block to the south. He was also an amazingly reliable source of Houston gossip.

"Gussie, any idea what's on fire? Our office boy said it was the bayou itself?"

His friend offered a hand.

"Afternoon, Henry. Yup. Your boy's right from what I hear. It's probably from the mills at Cheney Junction. You know there's a good inch of oil floating on top of the water all the time. Every operation out there dumps their waste willy nilly. Word is some delinquents tossed matches to it till it caught."

Fein was aghast.

"My God. Imagine if that happened at the Foot of Main."

While Henry Fein got the lowdown, the rest of the firm was straining at the bit to join the throngs headed west for a free Sunday afternoon show. When J.B. felt sufficiently assured by Sonny that the prep for Harris County was in hand, he motioned the young clerks to go. He himself walked back across the street and locked the offices.

His intention was to catch a crowded car out to find the spectacle himself, but as he strolled towards the streetcar stop at Main, he spied the sign for the Big Casino just beyond. His curiosity was suddenly nudged aside by hunger. He had never gotten the sandwiches he ordered. If he missed it, Duckworth figured he could read about it in the morning *Post*. Meanwhile, it was time for oysters and beer.

Chapter 28

J.B. Duckworth bid farewell to Maizy with some vigorous scratches and sent her home with his brother, John. It was a leisurely six or seven block walk to the Grand Central Station, and the perfect fall weather was something to savor after the steamy summer. Duckworth imagined that every Houstonian since the Indians had looked forward to this perfect time of year.

As he strolled down Franklin Street approaching the big train depot, the foot traffic thickened, and J.B. soaked in the sights. Old hack men smoked outside the busy front doors. An arriving woman shooed four untidy children in front of her like grass stained ducklings. The aroma of the chili cart tempted.

He walked past the colored waiting room just behind a porter who turned into the cramped space then ducked into the bathroom on a trot. J.B. glanced inside at the poor souls forced to jockey for a few benches, holding food on their laps. A well-dressed woman leaned against the wall eating a bunch of grapes.

Duckworth disliked waiting rooms. He thought waiting for anything to be a waste of time. The day's minutes should be utilized whether it was for work or relaxation, and sitting in a train station qualified as neither. Consequently, he tried to time things so that he walked through the front door and could pass directly to the ticket window and then the platform. This Sunday afternoon, he had succeeded.

It was a longer train, bound for destinations far west - San Antonio, El Paso and beyond, though the vast majority of travelers would have descended long before those places. J.B. found his seat in the first of the White passenger cars with only the Jim Crow car and the U.S. Mail between himself and the locomotive and tender. Hopefully the cinders coming in through the windows would be minimal.

If he looked out those windows rather than at his notes and papers, J.B. would have seen the city quickly fade to farms and ranches. White-faced cattle grazed, and occasionally, game looking horses gamboled. Knots of hardwoods rose here and there from the coastal prairie. An early V of wood ducks passed overhead, and a county road gang smoothed the gravel barely a hundred yards south of the tracks. The studious lawyer saw none of it. He only listened to the noises of the train and read.

After dropping his grip in the Richmond hotel room that would be home for the next few days, Duckworth brushed the train grime from his jacket then headed directly to the county jail. Dark was falling, and there was still trial strategy to be discussed on this eve of opening remarks.

J.B.'s knock on the jailhouse door was answered by the same crabby deputy that he had dealt with previously, but the man's surly visage showed a slight crack when he noticed that the visitor held two bottles of Old Taylor whiskey.

At his lawyer's request, Burt Smith had gotten a message to Fred Shaw and Chappie Dineen, and the guards arrived at the jail about dusk, not long after Duckworth, anxious to help their friend. Shaw was the new sergeant at Camp #3. Though he was Burt Smith's replacement, the jailed guard considered Shaw his closest friend.

Sheriff Hickley led them upstairs to where Duckworth already sat with Smith in the unlocked cell. He dragged in another chair for the burly Shaw. The rangier Dineen sat next to Burt Smith on the bunk.

Brief pleasantries were dispensed with then J.B. began gathering information. He tried to keep things conversational, but there was definitely a list of questions to get through. In relaying the general feel of life at Sartartia these days, the guards spoke of hostility between the Ennis family and the camp guards since the killing of their brother Caswell.

"Well, it ain't exactly helped."

Chappie Dineen laughed as he spoke.

"Yeah, Burt, you really fucked things up for all of us."

Dineen punctuated his fake reprimand with a playful punch of the air in Smith's general direction. Burt Smith smiled sadly and faintly shook his head. The insulting camaraderie reminded him of better days.

Duckworth asked several more questions about the state of the plantation operation since Cass Ennis' death. When he reached the current management hierarchy, Fred Shaw's response was something of a surprise.

"The kid took over."

"Emmett?" J.B. asked with raised eyebrows.

Chappie Dineen nodded.

"Yep. He don't know his ass from hog bacon."

Shaw added reinforcement.

"And he's a surly little fucker to boot."

With a philosophical air, Dineen summarized his personal conclusions about young Ennis and others.

"A college sure can churn out some puddin' heads, can't they?"

Duckworth was slightly incredulous.

"So, he's running things? Emmett is?"

Sergeant Shaw offered details.

"Well, that's who we ride with, though it sure ain't every day like it was before. If you get down to brass tacks, the banks all got together and appointed a receiver, but we only see him once a month or thereabouts. I can't even tell you his name."

Chappie Dineen took a healthy slug from his whiskey before offering clarification.

"Don't get Fred wrong. The lack of meddling suits us just fine."

At roughly half past ten, the group finished the bottle and began to make stirrings about calling it a night. J.B. was hungry and hoping against hope that he could find something to scrounge in the sleepy town.

With uncanny timing, the four men heard footsteps trudging up the metal stairs. Sheriff Hickley poked his head around the corner. He was holding another small chair and a coffee mug.

"Mind if I join you?"

Without waiting for a response, Hickley sat the chair down in the doorway, reached for the second bottle of whiskey, unscrewed the stopper and poured a good measure of Old Taylor into his cup. The night deputy reached over his boss' back and handed a plate of four hearty sandwiches to Fred Shaw whose chair was closest to the door. The deputy then departed without a word, but Hickley explained.

"As long as you boys have been flapping your gums, I reckoned y'all had worked up an appetite."

The sandwiches were basic, roast pork with a piquant mustard, but famished as he was, J.B. classified them as delicious.

"I had one down in my quarters, so they're all yours," the sheriff added with a smile.

Apparently, the whiskey had ginned up hunger in everyone. For the next three minutes, there were only the sounds of chewing, smacking and gulping. As the last of the sandwiches disappeared, Smith and Shaw each offered a lusty belch. An answering burp came from the communal cell, reminding everyone that they were not alone.

Chappie Dineen was the next to bring up something of substance.

"There's likely nothing to it, but there was a story going around back in the summer that Emmett tried to bribe a deputy to cut Burt's throat. Like I said, I personally don't give it much truck, but us guards have been trying to keep an eye either way."

Dineen poked his buddy Smith in the shoulder.

"Not that we wouldn't have been visiting you anyhow."

Duckworth turned to Hickley.

"'How about it, sheriff? Are people safe in your jail?"

Hickley laughed.

"We spend most of our effort trying to keep fellows from breaking out, not breaking in."

The lawyer's scowl prompted clarification.

"Yes. I think Burt's out of harm's way."

Over the next half hour, the men went over the witnesses, talking about potential weak spots or unexpected pitfalls. Multiple times, Ed Hickley inserted his own comment or inquiry. As they mounted, the questions made Duckworth more than a little disquieted. Eventually, after the sheriff asked how a particular legal point would be played, he looked at Hickley.

"I know nothing in a jail is private, but I'm not looking to give away our whole trial strategy in a felled swoop."

Burt Smith, whose life was on the line and who had spent the last five months with little else to do besides dissect his chances in court, was the first to float the notion that the Ennises might have spies. There were grumbles and sideways glances from Duckworth and the three prison men.

Fred Shaw looked at his shoes before saying anything.

"It ain't that far fetched. I know Captain Veale has been getting an envelope from the big house for many years. Now, that likely ended with Cass being shot. Emmett sure don't strike me as sharp enough, but I reckon the point is that it's happened before. All the way back to old man Ennis. I've heard the tales. I know you have, too, Burt."

Smith nodded slowly then raised his eyes to Ed Hickley.

"Could something like that be happening here at your jail, sheriff? Is there anyone here who could be talking to the Ennises?"

Hickley leaned back in his chair and offered his usual devil-may-care grin.

"I don't follow my deputies home, so I don't rightly know."

He took another swallow of Old Taylor from the blue ceramic mug, but Duckworth was not ready to accept that glibness as an answer.

"What about you, sheriff? You have any dealings with the Ennis family? Hospitality aside, I can't help but mention that having the county sheriff sit in on a defense conference is not the usual procedure."

Ed Hickley gave a self-assured and dismissive wave of the hand. This time it was Burt Smith who pressed things further.

"Yeah, Ed. That's an excellent question. Are you sure you're impartial?"

"Shit, Burt, I'm not on the jury. I just got to make sure your ass shows up in front of Judge Thompson."

The walk back through downtown Richmond was quiet. Very different from midnight in the heart of Houston. The bass croak of bull frogs was continuous, and from somewhere toward the river the long whinny of a screech owl floated in. The only human noises were the late revelers at some bar along the tracks.

When Duckworth passed the courthouse square where he would go into battle in a few hours, he noticed a dark figure sitting on the steps. As he strolled the last deserted block, he listened in vain for footsteps behind him.

Only a few minutes after he entered his room, there was a soft knock on the door. A wary J.B. Duckworth cracked it open. He was turned sideways, partially behind the door with his right hand held behind his back.

It took a moment to register the man's face, but when he did, J.B. opened the door wide and motioned his visitor inside. As he turned, Duckworth laid his heavy pistol on the dresser with a thunk.

Ed Bertrand sat down in a straight backed chair only slightly nicer than the ones that had been in the jail cell. Duckworth sat on the bed.

"What can I do for, Mr. Bertrand?"

As Bertrand began talking, Duckworth held up a bottle, received a nod, and poured two drinks.

"I suppose you could say that I'm here because of George Purdy. Not that I knew him well," Bertrand said.

"Have you heard from him?"

"I got one letter more than a year ago. He was headed up north, or California maybe. If he's still living,... I know he'll never be the same man. That family..."

Bertrand's voice died away, and he looked down at his fidgeting hands. J.B.'s next question eased the tension.

"How are you doing Mr. Bertrand? I noticed you were no longer at Sartartia."

Bertrand gave a rueful laugh. When he resumed speaking, he was more focused.

"No. I got run off the Ennis place after the last trial when they no longer needed me for a witness. They blamed me for not shooting Purdy after the fact. Cass Ennis seriously expected me to just gun him down like a dog turned bad."

J.B. offered his visitor an encouraging look, but he noted that this was not the confident man he had seen on the stand a few years before. He nudged Bertrand to continue.

"And now?"

"I'm in Matagorda County as hired hand now. The missus takes in sewing. I took the late train up because the whole thing wouldn't stop nagging at me. If there was anything I could help with,... well, I didn't want to have regrets later."

"Much obliged. Let me ask you a question, Mr. Bertrand. Did you know if Will Ennis was giving payoffs to prison guards at Sartartia?"

"The old man was, but Will had stopped that. Or at least slowed it down. He was determined to run a modern plantation, he said. Carrying on as if he gave a rat's ass about the people beneath him."

Bertrand waved away his brief digression and then kept talking.

"The straight answer to your question is yes. The Ennis family has long been giving something extra to at least the guard captain, I reckon."

Upon confirmation of this practice, J.B. gave his moustache a thoughtful smoothing.

The two men finished their whiskeys unhurriedly while Bertrand continued the frank but bitter assessment of his former employers. Finally, Duckworth thanked his guest but told him that sleep was in order. As they shook hands at the door, Ed Bertrand held the grip a beat longer than normal and looked intently at the lawyer.

"Tread easy. They are a family of serpents, Mr. Duckworth."

"I appreciate the warning, Mr. Bertrand, but I believe that sometimes a man just has to thump the tiger in the balls."

Chapter 29

Richmond, Texas

The newspaper men were thick. Shoulder to shoulder on the back bench, pencils and pads in hand, were reporters from the two Houston dailies, plus the *Galveston News* and the *Richmond Coaster*. Even the *San Antonio Express* had a representative thanks to the Ennis family's ties to the Alamo City.

At the opposite corner of the Fort Bend County courtroom, conspicuously seated behind the prosecutor's table, were the two surviving Ennis brothers and Caswell's widow, Nelly. Emmett and Leigh, both wearing sour expressions, could hardly help thinking of the trial for their brother Will's killer. The distaste was especially clear on Emmett who looked as if he despised everyone and everything.

Nelly wore a fashionable black hat and veil, perhaps as much for effect on the jury as to mask her grief. Her fingers worried at an embroidered handkerchief. The two girls were at home with Letha Ward, the woman who grieved most for her Cass. The other spectator benches were filled, and people squirmed, all anxious to hear Judge Thompson's opening gavel.

District Judge Wells Thompson was a Matagorda County man with a major political record in these parts. He had served as a state senator and even two years as lieutenant governor back in what may as well have been a lifetime ago. Now he was 67 years old, completely unpredictable, and as cantankerous a son of a bitch who ever wore robes. J.B., who had appeared before him many times, considered Wells Thompson to be a thorn in his flesh before a trial even started.

The competing attorneys busied themselves at the front tables. Bill Davidson, a grizzled Civil War veteran even older than the judge, was Fort Bend County Attorney, and he had finagled his way into prosecuting the case. Though he had been practicing law in Richmond for almost thirty years, he still carried an overwhelming patina of his native Mississippi. Oozing graciousness to those he liked and dripping condescension on those he did not, Davidson was an open book. He did not care for J.B. Duckworth.

Burt Smith had entered the courtroom a quarter hour earlier, wearing a new suit of clothes courtesy of Duckworth & Fein. Smith had a song stuck in his head, and it threatened to render him senseless. With all the jail windows open, he had heard it repeatedly from the Sheriff's Quarters for three days running, and this morning, of all times, it lodged itself firmly in his brain. The culprit was almost certainly the Hickley daughter who had seemingly made a career out of playing Billy Murray's "In My Merry Oldsmobile" on the Edison. Burt doubted if there was even such a car in all of Fort Bend County. He surely had never seen one, but if it ever arrived, he had already gotten his fill of it.

Next to him at the table, Duckworth felt almost equally discombobulated. It had been a noisy night at the Exchange. After Ed Bertrand departed, J.B., feeling sufficiently primed with Old Taylor, had climbed into the lumpy bed. The first thing that prevented him from drifting off was the music from out back of the Railroad Street bagnios and honkatonks. Soon that racket was superseded by a drunken fist fight in the alley. As much as he desired a fresh breeze, Duckworth finally closed the window, only to be subjected to the man in next room farting incessantly and a barrage of snoring from all sides.

When he awoke from the fitful night, J.B. sincerely hoped that today would be an improvement. He ran water from the room sink and splashed it on his face then visited the very pungent outhouse in the little lot behind the hotel. He now sat next to his client waiting to find out if such wishes came true.

When called to order a little past nine, first Davidson then Duckworth delivered brief and largely unremarkable openings. J.B., in rather rumpled suit pants, laid out his usual foundation for self-defense, but in his heart, he knew this was a deck stacked against him. Cass Ennis' knife was yet to be found.

Davidson began the prosecution case with witnesses chosen to establish the excellent character of Caswell Ennis. Three longtime businessmen in the county, chosen because they were recognizable to the jurors, extolled the virtues of the departed. It was certainly the lack of sleep, but as Davidson guided the men's testimony, J.B. found himself mesmerized by the prosecutor's wattle.

Looking over the long witness list, Duckworth decided to be brief. He wanted to minimize Davidson's oratory. J.B. confined his attempts to impeach each man to one topic apiece. Was the deceased not a man who had developed a sour disposition? Had not Ennis been asked to leave the state university?

When the third of the character witnesses, a long timed pharmacist named Jim Winston took the stand, J.B. had another insinuation at the ready. He felt it was tailor made for the pencil-necked druggist with jug handle ears.

Since it was an open secret, Duckworth knew fully well about Naomi and the illegitimate son, but there were some lines even he tried to avoid unless it became a necessity. Not that he gave a feather or a fig about the reputation of Cass Ennis, but because the more blue nosed on the jury may well hold it against him. Railroad Street in the abstract was fair game, but for the moment he would keep it vague and hold the quadroon toddler in his vest pocket.

"Mr. Winston, do you also frequent the establishments on Railroad Street like Mr. Ennis did?"

With his mouth agape, Winston did not produce an immediate answer, only a mild gurgling noise. J.B. filled the silence.

"Perhaps y'all went together."

Judge Thompson gaveled away the widespread laughter and shot Duckworth a schoolmarm's stare.

Next Davidson introduced the dying declaration. Thompson allowed him to read it to the jury. For all of the exaggerated courtliness that Duckworth found so irritating, Davidson summoned up his best dramatic skills as he imparted the alleged last words like a Mississippi Sarah Bernhardt. Every syllable damning Burt Smith's chances at acquittal.

J.B. watched the jury closely during the reading of the statement. More than half the men were leaning forward slightly in their chairs. As Davidson read the claim that Cass Ennis begged for his life, juror number six, a Richmond butcher named Nash, solemnly shook his head.

As soon as the declaration was duly entered, the lawyer Albert Russell was called. He attested to the deathbed statement and explained the circumstances in lurid detail. He talked of loved ones coming and going from the death room. Whatever coaching Davidson had given Russell paid off as the man on the stand played at the emotions of most everyone in the room.

Duckworth could only sigh. The shyster Russell had the jury eating out of his hand like so many docile puppies. As he told of the final moments shared between Nelly Ennis and her fading husband, several of the men in the box worked their mouths tightly. One juror, an elderly farmer who wore a threadbare jacket, appeared to be biting his lip and, at one point, wiped at the corner of his eye, unable to check himself entirely.

Nelly herself dabbed her handkerchief underneath the veil, though Duckworth saw no actual tears. He also noted that the widow was not on the witness list.

Duckworth took his time standing after Davidson sat. He rummaged absently through the few papers on the table in front of him, then rose without anything in his hands. He approached the witness chair slowly and expelled air through his nostrils like an irritated bull.

"Mr. Russell, I have a serious problem with this death bed statement. Cass Ennis had taken a bullet to the chest and two in the gut, all at extremely close range."

J.B. paused to slap himself hard in the abdomen three times. The claps were heard around the room.

"Imagine that you've got three grievous bullet wounds, mortal wounds, and then you've been thrown into a buckboard and ridden over the field roads, then you're carried up a flight of stairs. You've lost a few pints of blood before the first doctor ever arrived. Don't you imagine that you'd be in excruciating pain?"

"Yes, Mr. Duckworth. I can assure you that Mr. Ennis was in horrible pain."

"And yet, you would have us believe that in all of that pain, with his very life blood seeping from him, he was still coherent enough to personally compose a detailed statement accusing my client?"

"But that is exactly what he did, Mr. Duckworth. Caswell Ennis was intent on seeing justice served."

"Did Caswell Ennis go to law school, Mr. Russell? This statement certainly sounds to me as if it was written by a member of the bar."

If Duckworth was hoping to score a big laugh with his brazen accusation, he was instead rewarded with only a few titters. Lawyer Russell summoned outrage.

"Shame on you, sir. Besmirching a dying man and my own reputation besides. I only recorded the words of Mr. Ennis."

Duckworth spent another fifteen minutes beating at the idea of mental incapacity. Logic demanded that conclusion, he said, but Russell was having none of it. The defense counsel could only hope that his endless suggestions scored some points.

As he started to walk to the defense table where Burt Smith sat rather forlornly, J.B. turned back to the witness once more.

"Mr. Russell, I notice that Doctor Morris, the man who was there to minister to Mr. Ennis in his final hours, is not on the witness list. Does that imply that Dr. Morris disagrees with your assessment of mental capacity?"

The prosecutor was instantly on his feet.

"Your honor, Dr. Morris is in high demand in Houston where he practices, and was not available to testify here. Sneaking in such a horrid assertion as part of Mr. Russell's testimony is beyond the pale."

Before Judge Thompson could admonish him, Duckworth apologized and sat down.

Bill Davidson's methodical plan was to wring every last drop of benefit from the heart-tugging final words. He called a string of witnesses who recalled signing Cass Ennis' dying declaration. If there were eleven signatories on that statement, it appeared that Davidson intended to call them all.

In each of his short cross examinations, J.B. tried again to introduce the concept of mental incapacity through his questions, but the prosecution witnesses never wavered. Not a one. Only Judge Thompson's late adjournment for dinner saved the defense from more squirming anxiety.

The final three witnesses to the dying statement led off after lunch. At one point, Duckworth tried to mock the repetitious process by adopting a singsong cadence as he asked the exact questions that he had put to the several preceding witnesses, but Judge Thompson vigorously gaveled him to a stop.

"You will not make sport in my courtroom, Mr. Duckworth. This is not a burlesque!"

J.B. offered a stage bow.

"Your honor."

Emmett Ennis was the next prosecution witness. Davidson began his time by having Caswell's brother yet again establish the veracity of the dying declaration. He even tried to head his opponent off at the pass by asking if Cass was in any way mentally impaired by his grievous physical wounds. Young Ennis said that his brother was quite lucid. He also included some heartfelt words about their final goodbye.

The prosecution then moved on to the main course for their star witness, questions about Sergeant Smith himself. Emmett adamantly asserted that there was ongoing animosity from the guards in general and Smith in particular. As Davidson had him recount alleged incidents, he worked himself to a froth over

Burt Smith. It culminated with him blurting out that it would not surprise him if Smith had planned for days to kill Cass.

This idea of premeditation was clearly a step too far, and it was seen in confusion on the faces of the jury. Prosecutor Davidson reined back his witness by softly suggesting to Emmett that he had misspoken.

Settled on a more even track, Emmett spoke of the specific issue that led to the fatal trouble in May. He claimed it all boiled down to the fact that Smith ignored the incompetence of certain inmates. Burt Smith coddled them, he said, let them get away with loafing the day away. The Ennis family was greatly put upon by this poor management and surly attitude.

Following several of the responses throughout his time in the chair, Ennis cast smugly defiant looks at Duckworth. At other moments, he confidently raised his chin toward his little brother, Leigh. Twice, he specifically sought the eyes of the men in the jury box. J.B. noted with resignation that several of the jurors returned the looks with what felt like solidarity.

Emmitt's eyes threw daggers at the defense lawyer as he stepped up for cross examination. J.B. looked back with a muted smile, kind eyes and a smoothing of his already perfect moustache.

"Mr. Ennis, is Sartatia profitable?"

For the next fifteen minutes, Duckworth led Emmett through a series of questions about receivership and debts. The early responses varied between combative rejoinders and childish obfuscation. Two or three times it appeared that the plantation's managing owner simply did not know the answer.

From there, the defense questions turned to the physical yield from the thousands of acres at Sartartia. Any time Emmett brightened over the success of the operation, J.B. peppered in a reminder that Smith and the other guards ran the labor force.

Soon, Ennis sensed that he was wading into trouble, and his freely offered responses turned to into attempts at stonewalling Duckworth's efforts. When the witness ceased supplying numbers, the defense lawyer had them at the ready.

"Well, let's take just one crop. How many acres did you have in cane last fall?"

"Eighteen hundred."

"And that yielded what?"

"I don't know exactly."

"Was it 36,000 tons?"

Ennis made a snicking noise before answering.

"Could be."

J.B., who had been looking at the jury as he reeled off the tonnage, whipped back toward the witness with incredulity.

"Could be?"

"Sounds about right."

Duckworth nodded solemnly.

"And Mr. Ennis, what is the going price for a ton of cane?"

Emmett, feeling that this was a moment to get off the ropes, sat straight in his chair, and his voice quickened.

"Well, we mill and process all of our own. We have three sugar mills, and we move cane by…"

Duckworth cut him off.

"But it still has value. What is a ton of cane worth?"

Ennis cast an evil eye toward the lawyer, and his face began to redden.

"Three dollars," he answered.

"So, three dollars a ton for 36,000 tons. That's $108,000."

Ennis started his protest, but Duckworth drowned him out.

"One hundred eight thousand dollars on just one of three major crops at Sartartia."

Emmett had quieted. Duckworth's words now registered clearly and unimpeded.

"One hundred eight thousand dollars on one crop, and a plantation in receivership nonetheless. It sure sounds to me like it was Cass Ennis who wasn't doing a very good job, not some poor convict or some underpaid guard."

With Emmett Ennis' self-control shattered and his threats ringing off the courtroom walls, Duckworth said he had nothing further and turned his back.

Chapter 30

After adjournment for the day, J.B. Duckworth locked some papers up in his hotel room then moved to a saloon around the corner. He sat at a table by himself, enjoying a cool beer, some cold chicken, and a chunk of rat cheese. The normally social lawyer relished his time alone in a town where he was likely known only by other members of the legal circle.

That was because at the moment, the solitude offered time to think. He needed to let his mind loose and see what tricks fell out. He watched the few pedestrians out the window. He eavesdropped on the men drinking at the bar. He yawned and stretched and drank more beer.

Some three hours into Duckworth's relaxation, just as his stomach was getting its fill of hops and barley, he had about given up on an epiphany. He was about to switch from beer to whiskey when a small Black boy entered the saloon. Duckworth was trying to catch the bartender's attention when he noticed the barkeep talking to the young lad instead. After a point of the finger, the boy approached J.B.'s table.

"Are you Mr. Duckworth, sir?"

"I am."

"Telegram for you, sir."

He handed the paper over and waited as J.B. fished a dime tip from his pocket.

Duckworth read the brief missive through twice, feeling his anger well. When he slapped the table top, several drinkers glanced over. J.B. did not notice. He was so mad that he was halfway out the door before he remembered to turn around and pay his tab.

As soon as Emmett Ennis alighted from the train at Sartartia, even before he went to the big house for his supper, he sent a summons to Convict Camp #1. It took less than twenty minutes before Sergeant Billy Pryor stepped into the plantation office. He was a swaggering Georgian in his mid-thirties, and after more than a decade on the place, he was well known to everyone. Emmett pointed to an open chair and wasted no time getting to the point.

"How are the guards going to testify?"

Pryor leaned his chair back on two legs.

"Smith is one of our own, but I'm in your corner."

"That's it? You're supposed to deliver. That was fully understood. I'm worried about the two other guards who were out there that morning."

"Yep. I'm working on Conner."

"This should be settled by now. How much is it going to take to get his story right?"

Fred Shaw had surmised correctly. The Ennis family had been bribing Texas prison guards for decades. They considered it a cost of doing business. Among the current state employees on the private payroll were Pryor and Captain Veale. They were handed a cash gift for Christmas and birthdays to play ball. In a good year there were a couple of additional envelopes handed out on the back porch of the big house or during a quick stop at the Sartartia office.

For the extra money in their pockets, guards on the Ennis dole were expected to push the prisoners a little harder when needed. Most every day, those in charge would make inmates work extra time beyond the 10 hour average day mandated by the state. Given the right circumstances, Captain Veale and his predecessor even kept a few men on the books for a few months longer than their sentence. If a prisoner's time was up in the middle of the cane harvest and juicing, it was understood that the man would not be going anywhere until the work was done.

Though neither voiced it, both Pryor and Ennis knew that if Burt Smith had gone along a little better, he would be getting some extra greenbacks himself. Instead, the sergeant was a doomed man bunged up in the Richmond Jail.

Emmett was not happy with the lackadaisical answers from Pryor, nor did he wish to look at the sergeant any longer. He waved the back of his hand toward the door.

Billy Pryor stood, but was not quite yet ready to go anywhere. Instead, he felt the need to impart a portion of wisdom and lament the loss of the good old days.

"Smith brung all of this shit down on his own head, of course. Fucking kid. Time was when people didn't get all bent out of shape over whipping and such. It's part of the job, and always will be. Hell, when I first started, you could even whip the women cons, if you'd a mind to."

He tipped his head to one side and offered Emmett a leer. Ennis answered with a hostile stare, but the guard was not through talking.

"The criminal class don't understand naught but force. You got one choice to manage them. Only one. Knock them down until they're pliable."

Pryor punctuated his remarks with a curt nod and strolled out the door.

Richmond was a small town. It took J.B. asking just two people in order to find out where the Fort Bend County attorney lived and only another seven minutes to stomp the four blocks south to the two-story house shaded beneath several live oaks. He stalked onto Bill Davidson's front porch at a few minutes past 8 P.M..

A middle-aged maid answered the door and informed Duckworth that the Davidsons had just finished their supper. Duckworth restrained himself as much as possible, but his request to see the old lawyer still sounded just shy of a demand. The maid left the door ever so slightly ajar when she retreated to find her employer.

When Davidson stepped onto the porch and saw the visitor, his face darkened. Duckworth did not wait for niceties.

"Emmett Ennis and his family are tampering with witnesses, and I want something done about it."

"Have you been drinking?"

"My drinking has nothing to do with it, goddamnit. That snake is meeting and colluding with a prison guard, one you're calling tomorrow morning. Now I asked you straight, are you behind this?"

Davidson shrank back as if slapped.

"No, I'm not behind this. How dare you!" he thundered. "And how would you know this anyway?"

"Don't you worry about how. That is not the point!"

Davidson had no intention of inviting Duckworth into his parlor even on a good day, but seeing his opponent show up uninvited, belligerent and half-inebriated cemented his resolve. Whatever business was to be conducted could take place right here on the porch. Bill Davidson settled back into a swing, and J.B. pulled over a stray chair as his tirade continued.

"It's witness tampering, and it's a felony. I wanted to give you first chance to fix it before I went to the judge."

Davidson chuckled.

"Bullshit. You knew that if you disturbed Thompson at eight o'clock at night, he'd flay you and eat you."

J.B. suppressed a smile.

"All right. What about the knife? Do you still have it, or did you throw it in the river? Do you really think you can get away with just suppressing something like that?"

As Davidson raised his voice to match Duckworth's, a curtain fluttered at a neighbor's house across Sixth Street.

"Oh, come on, Duckworth. How do you even know there was a knife? The only thing you've got is the word of a murderer."

J.B. was standing now. Frustration had gotten the best of him.

"Damn it, Bill! You know these people. The Ennises of the world. They don't think they owe a goddamned thing to the law. If you're not hiding that knife, then they are!"

Duckworth spread his arms wide as he expressed his outrage. As he did so, his suit jacket rode up, revealing the handle of the pistol tucked into his waist band.

If Bill Davidson was the least bit alarmed, he did not show it. Instead, his next comment was nothing but smug.

"You should have tried to move this trial out of the county. Your nonsense worked before, but this time we got you on our home turf."

Duckworth was calm now. His voice was quiet.

"We'll see. I still know a lot of people here, too."

"This is not Houston. J.B.. People here won't stand for a criminal to walk free."

"You want to know what's criminal? That prosecutors, here and all over the country, see their only two jobs as protecting the rich and proving police assumptions to be correct. There is no interest in justice. You, Bill, don't give the tiniest rat's ass about justice, and it leaves defense lawyers like me as the sole protection for right and wrong."

It sounded good, and up until the last sentence, it might even be true. In any event, it was J.B. Duckworth's parting shot. Without a farewell, he turned and headed back for the hotel.

For the second night in a row, there was an unexpected knock on Duckworth's hotel door, but this one was definitely louder and rougher than before. The lawyer laid his notes aside and downed the last swallow from his whiskey glass. Before J.B. could answer, there was a second round of banging. As he warily opened the door, he realized his pistol was on the dresser.

The beefy county deputy pushed into the room.

"You're under arrest, Duckworth. Come with me."

J.B. stood there, disconcerted and gathering his wits before speaking.

"What am I charged with?"

"Sheriff will sort it out in the morning. All I know is they said you pulled a gun on the county attorney, and smelling of you, you probably did."

At the lawyer's request, the deputy allowed him to put on his coat and shoes. He also turned down the cock on the gas lamp. The big man eyed the lawyer's gun but made no move to pick it up. They stepped into the hall, and J.B. locked the door behind him.

With a satisfied sneer plastered to his face, the lawman dragged Duckworth down the stairs. Other guests opened their doors to watch the spectacle. A few were already thinking of embellishments to the stories they would tell when they got home. In the lobby, the dyspeptic desk clerk asked about the bill as the deputy gave Duckworth a firm push onto Morton Street.

At the county jail, the deputy shoved Duckworth into the communal cell. It was only ten o'clock, but the other three men inside were already sleeping. A solid steel wall and eighteen feet separated the big tank from the cramped private cell that held his client. J.B. considered yelling something to Burt Smith, but saw no point in it. He had no idea if he would even be out by the morning. With a sigh of resignation, he laid claim to the big cell's one free corner. He would either be in court by nine or he would not.

Though a blanket on an unforgiving steel floor will never be described as comfortable, the room was nice and cool, if more than a bit malodorous. Surprisingly, his three fellow inmates were quiet sleepers. J.B. shirked his coat and folded it neatly to make a pillow. He was dead tired. His shoes remained on since he wanted to be sure they were still there in the morning. Duckworth stretched out on his side, his back to the wall, and slept at least as well as he had the previous night in the hotel.

Chapter 31

Duckworth walked out of jail at 7:10 in the morning. He had spent nine hours in the cells. His joints hurt something awful, and his tongue had sprouted fur, but as he tried to stretch away his stiffness, he realized that he had slept uninterrupted until daybreak. It was one small personal victory.

His release, which was accompanied by a few jokes and what may have been an apology from Ed Hickley, gave him enough time to go back to the Exchange for a fresh shirt and the wash basin followed by three eggs and toast at a nearby cafe. He was relieved to find his hotel room undisturbed. As he ate and waited for a slight throbbing in his head to subside, J.B. read through his notes yet again.

Judge Thompson had blown his top when he heard. The sheriff himself had come to the judge's hotel room even before breakfast to inform him of the night's developments. A second after ordering Duckworth's release, Thompson, in an immediate turn, had sent the hotel's porter racing for the Davidson household. That is why, at 6:55, even before J.B. Duckworth exited the hoosegow, Fort Bend County's prosecutor was enduring a screaming fulmination from the district judge.

By all appearances, Thompson had not even combed his hair before coming to his courthouse office to unload on Davidson. His unkempt mane would have done a lion proud, and it made the judge look even more spectral than usual. He had no necktie, his shirt was a button off, and he was yelling like a scalded banshee.

"This is a high-profile trial. An important murder trial. In case you slept through the first day, there were reporters from half the newspapers in Texas out there. And you thought you'd just throw your opposing counsel in the clink?

This is pure fodder for ridicule! And if it is tomorrow's headline, I'll see to it that it's your name sullied, not mine!"

Davidson had tried remorse, then self-reproach. By the time he got a word in, he had arrived at indignance.

"Carrying a gun is illegal, your honor."

"So is being an addlepated dulbert. Or it ought to be. At least among members of the bar. Did he aim it at you? Threaten you?"

Only the stone deaf among anyone on the second floor of the courthouse could have missed hearing Wells Thompson's hollering. County Attorney Davidson was wholly discomfited.

"No, sir."

"Did he shoot you?"

Davidson's answer was barely audible.

"No."

"Then he showed more by God restraint than I would have. Get the hell out of my chambers, you clod."

As a result of the early morning's events, neither lawyer was at his best when he entered the courtroom. Bill Davidson could not help but glance around and wonder who had overheard, and perhaps relished, the loud dressing down he had received earlier.

Duckworth was extremely surprised to see Sonny Schlottmann sitting at the defense table. The junior partner had strolled into the courtroom just minutes before J.B., having been alerted to his boss' predicament thanks to a dawn phone call from Sheriff Hickley.

The prosecution had three witnesses left. By the time he had cross examined the first one, the blacksmith who had been working in the yard of Camp #3, Duckworth steeled himself for the two who would follow. His luck had not changed.

Bill Davidson's hope was to button up any wild notion that Cass Ennis had a knife before his defense opponent could even broach the subject. He made a fine start down that path with Walker Carey, one of Sartartia's blacksmiths. That man testified that he had seen no knife or any other weapon when he observed the distant argument on horseback that day.

Next, the prosecutor played an ace. He asked about seeing the victim up close after the shooting. Carey looked directly at the jurymen and recounted a bloody and dazed Ennis slipping from his horse and holding himself up by grasping the stirrup.

"And he spoke to you and Sergeant Pryor?" Davidson asked.

"Yes, sir. He did."

"What were Mr. Ennis' exact words?"

"He said 'Why did he shoot me? I'm gonna die.' Then he staggered out in the yard a piece and fell over."

Davidson had his witness repeat the phrase "Why did he shoot me." It was not precisely the wording of the dying statement, but it was damn close. Duckworth knew that he would be hearing that as a main point in the prosecution's closing argument, but J.B. also hoped to gain a little ground of his own.

"How did Mr. Ennis sound when he spoke to you, Mr. Carey?"

The blacksmith narrowed his eyes.

"What do you mean?"

"Did he sound strong? Normal?"

"Well, no. He'd been shot, of course. I could barely make out his words. He was ..."

Carey searched for the word.

"...raspy, I reckon you'd call it. Hard to understand."

J.B. gave a sympathetic nod.

"And you said he could only stand under his own power if he was holding on to his stirrup?"

"Yep. That's how it looked."

"So, would you imagine then, Mr. Carey, that a man in such bad shape could have dictated a complicated legal document?"

Davidson's exasperated shout covered the last few words of Duckworth's question.

"Your honor, Mr. Carey was not in the house when the dying declaration of Mr. Ennis was made. Defense counsel knows that. It is..."

Like a longtime spouse, Judge Thompson finished the objection for the prosecutor.

"... an improper question. Indeed, it is. The jury will pay no attention to that. No hijinks, Mr. Duckworth."

No one ever accused Joe Conner of being showy. He could sink into the background to such an extent that it would throw off the head count for a crowd of four. To Bill Davidson, however, he was another person who could reinforce the answers he wanted the jury to hear.

The guard, clearly uncomfortable on the witness seat, spoke so softly that the judge asked him to speak up or repeat an answer four separate times. By the last one, Thompson showed obvious frustration, but the jury heard the words that the prosecution most sought. Conner could not say with any confidence whatsoever that Cass Ennis pulled a knife. It hardly mattered to opposing counsel. By the time Davidson finished with Conner, J.B. Duckworth was focused entirely on the final prosecution witness.

The minute Billy Pryor was called, the defense attorney was on his feet requesting a sidebar conference.

"This witness was tampered with by the Ennis family, Judge. He should not be allowed on the stand."

Davidson pushed back.

"We have no idea what transpired, your honor."

"He's a dirty witness. Bought and paid for."

Wells Thompson slapped his palm against the bench, shutting Duckworth's plea down.

"That was just hearsay as far as the court knows. You get your chance on cross examination. Ask the boy then. Just don't expect me to do your work for you, Mr. Duckworth."

The substance of Pryor's testimony was not dissimilar to Conner's, almost identical, in fact. The difference was that Pryor exuded an all-knowing swagger. Where Emmett Ennis looked defiantly at the jurors, Billy Pryor gave them an exaggerated verbal wink, as if they were all saloon patrons in on the same joke. It was infuriating.

As soon as Duckworth got the opportunity to cross examine, he went straight for Pryor's credibility.

"Did you meet with Emmett Ennis yesterday evening?"

"Yes, sir, I work on his farm."

"Did you discuss this case?"

With a big grin directed past Duckworth to the spectators, the sergeant answered.

"I can't recollect. I've slept since then."

The lawyer stepped closer to the witness chair, trying to block his sightline to the jury.

"Let's try something else, then. Does the Ennis family give you bribes, Mr. Pryor."

"Bribes?"

"Extra pay."

Pryor only increased his mocking tone.

"Oh, no, Mister Duckworth. I am an employee of the State of Texas."

"So, you'll swear that no one in the Ennis Family has ever given you money."

Billy Pryor chuckled.

"Well, now, they are very generous folks. I might get a dollar here and there to spend around town, so I can't swear to that exactly."

The defense lawyer asked several questions about the things the Ennises expected for the extra pay, but Pryor gave him no satisfaction. At one point, Duckworth complimented him on earning his pocket money here on the stand.

When that dry avenue reached an end, J.B. began to pick away at Ennis' outburst on the morning of the shooting. The lawyer asked questions in quick succession about the flashes of anger and wanted to know why the two men had stopped so soon into their inspection ride. Still Pryor gave him nothing useful. When asked about a knife being pulled, the sergeant flatly denied such a thing took place. The lawyer pressed harder.

"What about the cut on his arm?"

Pryor tossed out another smug response.

"I sure can't say that I saw one."

J.B. let his rising temper release with the hope that it would work for him. His voice grew louder and more strident.

"Burt Smith had a nasty four inch cut on his forearm. A deep cut. It soaked his shirt in blood. Where do you think that came from Mr. Pryor?"

"I couldn't say anything about that either. I didn't see it."

"Maybe it was a four inch long mosquito bite? I know they are bad in the Brazos Bottom."

Pryor shook his head and continued to clown.

"They sure are, sir. Mosquitoes as big as crows."

Duckworth took another step closer to the witness chair.

"Did you dispose of Cass Ennis' knife, Mr. Pryor?"

"Nope."

"You deny getting rid of the weapon that Ennis used to attack my client?"

"I wouldn't do anything like that. I just guard the prisoners."

As the courtroom cleared for the noon break, John Hooper, the *Houston Post* reporter who routinely waved the flag for his occasional drinking buddy, the great J.B. Duckworth, approached his lawyer friend.

"J.B., forgive my saying so, but I've covered several dozen of your trials, and I'd have to say you've got a pretty high wall to scale this time, maybe even a moat to cross, to stay with the metaphor."

Duckworth offered a brave smile.

"You're not wrong, John. I am looking straight up on this one. But you know how magicians pull a live canary out from an empty top hat. Sonny and I are fixing to put our heads together and find ourselves a canary. I'll see you for dinner tonight."

J.B. clapped the young reporter on the shoulder and walked into the courthouse lobby to catch up with Schlottmann. He wondered to himself if he was truly out of flashy tricks this time.

J.B. and Sonny walked across the street to a small café and secured a back table. Duckworth had made up his mind to do something no one was going to like, and he did not want to tip his hand just yet. Though none of the adjacent seats were occupied, J.B. leaned in close.

"I don't need you here, but I want you to stop at Sartartia on your way back to town and arrange for one of the inmates to be in court to testify tomorrow morning. You can write up a subpoena and have Sheriff Hickley and serve it this afternoon. Actually, get two copies. Go directly to the guard captain, and make sure the plantation foreman is there at the same time. Neither can be trusted, but if they both receive it, then it's harder for them to deny."

Schlottmann's mouth flopped open like a catfish a time or two before he spoke.

"The convicts at Sartartia are all colored, J.B."

"You don't think I know that. I've got no choice. They're the only people left who saw this killing. If I can't prove that Caswell Ennis pulled a knife on our client, he is going to swing in that jailhouse across the tracks."

Schlottmann sighed heavily.

"We went over this on Sunday. We agreed. This will make the firm look like a bunch of idiots. We'll be a laughing stock, and you've got to know in your heart that it won't help us win."

Duckworth continued giving directions as if he had not heard Sonny's objections at all.

"I'll get Hickley to send a deputy out tomorrow morning, first thing, to make sure he shows up."

Sonny addressed his boss sarcastically.

"You want all of them J.B.? We could have a whole chain gang."

"No, just one. And make sure it's one who scares easy."

Sonny was still exasperated, but he had been around his senior partner long enough to recognize when an argument was lost. Still, he voiced his opposition one more time.

"This judge is as Confederate as they come. He was personally removed from office after the war by Phillip goddamned Sheridan, for Christ's sake. And you want to run a colored witness up in front of him?"

"I've only got to convince the jury. As long as the judge doesn't keep him off the stand, I think I have a plan to do that."

Schlottmann flashed a Cheshire grin.

"That's a big enough if that I am willing to throw two dollars at the notion that no colored convict sits his ass in Wells Thompson's witness chair."

Duckworth extended his hand.

In the afternoon, the defense got the chance to start their case. J.B. prided himself on reading jurors' faces, and he did not at all like what he had been seeing. If he believed in such mumbo jumbo, this would be a moment for prayer. Since he most assuredly did not, he silently asked the legal gods to sprinkle a bit of mojo over his paltry witness list.

In many trials, the defense begins with a parade of credible, friendly faces who will testify that their client is a wonderful person who loves their mother, goes to church every Sunday, and cares for neglected kittens. In the case of B.C. Smith, that should have been his other guard friends, but pressure and some well-placed dollars had winnowed that list down to only two true souls.

J.B. would normally call witnesses to swear that the alleged victim was a scoundrel who rumor said may or may not have boiled children alive, but, unlike his half-brother Will, Caswell Ennis was by all accounts a likeable, devil may care fellow. It was only recently that gloom and doubt overtook him, finally evaporating into a residue of rage.

Facing these challenges, the bare minimum for Duckworth was to show that at least Burt Smith's wife thought he was first rate, so that is where he began. Ivy Smith heaped praise on her husband, describing him as loving and kind. She teared up at the right places and recounted how difficult life had been without him. With no husband working at the camp, she was dispossessed. She was back to living at her mother's here in Richmond, and the dreams of starting a family were dashed. Ivy Smith closed her time in the witness chair by looking past the defense lawyer and making a small plea directly to the jurors. The faces of the twelve men remained stony.

The two Sartartia guards who were still willing to support their friend in his time of need came next. Fred Shaw and Chappie Dineen each told of a steady friend, a hard worker who brooked no trouble, nor did he seek it. In their own ways, each man was resolute in saying that there was no possibility that Sergeant Burt Smith would fire a gun at another man unless he was in fear for his life.

Fred Shaw had not been present for the fight, but Ivy Smith and guard Dineen each told Duckworth that they believed Cass Ennis held something in his hand prior to the fatal gun shots. Under Bill Davidson's cross examination, however, neither could be certain.

When Chappie Dineen stepped away from the witness chair, J.B. swiveled to face Wells Thompson.

"Judge, I am going to call the defendant next, and since I plan to have him on the stand for a considerable length of time, I would like to get a fresh start at Mr. Smith tomorrow morning."

The judge, permanently predisposed against coddling defense counselors, frowned and lifted a pocket watch off of the bench top in front of him. He started to shake his head.

"It's barely gone three o'clock, Mr. Duckworth."

"You are so right, your honor, but I had a long night."

With that remark, J.B. turned slowly and obviously toward Bill Davidson at the prosecution table. The judge followed suit. So far, no one in the press seemed to have caught wind of Duckworth's trip to the Fort Bend jail. J.B. imagined a slow-turning thought process going on in the head of Wells Thompson as he stared thoughtfully at the prosecutor. Finally, the judge growled a harrumph and picked up his gavel.

"All right. We are adjourned until nine o'clock tomorrow morning."

Chapter 32

Burt Smith had already taken off his coat and draped it over the back of his chair. He was now in the process of rolling up his sleeve. His lawyer knew that the only glimmer for Smith was convincing the jury that Cass Ennis had escalated the fight that day in Camp Three. With no knife to show anyone, the scar was the only physical evidence he had, and eight to twelve feet away from the box was too far to make an impression.

"Judge, I'd like permission for Mr. Smith to show his scar to the jurors."

Wells Thompson closed his eyes and scowled, but in the end, he gave Duckworth a small nod. The witness stepped from his chair to show his forearm to the jury. Twenty four eyes inspected the four inch long slice that was raised and still a livid red. The unsettling appearance of the gash may have been due to poor wound care at the county jail, but the vigorous rubbing his lawyer told him to give it just before he entered the courtroom certainly had not hurt.

Smith weaved a detailed account of the words that passed between him and Ennis. The guard told of his utter shock at the knife being pulled, of throwing out his arm to ward off the stabbing motion and of the bite of the blade into his flesh. Duckworth cast a few sidelong looks at the jury when he dared, and he finally saw something akin to rapt attention on at least some of the men's faces. He pressed on.

"The cut on your arm looks bad, Burt. Does it still bother you?"

Smith tightened his lips together.

"It does a little. It tingles from time to time. I can't forget it's there for too long."

J.B. had one more goal to achieve on this subject. He wanted to cast as much doubt as possible on the truthfulness of the Ennis Family.

"What do you think happened to the knife?"

"I don't know. Mr. Ennis dropped it in the dirt where we were, just like I told you. I saw it there, under the horses' feet while they skittered and nickered. It was well trampled ground. If it hasn't been found, it's only because someone picked it up and threw it away."

Smith could not help himself from looking at Emmett Ennis behind the prosecution table. Not surprisingly, he was rewarded with a glare.

Duckworth's plan was to open the day with the knife and the cut. He wanted to cast everything else in that light. If he could get the jury to start thinking about self-defense even a little bit, then all that followed might be viewed differently.

Once the knife wound was out there, J.B. guided Smith through the confrontations that came during the last two days of Cass Ennis' life. The growing fury, the baffling outrage and finally the lash of violence through the slashing blade. Considered as gospel, it was a portrait of building madness, but at the moment, Burt Smith's was a lonesome voice. If Cass Ennis' frustration had manifested in only a verbal altercation, no matter how heated, it was hardly justification for four shots fired.

Smith's testimony ended about ninety minutes after the court's day started. The last questions were about the effects that incarceration brought to Burt's life. He spoke about the separation from his wife and friends and the overall loss of freedom. The impactful line J.B. saved for the end was something that was shaped during conversations in the little jail cell.

"Burt, is there one thing that you've missed the most over the last half year?"

Smith started nodding before he answered.

"Yes, sir. I'd have to say it's my job. Not being able to earn a living and provide for my family. That's kind of a man's reason to be in the world, ain't it? To have that taken from you is hard."

Prosecutor Davidson asked if there was any concern over Cass Ennis being similarly deprived, but his question lacked the simple sincerity that Burt Smith had just offered about his own situation.

J.B. thought it was good, but it was still only the word of the accused trying to save his own neck.

Next, the defense lawyer spent five minutes with the pinch-faced deputy who had bandaged the cut on Smith's arm. He adequately described the depth of the wound, the large amount of blood and the wincing that the guard had done while the gash was cleaned.

"Did that appear to be a knife wound to you deputy?" Duckworth asked him.

"Yes, sir. No question."

It was a reinforcing moment that lasted for less than two minutes until Bill Davidson asked his sole question of the witness.

"Deputy, are you also a medical doctor?"

J.B. slowly rose to his feet and requested a moment to redirect.

"You're not a doctor, but as a long time deputy sheriff, how many knife wounds have you seen in the course of your duties?"

"Oh, over the course of twelve years, I'd say several hundred. It's one of the most common things we run across."

Duckworth sat down satisfied for the first time that he had won a major point. He knew it was not enough. And he knew that the entire trial hinged on what was about to occur.

It was quarter till eleven. The timing was just as J.B. Duckworth planned. If his gambit worked, the jury would have the entire lunch break to consider his final witness. If it did not, then Duckworth might get to sleep in his own bed tonight. Though in that eventuality, Burt Smith did not fare well.

"The defense would like to call Harry Duplantis, your honor."

The fat deputy from the jail opened the side door to the courtroom, and Duplantis, his hands chained before him, was led inside. The murmurs from all around the courtroom became louder until they could be called a crescendo.

At the moment everyone expected Wells Thompson to begin pounding his gavel, it was the judge's unmistakable voice that rang out instead.

"Hell, no. I am not letting some darkie testify in my courtroom."

Duckworth and Davidson were both already walking toward the bench before each man began asking permission to approach. Thompson waved them ahead. All three voices were raised well beyond the normal volume of a sidebar. The two lawyers had their backs turned to the gallery, but Thompson's words carried as if he was on an election stump.

"The only colored allowed on the main floor in this chamber are the accused."

For a solid three minutes that ignored all legal decorum, Wells Thompson stubbornly refused to let a Black man testify. Throughout that time, J.B. Duckworth repeated that Thompson was grievously hurting the defense's case and the conversation should be moved to the judge's office. Finally, Thompson agreed.

The private location only made the judge more intransigent. He pointed behind him as he raged.

"Folks fought a gun battle on the streets right out that window to rid this county of Negro interference in matters of the court! Why the holy hell would I change that now?"

Duckworth's words were steady.

"You'll be overturned on appeal, judge. That's why. Nobody wants to be overturned. The equal jury law was just upheld by the state court three years ago. A Negro can serve on a Texas jury, and by extension, the Supreme Court is saying that he can testify in a Texas trial."

Thompson boomed back at him.

"I am the law that matters in my courtroom, Mr. Duckworth. The only law."

With that the old jurist began to rise from his chair as if he was a twenty-year old about to administer a well-earned licking. Duckworth blinked but pressed on, and Thompson, quickly remembering his age, resumed his seat.

"Negroes are citizens of the United States, Judge, and like it or not, that includes Richmond, Texas."

The county attorney had been a silent observer thus far, but he now spoke.

"It's fine with me, your honor. I won't object."

With a smirk, he looked at Duckworth.

"It's your hanging."

Davidson even punctuated his comment with a small giggle.

Judge Thompson regarded the two lawyers with hatred, but he finally demurred. To prove that his disdain for the other men was not equal, he added one last word.

"Goddamn you, Duckworth."

J.B. positioned himself several paces away from his witness. Part of it was calculated to show detachment from a Negro, but part of it was because Harry Duplantis smelled ripe. Even if the man himself had seen water in the last few days, his convict garb was another story. Lord only knew how often those clothes saw the inside of a wash pot.

Duckworth suspected that whichever guards at Sartartia sent Duplantis into Richmond, they had deliberately neglected his hygiene to voice their displeasure at the entire spectacle of one of their inmates being summoned to court. J.B. was equally certain that none of the jurors had bathed last night, either.

"Can you please tell us your name?"

For hundreds of years, for generations, Blacks across the United States, particularly in the South, had been trained to avoid eye contact with Whites. It was not a matter of courtesy or respect. It was self-preservation. It was ingrained through a million slaps and rebukes. Consequently, Harry fixed his gaze on Duckworth's right shoulder. His voice was reluctant, but loud enough to be heard.

"Harry Duplantis, sir."

"Where are you from Harry?"

"Down around Cuero, sir."

"Why are you a convict at Sartartia?"

"House burglary, sir. I was convicted of house burglary."

"Now, Harry, I want you to be very honest with all of us. Did you do it?"

Harry Duplantis never wavered, but this time, he lifted his dark eyes a trifle, enough that he was staring directly at J.B. Duckworth.

"Yes, sir. I reckon I did."

With that, his small moment of defiance was over. He had owned up.

J.B. offered Harry an encouraging smile then took ample time to smooth his moustache before continuing.

"How do the guards treat the prisoners out at the camp, Harry?"

"They all treat us just fine, boss."

"Do any of the bosses ever whip the convicts?"

"I can't rightly recall."

Duckworth pulled out his incredulity.

"You can't recall men being whipped? Knocking skin off their back, blood running?"

"If they did, one of the men must've been shucking work."

J.B. paused to stroll back to the defense table for a glance at imaginary papers. Burt Smith desperately sought eye contact with his attorney, but there was none. Tension eased from the room like taut muscles in a saloon. J.B. turned back to the witness.

"Now, Harry, when I'm done asking you questions, the prosecutor over there will try to make you out to be some hardened criminal, so what do you say we just head that whole thing off at the pass?"

At the other table, Bill Davidson shifted in his seat.

"This is not your first time in the prison camps, is it?"

"No, sir, boss."

The convict paused for a moment before adding more.

"This is my third time."

Duplantis cast his eyes to the floor involuntarily.

J.B. made Harry Duplantis lay out his crimes one by one. When he was a younger man, Harry had been leased out at the Sartartia farm for a year for vagrancy. That was back when Will Ennis was in charge. Then there was another stint at a farm in Brazoria County. Robbery.

It was the vagrancy count that J.B. pursued.

"You said you got a year for vagrancy? What does that mean?"

"I was drinking out back of a store in Cuero."

"Why didn't you drink at home?"

"My grandpa didn't want no part of me, wouldn't allow me in the house."

"So, because you were on the outs with your grandpa, you were thrown in a prison camp for a year?"

"Little more when it was said and done, boss."

"More than a year just for drinking with your friends? That doesn't sound fair at all, does it?"

"It's just the way it is, boss.""That must have made you awfully mad, Harry. Losing a year of your life just for having a drink. That must have made you powerfully mad."

Harry Duplantis, not hearing a question, said nothing. Duckworth looked at the jury then back at his witness.

"What was the camp at Sartartia like when you were there before?"

"There weren't so many convicts back then."

"But you knew Sergeant Smith from before?"

"'I don't recollect him, boss."

"You don't recollect him? You were in a small labor camp. How could you not recollect him?"

Harry Duplantis stammered.

"Maybe he wasn't no sergeant, then. Maybe he was a guard in another part of the plantation."

Harry was in a total quandary. He had been lured in, accepting that the attorney was on his side. He should have known better, and attorney Duckworth was not about to let him off the hook. Each rapid question carried more urgency.

"Didn't he beat skin off your legs on one occasion?"

"No, sir, boss."

"Didn't he whip you?"

"No, sir, boss."

"You don't like Sergeant Smith do you?"

"I like him, fine, sir."

"The fact is that you don't like the guards at all. They abuse you and beat you, and you don't like them, isn't that true?"

Duplantis snuck one look at guards Shaw and Dineen in the courtroom before answering.

"They treat us real fair, boss."

Duckworth stepped closer.

"On the day Sergeant Smith shot Caswell Ennis, you were there in the camp yard?"

"Yes, sir."

"Were you standing between the shooting and the guards?"

"Yes, sir."

"How much closer?"

"Oh, maybe twenty, thirty yards closer."

"And being closer to the fight between those two men, did you see Caswell Ennis with a knife?"

"I can't say, sir."

"Did Mr. Ennis have a knife?"

Duplantis looked franticly into the courtroom gallery. The Ennis Brothers returned withering frowns from behind the prosecution table. On the other side, the looks from Guards Shaw and Dineen blazed. Directly in front of him, lawyer Duckworth was almost screaming.

"Did he have a knife?"

"Yes, sir."

Though it was not audible, there came a general sense that the room had taken a collective breath. Duckworth lowered his voice to a steady baritone.

"And you say that in spite of any grudge you hold against Sergeant Smith? Knowing that if you told us here today that Caswell Ennis was unarmed, you could fix Sergeant Smith up real good?"

"Ain't no grudge, sir."

"No matter what he did to you, and this being a chance to get back at him, you still say that Cass Ennis pulled a knife and stabbed at Sergeant Smith?"

For the second time that morning, Harry Duplantis looked J.B. Duckworth square in the face.

"Yes, sir. I do."

Duckworth turned to the jury and made slow eye contact with each of the twelve men, then he sat down at the defense table and clapped Burt Smith on the shoulder.

Chapter 33

He might be pompous and irritating, but after several decades in the law, Bill Davidson knew how to hammer the basics. In this case, the basics amounted to the perfectly crafted dying declaration and almost a dozen people who attested to it. Caswell Ennis was unarmed when Sergeant Burt Smith gunned him down. If Smith had been carrying more bullets, he would have reloaded and kept firing.

For twenty minutes, the prosecutor painted an act of hate-filled temper. He described an unreasonable guard resentful of authority. There was no evidence that contradicted the case he was laying out. A jury could not free a man based on some imaginary knife, and they certainly could not act upon the testimony of a Negro criminal, a three time inmate. To even bring that derelict into this courtroom was an affront to every law-abiding White man in the county.

The prosecutor brought his message home. Burt Smith was a man gone crazy, and he had killed poor Cass Ennis for no purpose. Widowed a fine woman and turned two precious little girls into orphans. It was cold-blooded murder, and that was that. The stoic resolve on the faces of the jurors filled Bill Davidson with satisfaction as he sat back down.

In his earliest days as a lawyer, J.B. Duckworth had been in love with words. He once spoke for almost three hours to sum up a complicated case, but as he grew older, he came to value brevity. Just enough words to make his point. With a thimble full of hard evidence, the challenge in this case might be to make sure he talked long enough. The courtroom was quiet as J.B. faced the jury.

"Bam! Bam! Bam! Three bullets just hit each of you gentlemen in the gut. The pain is unbearable, and your blood is pouring out into the dirt. Your wife is hollering like a hog being butchered. Your relatives are sobbing at your bedside. More blood is coming out than you realized was inside you, and as you get weaker, you know every breath may be your last. And yet, to believe the noble prosecutor, you take this time to dictate a legal document.

"'I wish to make a statement of all the facts surrounding the shooting of myself by B.C Smith... before the world ere I go to meet my God.'

"Come on, gentlemen."

Duckworth tucked his chin and let that sink in with the jurors. He reminded everyone that the Ennis family lawyer was in the room and suggested that it was Attorney Russell who had dictated the vaunted dying declaration, not the gasping man on his last legs.

The lawyer then turned to the knife. The missing knife was the key to this entire case.

"Clearly it was picked up. It was thrown away," Duckworth offered. "It's probably well sunk into the Brazos River mud long ago. You or I will never find that knife. Whether it was Emmett Ennis or Billy Pryor or someone else, the Ennis family demanded a conviction this time, and they were more than willing to falsify or tamper with evidence to get it.

"What doesn't lie, though, is the cut on Burt Smith's arm. A Fort Bend County deputy sheriff, a man who has been fighting criminals for most of his life, told you that he tended to a nasty knife wound on Burt Smith's left forearm immediately following the fight. That deputy has no reason to lie. A convict named Harry Duplantis admitted he saw the knife even when he knew telling that story could save a man he feared and disliked. Negro or not, that scared convict had no reason to lie. In fact, he had a dozen reasons to not tell the truth.

"No, gentlemen, if you use the cut on Burt Smith's arm to establish that there was a knife, and how else could the cut have gotten there, deep cuts don't just appear on their own, then this is a case of self-defense, as clear as the finest crystal."

Duckworth took a breath and a few paces.

"And let's talk about the right of a man to defend himself. It's one of the most fundamental rights of mankind."

As he delivered the words, Duckworth pointed straight at the jurors he judged to be most opposed to his client.

"You and I have families, too. And we would never sit still, none of us, and let some angry madman end our lives and deprive us of the chance to hold our wives again or to hug our little children. Caswell Ennis tried to stab Burt Smith with a knife. He cut his arm deeply, and if Burt Smith had not stopped him, it would be Burt moldering in a grave across the tracks. But Burt Smith defended himself just the same as you would. Or you. Or you. Or you."

By the time he was 29 years old, J.B. Duckworth had decided that he had taken enough shit from life. Consequently, he swore off all future uses for humility. After many ensuing years, he had largely stopped admitting any vulnerability even to himself. Yet when he wrapped up his closing arguments in the case of *Texas v. Smith*, a few little beads of doubt trickled down his spine nonetheless.

J.B. proffered a platitude about their chances, then Sheriff Hickley, who had been in court mostly to watch the closing arguments, personally led Burt Smith out the door toward the back stairs. Smith would wait out the deliberations back in his cell.

As he gathered up his few papers in the emptying courtroom, Duckworth noticed John Hooper waiting just across the gallery rail. The two walked together to the café down Morton Street where they ordered beers and an early supper. Cold sandwiches and potato salad.

Hooper tried to downplay his line of work when socializing with Duckworth even though he knew the lawyer was often the source of golden news copy. At the café table, he made small talk, and the two laughed about the escapades of mutual acquaintances. With ample niceties observed, the reporter finally posed the questions on his mind.

"You never fail to amaze me with your inside information, J.B., but Sartartia is not like Houston. It's a flyspeck. There are no neighbors to grease. No one lives at the place but family and sycophants, but still, there were times during this trial that you knew things about the family. How?"

"Let's just say there is one man in the Ennis household who believes in justice."

John Hooper had never been to the Ennis home, but then again, neither had Duckworth. Hooper put it down to the mysterious and unknown ways of defense attorneys and altered his tack a few degrees.

"I guess the guards told you about the earlier trouble between Smith and that con. That was masterful even if you never quite did get him to confess to it."

Duckworth's grin was enigmatic. He would hold his secret close, but he so wanted to let at least one person in on the joke. The repeated asking of the questions did all the persuading the defense needed. If he was prone to such sentiments, J.B. might have even felt sorry for Harry Duplantis up there on the stand, a frightened deer and the lawyer the wolf, growling to make you admit something that never happened. In the world of a colored convict, it must feel like everyone is against you every day.

J.B. Duckworth held his quiet smile as he leaned back in his chair and took another healthy swallow from his beer. Even the dabs at his moustache did not wipe it off his face.

The setting sun through the blinds made lines on the right side of the spectators' faces as they and the lawyers awaited news of Burt Smith's fate. A few squinted. In less than ten minutes, the light would be gone.

The old saw was that if the jurors were looking at the defendant when they settled back in, the verdict was not guilty. J.B. knew that to be so much horse shit. It was human nature to question a big decision. There were always at least a few jurors taking the measure of the person they had just freed or condemned. They wondered if they did the right thing.

Yet, there was something more ethereal at play when a verdict was delivered, something undefined. J.B. was convinced that nine times out of ten he could gauge the air around a jury, and as these twelve men filed back to their seats, this one felt clear. It was an acquittal. His heart quickened its beats.

To Duckworth on this evening in Richmond, the reading by the foreman was a small formality.

Emmett Ennis rose from his seat before Wells Thompson's parting words and stomped out of the room without even a glance at his fellow men. His little brother Leigh followed with a look of utter confusion and budding heartbreak. The family had filled their basket with revenge, and when they looked down, it was empty.

Fred Shaw was the only guard left in the courtroom, and once the final gavel fell, he stepped up to shake his friend's hand, but he was blocked out by a long and teary hug that Ivy Smith laid on her husband. Shaw stood by beaming as he waited. They comprised the entire contingent for the defendant.

As the three of them made to walk out into the perfect evening, Duckworth asked Burt if he had a moment. The newly free man pulled away from his wife and followed his attorney into the small anteroom where prisoners waited to enter court. J.B. was quick to his point.

"I just wanted to reiterate that we wish we could've gotten bail for you. We tried."

Burt Smith appreciated hearing that sentiment. He was overwhelmingly relieved to be out, but he was also a little curious.

"Was Thompson on the Ennis payroll, too?"

"I doubt it. He's just a pure no good bastard."

The two men shared a small smile before the lawyer added one final thought.

"Watch yourself, Burt. There are still two Ennis Brothers left."

"Don't worry about me, Mr. Duckworth. My guess is that the Ennis Family is as done as done can be. They thought they were bigger than the State of Texas, but that was proved wrong. Even around here, the real power is in Richmond, and these old boys hold little truck with what happens on the east side of the river."

Duckworth nodded and extended his hand.

"Stay out of trouble."

Those were the standard parting words that J.B. had offered to a thousand clients. Four words that signified the last of his investment, but this time, he pulled his hand off the brass doorknob and turned back.

"What are you going to do now?"

Smith shrugged his shoulders.

"Oh, I don't know. I think I'm done with the prison system, though. It doesn't exactly bring out the best in a man."

"I do think you were provoked, Burt." Duckworth said. "It wasn't a square deal, but I hope you won't carry the bitterness with you forever. The anger – for me, it's motivation, but you can do better. That resentment is unseemly."

J.B.'s eyes twinkled as his great moustache rose at the corners.

"Well, I'm off to catch my train. I've got to keep the world safe from scoundrels."

Burt Smith let out a short chuckle.

"From them or for them?" Smith asked.

"Whoever's paying."

Historical Notes

Like the disclaimer says, this is a work of fiction. The characters are my creation alone, even when I used real names. But what takes place in the book is steeped in history. That includes the murders which are based on real cases. I used newspapers and court records for those cases and many other legal cases in creating the action. Though I am most decidedly not an attorney, I did research court procedure in the first decade of the twentieth century in Texas. Most of all I utilized my previous works of historical non-fiction in deciding how the cases would go. I hope they ring true to the time period.

Several of the characters are based on real people, beginning with the three partners at Duckworth's firm. That includes Henry Fein. At the time period, many, dare I say most, of the largest American law firms did not even consider hiring Jewish attorneys, but there were a few at firms such as Duckworth's. Henry Fein is based on a man who was one of those in Houston, and his life story is very similar.

Though Harry Duplantis is completely fictional, there was Texas case law that at least nominally addressed the practice in most Texas counties that would have omitted any African-Americans from a jury pool. The lawyer on whom Duckworth is based did successfully appeal cases on behalf of his Black clients by arguing that an all-White jury was not a jury of peers. I extended the rulings to a witness, hopefully with plausibility.

The real people who share names with my characters were dead a century or more before now, and I did not know them personally. I have, however, used the historical record to create their personalities and actions in a manner that I find reasonable based on what is knowable. There is plentiful research behind my choices. In a few cases where characters were patterned after a combination of real people, I altered the name slightly to clearly differentiate from the historical figure.

Many of the places included in these pages were real. I tried to let the characters stay in real hotels, drink in real bars, and talk to real bar owners whenever possible. For example, the Mexican-born tailor in Richmond was a real person who had a shop just where I put it. The Houston police chief who so disliked Duckworth was also a real person who truly did have a background in blacksmithing, and his police station was just as described based on available photographs. West End Baseball Park opened in April of 1905. I would have enjoyed catching a game there. There are many other such instances.

Houston, as the soon-to-be third largest city in the U.S., has changed a touch since the start of the 1900s, but a few of the buildings I mention still exist, and the street grid is the same, at least in the central business district. Downtown Houston nearest the bayou is still a fascinating place worth exploration. As an aside, that city where I grew up is also arguably the best food city in the country.

Richmond, though now suburban Houston, maintains a few streets that have a feel slightly truer to the time period of the book. Sadly, there are many large blank spots in that canvas where buildings once crowded each other. The same goes for Wharton. In 2024, empty lots were in no short supply.

There are about three blocks on Morton Street in Richmond where you can squint and still imagine 1905. The old, beautifully restored courthouses in Richmond and Houston came along just after the action in this book takes place, so the buildings Duckworth used in those two cities were different. The one on the square in Wharton, however, is the same one where Duckworth tried his case.

The part of this book that is most real is the convict leasing system. Such systems were in place throughout the South, and information suggests several were worse than the one in Texas, but that is a matter of degrees of a bad thing.

The lease system in Texas started two years after the Confederacy's surrender out of a dire need for money on the part of the state government. It privatized the whole prison system and allowed the parties who took it over to lease out the state's inmates and pocket the proceeds. About half of the entire prison population got leased to third parties.

The first two times the state awarded contracts, it was filled with trouble. The contractors cut costs on feeding and caring for the prisoners to the point where Texas, never an unflinching advocate of inmate rights, was forced to nullify the deals. Inspections in those first years found a large number of the leased convicts to be malnourished and wearing clothing that barely covered them after weeks without being changed. Men regularly endured beatings, and the inmates, like Harry Duplantis in this book, were extremely hesitant to speak up about any abuse.

The third time Texas signed a private prison deal was different, at least economically. Two Fort Bend County business partners took over the prison system in 1875 and turned the idea into a monetary success. State inspectors seemed satisfied with the results, though they were almost certainly not getting a true picture. The partners invested in the prison infrastructure and leased the convicts out to private farms, railroads and industries, including their own. The two were so successful that in 1883, the state took back the prison system in order to keep more money for themselves.

Throughout the life of the leasing system, the demand for inexpensive convict labor sometimes outpaced the supply. Large landowners and industrialists could no longer simply buy workers as they had under slavery, and make no mistake that enslaved laborers were not only on plantations. They worked in southern industry, unloaded ships on southern docks and built southern railroads.

After the Civil War, many Texas counties regularly doled out harsh sentences for misdemeanor offenses, and a disproportionate percentage of the recipients of these punishments were African-American males. Though Blacks made up roughly a third of the overall population of Texas, they always topped 50%, and sometimes 60%, of the state's prisoners. Stealing a pocket watch or even vagrancy sometimes earned a Black man in Texas a two to three year term at hard labor. State policy set the cost of leasing a Black convict higher than a White because the lessor and lessee both knew that they would be worked harder. The sugar plantations southwest of Houston exclusively used African-Americans while White convicts were more likely to work building railroads.

Unlike some current hyperbole would suggest, and as brutal as the convict lease system was, it did not impact all Blacks in the South as did slavery. It was, however, a horrid system. The population of Texas prisons during this period was between three and four thousand inmates. Ninety-five percent were male, and half of those were leased convicts. The death rate among those men was about three to four percent. In 2019, for example, the death rate across state prisons in the U.S. was 0.33%, so these men were ten times more likely to die during their imprisonment than inmates now.

The Progressive Era, which very often failed to live up to its name, did prove to be the undoing of the system, at least in Texas. The state outlawed convict leasing in 1910, and the law took full effect two years later. It was replaced with state-owned and state-operated prison farms, so for the prisoners, there was not a great deal of difference. The profits simply accrued to the State of Texas instead of a private business.

The eastern part of Sartartia, which was a very real plantation operating during this time period, got rolled into what became Sugar Land, a thriving Houston suburb. Most of Sartartia became the Central Unit of the Texas Prison System that housed prisoners who worked in the fields for many more decades. Prison farms on that land after 1912 were segregated into White, Black and Latino populations.

Today, you can drive down I-69 or US 90A through east Fort Bend County just southwest of Sugar Land and pass through the very heart of what was once Sartartia. You will find it smothered with upscale suburban housing and a few golf courses. In early 2018, during construction of a new school in the school district from which I graduated high school, a cemetery was unearthed. It was used to bury Black convicts during the leasing system. Over the next months, a total of 95 unidentified graves were discovered. The remains were reburied at the site in November 2019, this time with community members present to offer respects. DNA research to identify those individuals continues.

Acknowledgements

Much of the research on this novel dates back to historical non-fiction work I did many years ago. During that time-consuming process I was helped greatly by Sarah Jackson who was then the Harris County Archivist and Francisco Heredia of the Harris County District Court Archives.

Several new folks provided details or answered questions during the time I was writing this novel. Those include: Bryan McAuley and Michael Moore formerly and currently of the Fort Bend County Historical Commission, Lt. Donald Kovar of the Richmond Police Department which currently operates out of the amazing old Fort Bend County Jail, Chris Godbold of the Fort Bend History Association and Ken Tisdell of LCG, who restored the Exchange Hotel property. Wharton County Museum staff were very helpful, and I am sure they would welcome you dropping in for a visit. R.S. "Bob" Shaw and Beaver Blake, longtime friends and former Texas prison guards were huge helps in providing some ins and outs of that world. Joni White at the Texas Prison Museum helped with images, and Jim Willett of the same museum shared stories a decade and a half ago that stuck in the back of my mind.

Though I didn't bug them in person, thanks must also go to the folks at Portal to Texas History and all of their member libraries who supplied many thousands of old newspapers to peruse. The same goes for those who make old Sanborn maps digitally available at the University of Texas Libraries. It especially is true of the digital city directories available from my forever friends at the Houston History Research Center, Houston Public Library. The world cannot survive in any sort of hospitable, intelligent, forward-moving form without libraries. Please support them in all ways.

Lastly, endless thanks go to my beta readers and editors for providing feedback and telling me that I am not out on some crazy limb. Those people include Elizabeth Price, Marsha Franty, Timothy Howard, Mark Kishego, Tony Cavender, and Eliot Tucker. Unlike me, those last two gentlemen have decades of experience as attorneys, and their thoughts on the legal profession were absolutely invaluable. My wife, Anne, read the book and provided copy editing at a reasonable price. Finally, Chris White, my pal since high school and a longtime professional author, has generously given his time so we could talk shop and swap ideas in hopes of making these labors of love profitable.

Coming in 2025

Book 2 in the Duckworth Historic Crime Novel Series

J.B. Duckworth is tasked with saving the carefree son of a small town Texas lawman, but the young man, who has established his own life among the drinking establishments of Houston, just might be guilty.

Please sign up for the newsletter at www.mikevancewriter.com to stay up to date on all of Mike's work, and don't forget to follow @mikevancewriter on social media. Above all, if you enjoyed reading The Devil's Lease, please spread the word. Thanks!